THE
NEAR
WITCH

V.E. SCHWAB

THE NEAR WITCH

TITAN BOOKS

The Near Witch
Hardback edition ISBN: 9781789091120
Paperback edition ISBN: 9781789091144
Ebook edition ISBN: 9781789091137

Published by Titan Books
A division of Titan Publishing Group Ltd
144 Southwark Street, London SE1 0UP
www.titanbooks.com

First Titan edition: March 2019
10 9 8 7 6 5 4 3 2 1

A CIP catalogue record for this title is available from the British Library.

Printed and bound in Great Britain by CPI Group Ltd.

To my mother and father, for never once doubting

INTRODUCTION

Many people long to tell a story.

Say to any group, "I write books," and at least half will respond that, one day, they plan to write one, too. One day, when they have the time. One day, when they have the focus. Some have even started, though few have gotten past the first chapter, or the third, or the fifth.

This isn't meant as a judgment (the world needs far more readers than writers). I only mean to say that it is no small feat, to write a book. And if you want anyone to read said book, The End is only the beginning. Next, if one has opted to participate in traditional publishing, one must find an agent, a publisher. Then comes revision, sometimes one round, sometimes half a dozen, all to ready the text for an audience, to earn that place on the shelves of a bookstore, and then, a reader's home.

With so many obstacles between the first flutter of an aspiring author's imagination and the final product, few stories get to live even a single life on shelves.

Almost none get to live *two*.

But *The Near Witch* has been afforded that luxury.

This is the book that, for me, began everything. It wasn't the first one I *wrote*—that dubious honor belongs to the plot-less, acid trip of a story I created when I was nineteen and simply longed to discover if I was capable of holding a story in my head for more than a dozen pages, capable of finding *The End*.

But *The Near Witch* is the first book that found its way to shelves, to readers.

This, for those who don't know, is a book about magic.

It is also a book about fear.

Specifically, about the fear of the inside toward the outside, the antagonism between those who belong, and those who don't. Little did I know then that it would become a theme so central to my work. That all my stories, from *A Darker Shade of Magic* to *Vicious*, *The Archived* to *This Savage Song*, would center on those who felt lost inside their own worlds, or found inside someone else's. But at twenty-one, as a second-semester senior at university, stealing hours in a coffee shop each night to write, and as a young adult on the cusp of graduation, and the unknown of life beyond school, I felt pressed between two chapters of my own life, and as if I belonged to neither.

That is the world in which this book was written.

It starts with a crack, a sputter, and a spark.

Those are the opening words of the book, but they could just as easily apply to my career as an author. *The Near Witch* was a small book, quiet and strange at a time when everything that sold well was loud and vaguely familiar, and though I tried to shield the fragile candle of its life, it was only a matter of time before the wind of publishing blew through, and snuffed it out.

Fortunately, my own flame was more resilient. I kept writing, kept publishing, kept bolstering the fire until it burned hot enough that the seasonal gusts of this wonderful, but fickle industry served to stoke the fire instead of quash it.

Over the next seven years, I wrote *fourteen* novels. With each one, the readership grew, the books found their audience, a little more with every release, and as the years passed, people began to ask about that first story.

The spark that started the fire.

It is bittersweet, to see a story wanted so long after it was gone, but I harbored a stubborn hope that one day, it would find its way back. Some part of me has been sheltering that matchstick ever since the flame went out.

And here we are.

Back at the beginning.

V.E. Schwab, 2018

1

It starts with a crack, a sputter, and a spark. The match hisses to life.

"Please," comes the small voice behind me.

"It's late, Wren," I say. The fire chews on the wooden stem in my hand. I touch the match to each of the three candles gathered on the low chest by the window. "It's time for bed."

With the candles all lit, I shake the match and the flame dies, leaving a trail of smoke that curls up against the darkened glass.

Everything seems different at night. Defined. Beyond the window, the world is full of shadows, all pressed together in harsh relief, somehow sharper than they ever were in daylight.

Sounds seem sharper, too, at night. A whistle. A crack. A child's whisper.

"Just one more," she pleads, hugging the covers close. I sigh, my back to my little sister, and run my fingers over the tops of the books stacked beside the candles. I feel myself bending.

"It can be a very short one," she says.

My hand rests against an old green book as the wind hums against the house.

"All right." I cannot deny my sister anything, it seems. "Just one," I add, turning back to the bed.

Wren sighs happily against her pillow, and I slip down beside her.

The candles paint pictures of light on the walls of our room. I take a deep breath.

"The wind on the moors is a tricky thing," I begin, and Wren's small body sinks deeper into the bed. I imagine she is listening more to the highs and lows of my voice than the words themselves. We both know the words by heart anyway—I from my father, and Wren from me.

"Of every aspect of the moor, the earth and stone and rain and fire, the wind is the strongest one in Near. Here on the outskirts of the village, the wind is always pressing close, making windows groan. It whispers and it howls and it sings. It can bend its voice and cast it into any shape, long and thin enough to slide beneath the door, stout enough to seem a thing of weight and breath and bone.

"The wind was here when you were born, when I was born, when our house was built, when the Council was formed, and even when the Near Witch lived," I say with a quiet smile, the way my father always did, because *this* is where the story starts.

"Long, long ago, the Near Witch lived in a small house on the farthest edge of the village, and she used to sing the hills to sleep."

Wren pulls the covers up.

"She was very old and very young, depending on which way she turned her head, for no one knows the age of witches. The moor streams were her blood and the moor grass was her skin, and her smile was kind and sharp at once, like the moon in the black, black night..."

I hardly ever get to the end of the story. Soon enough Wren is a pile of blankets and quiet breath, shifting in her heavy dreams beside me. The three candles are still burning on the chest, leaning into one another, dripping and pooling on the wood.

Wren is afraid of the dark. I used to leave the candles lit all night, but she falls asleep so fast, and if she does wake, she often finds her way, eyes closed, into our mother's room. Now I tend to stay up until she's drifted off, and then blow the candles out. No need to waste them, or set the house on fire. I slide from the bed, my bare feet settling on the old wood floor.

When I reach the candles, my eyes wander down to the puddles of wax, dotted with tiny fingerprints where Wren likes to stand on her tiptoes and draw patterns in the pools while the wax is warm. I brush my own fingers over them absently, when something, a sliver of movement, draws my eyes up to the window. There's nothing there. Outside, the night is still and streaked with silver threads of light, and the wind is breathing against the glass, a wobbling hum that causes the old wooden frame to groan.

My fingertips drift up from the wax to the windowsill, feeling the wind through the walls of our house. It's getting stronger.

When I was small, the wind sang me lullabies. Lilting,

humming, high-pitched things, filling the space around me
so that even when all seemed quiet, it wasn't. This is a wind
I have lived with.

But tonight it's different. As if there's a new thread of
music woven in, lower and sadder than the rest. Our house
sits at the northern edge of the village of Near, and beyond
the weathered glass the moor rolls away like a spool of
fabric: hill after hill of wild grass, dotted by rocks, and a
rare river or two. There is no end in sight, and the world
seems painted in black and white, crisp and still. A few trees
jut out of the earth amid the rocks and weeds, but even in
this wind it is all strangely static. But I'd swear I saw—

Again something moves.

This time my eyes are keen enough to catch it. At the
edge of our yard, the invisible line where the village ends
and the moor picks up, a shape moves against the painted
night. A shadow twitches and steps forward, catching a
slice of moonlight.

I squint, pressing my hands against the cool glass. The
shape is a body, but drawn too thin, like the wind is
pulling at it, tugging slivers away. The moonlight cuts
across the front of the form, over fabric and skin, a throat,
a jaw, a cheekbone.

There are no strangers in the town of Near. I have seen
every face a thousand times. But not this one.

The figure just stands there, looking out to the side. And
yet, he is not *all* there. There is something in the way the
cool blue-white moon lights his face that makes me think I
could brush my fingers right through it. His form is
smudged at the edges, blurring into the night on either side,

as if he's moving very fast, but it must be the weathered glass, because he's not moving at all. He is just standing there, looking at nothing.

The candles flicker beside me, and on the moor, the wind picks up and the stranger's body seems to ripple, fade. Before I know it, I am pressing myself against the window, reaching for the latch to throw it open, to speak, to call the form back, when he moves. He turns his face toward the house and the window, and toward me.

I catch my breath as the stranger's eyes find mine. Eyes as dark as river stones and yet somehow shining, soaking up moonlight. Eyes that widen a fraction as they meet my own. A single, long, unblinking look. And then in an instant the stranger seems to break apart, a sharp gust of wind tears through, and the shutters slam closed against the glass.

The sound wakes Wren, who mumbles and peels her half-sleeping form from between the sheets, stumbling through the moonlit room. She doesn't even see me standing at the window, staring at the wooden slats that have blotted out the stranger and the moor. I hear her pad across the threshold, slide open our mother's door, and disappear within. The room is suddenly quiet. I pry the window open, the wood protesting as it drags against itself, and throw the shutters back.

The stranger is gone.

I feel like there should be a mark in the air where he was wiped away. But there is no trace. No matter how much I stare, there is nothing but trees, and rocks, and rolling hills.

I stare out at this empty landscape, and it seems impossible that I saw him, saw anyone. After all, there are no strangers in the town of Near. There haven't been since long ago, before I was born, before the house was built, before the Council... And he didn't even seem real, didn't seem *there*. I rub my eyes, and realize I've been holding my breath.

I use the air to blow the candles out.

2

"Lexi."

The light creeps in between the sheets. I pull the blankets up, try to recreate the darkness, and find my mind wandering to the night before, to shadowed forms on the moonlit moor.

"Lexi," my mother's voice calls again, this time penetrating the cocoon of blankets. It burrows in beside me along with the morning light. The night-washed memory seems to bleed away.

From my nest I hear the thudding of feet on wood, followed by an airborne pause. I brace myself, staying perfectly still as the body catapults itself onto the bed. Small fingers tap the blankets covering me.

"Lexi," says a new voice, a higher-pitched version of my mother's. "Get up now." Still I feign sleep. "Lexi?"

I shoot my arms out, reaching through the linens for my sister, trapping her in a blanketed hug.

"Got you!" I call. Wren lets out a playful little cry. She wriggles free and I wrestle the blankets off. My dark hair nests around my face. I can feel it, the climbing tendrils already unruly, as Wren sits at the edge of the bed and laughs in her chirping way. Her hair is blond and stock straight. It never leaves the sides of her face, never shifts from her shoulders. I bury my fingers in it, try to mess it up, but she only laughs and shakes her head, and the hair settles, perfect and smooth again.

These are our morning rituals.

Wren hops off and wanders into the kitchen. I'm up and heading to the chest to fetch some clothes, when my eyes flick to the window, examining the glass and the morning beyond. The moor, with its tangled grass and scattered rocks, looks so soft and open, laid out in the light of day. It is a different world in the gray morning. I can't help but wonder if what I saw last night was just a dream. If *he* was just a dream.

I touch my fingers to the glass to test the warmth of the day. It is the farthest edge of summer, that brief time where the days can be pleasant, even warm, or crisp and cold. The glass is cool, but my fingertips make only small halos of steam. I pull away.

I do my best to uncoil my hair from my forehead, and wrestle it back into a plait.

"Lexi!" my mother calls again. The bread must be ready.

I pull on a long simple dress, cinching the waist. What I wouldn't give for pants. I'm fairly certain my father would have fallen for my mother if she wore britches and a hunting hat, even once she'd reached sixteen, marrying age. My age. *Marrying age*, I scoff, eyeing a pair of girlish slippers despairingly. They're pale green, thin-soled, and they make a very poor substitute for my father's old leather boots.

I stare at my bare feet, marked by the miles they've walked across the rough moor. I'd rather stay here and deliver my mother's bread, rather grow old and crooked like Magda and Dreska Thorne, than be bound up in skirts and slippers and married off to a village boy. I slide the slippers on.

I'm dressed, but can't shake the feeling I'm missing something. I turn to the small wooden table by my bed and exhale, eyes finding my father's knife sheathed on its dark leather strap, the handle worn from his grip. I like to place my narrow fingers in the impressions. It's like I can feel his hand in mine. I used to wear it every day, until Otto's glares got heavy enough, and even then I'd sometimes chance it. I must be feeling bold today, because my fingers close around the knife, and the weight of it feels good. I slip it around my waist like a belt, the guarded blade against my lower back, and feel safe again. Clothed.

"Lexi, come on!" my mother calls, and I wonder what on earth the hurry could be, since the morning loaves will cool before I ever reach the purchasers, but then a second voice reaches me through the walls, a low, tense muttering that tangles with my mother's higher tone. Otto. The smell of slightly burned bread greets me as I enter the kitchen.

"Good morning," I say, meeting the two pairs of eyes, one pale and tired, but unblinking, the other dark and furrowed. My uncle's eyes are so much like my father's—the same rich brown, framed by dark lashes—but where my father's were always dancing, Otto's are fenced by lines, always still. He hunches forward, his broad shoulders draped over his coffee.

I cross the room and kiss my mother's cheek.

"About time," says my uncle. Wren skips in behind me and throws her arms around his waist. He softens a fraction, running his hand lightly over her hair, and then she's gone, a slip of fabric through the doorway. Otto turns his attention back to me, as if waiting for an answer, an explanation.

"What's the rush?" I ask as my mother's eyes flick to my waist and the leather strap against my dress, but she says nothing, only turns and glides over to the oven. My mother's feet rarely touch the ground. She's not beautiful or charming, except in that way all mothers are to their daughters, but she just flows.

These, too, are morning rituals. My mother's kiss. Otto's appearance in our kitchen, regular enough that he could leave his shadow here. His stern eyes as he gives me a sweeping look, snagging on my father's knife. I wait for him to comment on it, but he doesn't.

"You're here early, Otto," I say, taking a slice of warm bread and a mug.

"Not early enough," he says. "The whole town's up and talking by now."

"And why is that?" I ask, pouring tea from a kettle beside the hearth.

My mother turns to us, flour painted across her hands. "We need to go into town."

"There's a stranger," Otto grunts into his cup. "Came through last night."

I fumble the kettle, nearly scalding my hands.

"A stranger?" I ask, steadying the pot. So it wasn't a dream or a phantom. There *was* someone there.

"I want to know what he's doing here," adds my uncle.

"He's still here?" I ask, struggling to keep the curiosity from flooding my voice. I take a sip of tea, burning my mouth. Otto offers a curt nod and drains his cup, and before I can bite my tongue, the questions bubble up.

"Where did he come from? Has anyone spoken to him?" I ask. "Where is he now?"

"Enough, Lexi." Otto's words cut through the warmth in the kitchen. "It's all rumors right now. Too many voices chattering at once." He's changing before my eyes, straightening, shifting from my uncle into the village Protector, as if the title has its own mass and weight. "I don't yet know for certain who the stranger is or where he's from or who's offered him shelter," he adds. "But I mean to find out."

So someone has offered him shelter. I bite my lip to swallow the smile. I bet I know who's hiding the stranger. What I want to know is *why*. I gulp my too-hot tea, suffering the heat of it all the way down to my stomach, eager to escape. I want to see if I'm right. And if I am, I want to get there before my uncle. Otto pushes himself up from the table.

"You go on ahead," I say, mustering an innocent smile.

Otto lets out a rough laugh. "I don't think so. Not today."

My face falls. "Why not?" I ask.

Otto's brow lowers over his eyes. "I know what you want, Lexi. You want to go hunt for him yourself. I won't have it."

"What can I say? I am my father's daughter."

Otto nods grimly. "That much is clear as glass. Now go get ready. We're *all* going into the village."

I lift an eyebrow. "Am I not ready?"

Otto leans across the table slowly. His dark eyes bear down on mine as if he can bully me with a glance. But his looks are not as strong as my mother's or my own, and they do not say nearly as many things. I stare calmly back, waiting for the last act of our morning rituals.

"Take that knife off. You look like a fool."

I ignore him, finish my bread, and turn to my mother. "I'll be in the yard when you two are ready." Otto's voice fills the space behind me as I leave.

" You should teach her properly, Amelia," he mutters.

"Your brother saw fit to teach her his trade," replies my mother, wrapping loaves of bread.

"It's not right, Amelia, for a girl, and certainly not one her age, to be out and about with boys' things. Don't think I haven't seen the boots. As bad as walking around barefoot. Has she been in town taking lessons? Helena Drake can stitch and cook and tend…" I can see him running his fingers through his dark hair, then immediately over his beard, tugging his face the way he always does when he's frustrated. *Not right. Not proper.*

I've just begun to tune them out when Wren appears in the yard out of nowhere. She really is like a bird. Flying off at a blink. Alighting at another. Good thing she's loud, or else her sudden appearances would be frightening.

"Where are we going?" she chirps, wrapping her arms around my waist.

"Into the village."

"What for?" She lets go of my dress and leans back to peer up at me.

"To sell you," I say, trying to keep a straight face. "Or maybe just to give you away."

My smile cracks.

Wren frowns. "I don't think that's why."

I sigh. The child may look like a bundle of light and joy, but she doesn't scare nearly as easily as a five-year-old should. She looks up, past my head, and so do I. The clouds overhead are clustering, coming together the way they do each day. Like a pilgrimage—that's the way my father put it. I slip free of my sister and turn away, toward Otto's house, and beyond it, hidden by hills, the village. I want to get there as soon as possible and see if my hunch about the stranger is correct.

"Let's go," calls my uncle, my mother in tow. Otto eyes the knife at my waist one last time, but only grumbles and sets off down the path. I smile and follow.

*

The town of Near is shaped like a circle. There's no wall around it, but everyone seems to know where it ends and where the countryside begins. Stone walls snake through the village, no higher than my waist and half swallowed by the weeds and wild grass. They wander past clusters of cottages scattered among empty hills or fields, until you reach the center of town, where the structures stand almost side by side. The center of town is filled with seamstresses and carpenters and those who can do their work shoulder to shoulder. Most of the villagers live close to the town square. No one ventures onto the moor if they can help it, but a few cottages, such as our own, and the Thorne sisters', dot the edges, sitting right up against the seam where Near meets the moor. Only hunters and witches live out this way, they say.

Soon the thickest circle of houses sprouts up into sight. The buildings, all cut stone trimmed in wood and topped with thatch, are huddled together. The newer houses are paler, the older ones darkened by storms and licked by moss and weed. Narrow, well-walked paths run between and around and through everything.

And I can see even from a distance that the center of Near is bustling with people.

News spreads like weeds in a place so small.

When we reach the town square, most of the villagers are already floating about, gossiping and grumbling in turn. As they arrive, they break up into clusters, splitting into smaller and smaller groups. It reminds me of the clouds in reverse. Otto breaks off to find Bo and the rest of his men, probably to dole out orders. My mother sees a few of the other mothers, and gives them a tired wave. She lets go of Wren's hand, and my sister flutters off into the crowd.

"Look after her," she says to me, already turning away, gliding in the direction of a group across the square.

I have other plans, but the protest dies in my throat. My mother doesn't beg. She just gives me the look. The look that says, *My husband is dead and my brother-in-law is demanding enough, and I have so little time to myself, and unless you want to be a burden on your poor mother, you'll be a good daughter and look after your sister.* All in a look. In some ways, my mother is a powerful woman. I nod and follow Wren, tuning my ears to the voices, almost all rumors, buzzing and bustling around me.

Wren leads me past Otto and Bo, the two talking in low tones. Bo, a narrow man with a slight limp, is several years younger than my uncle. His nose is long, and his brown hair curls across his forehead but recedes to either side, making him look pointed.

"...saw him by my house," Bo is saying. "Early enough that it wasn't too dark, late enough that I didn't trust my eyes entirely..."

Wren has strayed far ahead now, and Otto casts a look up at me, giving a sideways jerk of his head. I turn and go, making note that Bo lives on the western edge of the village, so the stranger must have circled Near in that direction. Catching up to Wren, I pass by two families from the southern part of town. I slow my pace, careful to keep my sister in my sight.

"No, John, I swear he towers like a bare tree..." hollers an older woman, holding her arms wide as a scarecrow.

"You're daft, Berth. I saw him, and he's old, very old, practically crumbling."

"He's a ghost."

"No such thing as a ghost! He's a halfling—part man, part crow."

"Hah! So there's no ghosts, but there's half-crow people? You didn't see him."

"I did, I swear."

"He must have been a witch," a younger woman joins in. The cluster quiets for a moment before John picks back up too emphatically, passing over the remark.

"No, if he was a crow-thing, then that's a good omen. Crows are good omens."

"Crows are terrible omens! You've lost your mind, John. I know I said it last week but I was wrong. Today you've really lost it..."

I've lost Wren.

I look around and finally see a slip of blond hair vanishing into a nearby circle of children. I reach the cluster and find my sister, a good head shorter than most of them but just as loud and twice as quick. They are joining hands, preparing to play a game. A girl a year older than Wren named Cecilia, all edges and elbows in a skirt the color of heather, takes my sister's hand. Cecilia has a scatter of freckles like muddy flecks across her face, vanishing along her cheekbones and into auburn curls. I watch her swing Wren's small hand back and forth until a shape stumbles into the dirt nearby, letting out a small sob.

Edgar Drake, a boy with a whitish-blond mop of hair, sits in the dirt, rubbing his palms together.

"Are you all right?" I ask, kneeling down and examining his scraped hands. He bites his lip and manages a nod as I clear the dirt away with my thumbs as gently as possible. He's Wren's age, but she seems unbreakable, and he is a patchwork of scratches from always falling down. His mother, the village seamstress, has patched his clothes as many times as she's patched him. Edgar keeps staring sadly at his fingers.

"What does Helena do," I ask, offering a smile, "to make it better?" Helena is my closest friend and Edgar's older sister, and she dotes on him incessantly.

"Kisses it," he murmurs, still biting his lip. I set an airy kiss on each palm. I wonder if I babied Wren like this, would she be so fragile, so shocked by a knick or scrape? Just then she lets out a raucous laugh and calls to us.

"Edgar, hurry!" she shouts, bouncing on her toes as she waits for the game to start. I help the boy up and he hurries over, nearly tripping again halfway there. Clumsy little boy. He reaches the circle and slides in beside Wren and squeezes her right hand, knocking her shoulder with his.

I watch as the game takes shape. This is the same one I used to play, Tyler on one side, Helena on the other. The spinning game. It starts with a song, the Witch's Rhyme. The song has been around as long as the bedtime stories of the Near Witch, and those have been around as long as the moor itself, it seems. It is a fearfully addictive tune, so much so that it seems the wind itself has taken to humming it. The children join hands. They begin to move in a slow circle as they sing.

> The wind on the moors is a'singing to me
> The grass, and the stones, and the far-off sea
> The crows all watching on the low stone wall
> The flowers in the yard all stretching tall
> To the garden we children went every day
> To hear the witch and watch her play

The children sing faster as they pick up speed. The game always reminds me of the way the wind whips up the fallen leaves, spinning them in tight, dizzying rings.

> She spoke to the earth and the earth it cracked
> Spoke to the wind and it whistled back
> Spoke to the river and the river whirled
> Spoke to the fire and the fire curled
> But little boy Jack he stayed too long
> Listened too close to the witch's song

Faster.

> *Six different flowers on the little boy's bed*
> *Her house it burned and the witch she fled*
> *Cast out, thrown out, on the moor*
> *Near Witch, Moor Witch, now no more*

And faster, still.

> *The witch still a'singing her hills to sleep*
> *Her voice is high and her voice is deep*
> *Under the door the sounds all sweep*
> *Through the glass the words all creep*
> *The Near Witch is a'singing to me*

The song starts over.

> *The wind on the moors is a'singing to me…*

The words circle round on themselves until eventually the children fall down, tired and laughing. The winner is the last one standing. Wren manages to stay up longer than most, but eventually even she topples into the dirt, breathless and smiling. The children rise unsteadily and prepare to play again as my mind turns slow circles over the mystery of the stranger, with his eyes that seemed to soak up moonlight, and his blurring edges.

Who is he? Why is he here? And there, softer in my head: *How did he vanish? How did he just break apart?*

I keep an eye on Wren while hovering on the outskirts of

conversations. Several people claim to have seen the shadowy form, but I do not believe them all. I accept that he passed west at Bo's, north by me. He seems to have walked the invisible line that separates Near from the moor, though how he recognized the boundary I do not know.

The children's laughter is replaced by a familiar voice, and I turn to find Helena sitting on one of the low walls that taper out along the edge of the square. A group of men and women crowd around her, perhaps the only villagers in the square who aren't talking. In fact, they are all silent, and Helena herself is the object of their attention. She catches my eye and winks before turning back to her audience.

"I saw him," she says. "It was dark, but I know it was him."

She pulls a ribbon from her hair and winds it around her wrist, letting white-blond strands, the same color as Edgar's, fall over her shoulders. Helena, who never manages to be loud enough, bold enough, is drenched in sun and soaking up every drop of the attention being paid her.

I frown. She isn't lying. Her pale cheeks always flush at the first wisp of a fib, but these words pour out smooth and sure, her cheeks their usual pink.

"He was tall, thin, with dark, dark hair that fell around his face."

The crowd murmurs collectively, growing as people peel themselves away from other groups. Word spreads through the town square that someone has had a good long look at the stranger. I press through the bodies until I am at her side, the questions bubbling up around us. I squeeze her arm.

"There you are!" she says, pulling me close.

"What's going on?" I ask, but my question is swallowed by a dozen others.

"Did he speak to you?"

"Which way was he headed?"

"How tall was he?"

"Give her air," I say, noticing my uncle over their heads, across the square. He has seen the gathering crowd around Helena, and is turning toward us to investigate. "A moment's air." I tug Helena aside.

"Did you really see him?" I hiss in her ear.

"I did!" she hisses back. "And Lexi, he was gorgeous. And strange. And young! If only you could have seen him, too."

"If only," I whisper. There are too many voices chirping about the stranger, and too many eyes looking for him. I won't add mine to them. Not yet.

The group around us has grown, and the questions redouble. Otto is crossing the square.

"Tell us, Helena."

"Tell us what you saw."

"Tell us where he is," says a male voice, his tone tinged with something more severe than curiosity. Bo.

Helena turns back to her audience to answer, but I grab her arm and pull her to me, a bit forcefully. She gives a small cry.

"Lexi!" she whispers. "Easy."

"Hel, it's important. Do you know where he is now?"

"Indeed," she says. Her eyes shine. "Don't you? Lexi the great tracker, surely you've deduced."

Otto is at the edge of the crowd, touching Bo's shoulder. The latter whispers something to him.

"Helena Drake," Otto calls over everyone. "A word."

She hops down from the wall. My fingers tighten around her arm.

"Don't tell him."

She looks back over her shoulder at me. "Why on earth not?"

"You know my uncle. All he wants is to see the stranger gone." Gone, and everything back the way it was, safe and same. Her pale brows knit. "Just a head start, Helena. Give me that. To warn him."

The crowd parts for my uncle. "Good day, Mr. Harris," Helena says.

Across the square, a bell sounds, followed by another, lower, and a third, lower still. The Council. Otto pauses, turning toward the noise. Three men as old as dirt wait at the door to one of the houses, standing on the steps to be seen. Master Eli, Master Tomas, and Master Matthew. Their voices are withered with age, and so they use their bells instead of shouting to draw their crowd close. They don't actually do anything but grow older. The Council started out as the three men who faced the Near Witch and cast her out. But these skeletal men on the steps are Council only in title, the inheritors of power. Still, there is something in their eyes, something cold and sharp that makes the children whisper and the adults look down.

People diligently make their way toward the old men. My uncle frowns, torn between questioning Helena and following the crowd. He huffs and pivots, walking back across the square. Helena casts one last look at me and bobs after him.

This is my only chance.

I slip out along the wall, away from my uncle and the cluster of villagers. Leaving the square, I catch sight of Wren with the other children. My mother is beside her now. Otto is taking his spot nearest the three old men, his Protector face on. I won't be missed.

"As you have heard," says Master Tomas over the quieting crowd. He is a head taller than even Otto, and his voice, though withered, has a remarkable way of traveling. "We have a stranger in our midst..."

I duck between two houses, picking up a path that leads east.

Helena's right: I do know where the stranger is.

Almost everyone had already gathered in the square when we arrived. Except for two. Not that they like to put in appearances. But the presence of a stranger should have been enough to bring even the Thorne sisters into Near. Unless they're the ones keeping him.

I weave through the lanes, heading east, until the sounds of the village die away and the wind picks up.

3

My father taught me a lot about witches.

Witches can call down rain or summon stones. They can make fire leap and dance. They can move the earth. They can control an element. The way Magda and Dreska Thorne can. I asked them once what they were, and they said *old*. *Old as rocks*. But that's not the whole of it. The Thorne sisters are witches, through and through. And witches are not so welcome here.

I make my way to the sisters' house. The path beneath my shoes is faint and narrow, but never fully fades, despite the fact that so few walk it. The way has worn itself into the earth. The sisters' cottage sits beyond a grove and atop a hill. I know how many steps it will take to reach their home, both from my own or from the center of Near, every kind of flower that grows on the way, every rise and fall of the ground.

My father used to take me there.

And even now that he's gone, I come this way. I've been to their cottage many times, drawn to their odd charm, to watch them gather weeds or to toss out a question or a cheerful hello. Everyone else in the village turns their back

on the sisters, pretends they are not here, and seems to do a
decent job of forgetting. But to me they are like gravity,
with their own strange pull, and whenever I have nowhere
to go, my feet take me toward their house. It's the same
gravity I felt at the window last night, pulling me to the
stranger on the moor, a kind of weight I've never fully
understood. But my father taught me to trust it as much as
my eyes, so I do.

I remember the first time he took me to see the sisters. I
must have been eight or so, older than Wren is now. The
whole house smelled of dirt, rich and heavy and fresh at
once. I remember Dreska's sharp green eyes, and Magda's
crooked smile, crooked spine, crooked everything. They've
never let me back inside, not since he died.

The trees creep up around me as I enter the grove.

I stop, knowing at once I'm not alone. Something is
breathing, moving, just beyond my sight. I hold my breath,
letting the breeze and the hush and the sighing moor slip
away into ambient noise. I scan with my ears, waiting for a
sound to emerge from the sea of whispers, scan with my
eyes, waiting for something to move.

My father taught me how to track, how to read the ground
and the trees. He taught me that everything has a language,
that if you knew the language, you could make the world
talk. *The grass and the dirt hold secrets*, he'd say. *The wind
and the water carry stories and warnings*. Everyone knows
that witches are born, not made, but growing up I used to
think he'd found some way to cheat, to coax the world to
work for him.

Something moves through the trees just to my right.

I spin as a cluster of branches peels itself away from a trunk. Not branches, I realize. Horns. A deer slips between the trees on stiltlike legs. I sigh and turn back to the path, when a shadow twitches, deeper in the grove.

A flash of dark fabric.

I blink, and it is gone, but I would swear I saw it, a glimpse of a gray cloak between the trees.

A sharp crack issues behind me, and I jump and spin to find Magda, small and hunched and staring at me. Her left eye is a cool blue, but her right eye is made of something dark and solid like rotted wood, and her two-toned gaze is inches from my face. I let out a breath I didn't know I'd been holding, as the old woman shakes her head, all silver hair and weathered skin. She chuckles, crooked fingers curving around her basket.

"You might be good at tracking, dearie, but you startle like a rabbit." She pokes me with a long bony finger. "No, not much for being tracked."

I glance back, but the shadow is gone.

"Hello, Magda," I say. "I was on my way to see you."

"I figured as much," she says, winking her good eye. For a moment only her dark eye stares back at me, and I shiver.

"Come on, then." She sets off through the grove, toward the hill and her house. "We'll have tea."

*

In three years, I have not been invited in.

Now Magda leads me back toward the cottage in silence as the clouds darken overhead. It is slow going because it takes three of her steps to match my one. The wind is up, and my hair is escaping its braid, curling defiantly around my face and neck as Magda totters along beside me.

I am a good head taller than she is, but I imagine she is a good head shorter than she once was, so it seems unfair to compare our heights. She moves more like a windblown leaf than an old woman, bouncing along the ground and changing course as we make our way up the hill to the house she shares with her sister.

Growing up in Near, I've heard a dozen stories about witches. My father hated those tales, told me they were made up by the Council to frighten people. "Fear is a strange thing," he used to say. "It has the power to make people close their eyes, turn away. Nothing good grows out of fear."

The cottage sits waiting for us, as warped as the two women it was built to hold, the spine of the structure cocked halfway up, the roofing on another angle entirely. None of the stacked stones look comfortable or well-seated, like the ones in the town center. This house is as old as Near itself, sagging over the centuries. It sits on the eastern edge of the village, bordered on one side by a low stone wall, and on the other by a dilapidated shed. Between the stone wall and the house are two rectangular patches. One is a small bordered stretch of dirt that Magda calls her garden, and the other is nothing more than a swatch of bare ground where nothing seems to grow. It might be the only place in Near not overrun by weeds. I don't like the second patch. It seems unnatural. Beyond the cottage, the moor takes hold, much the way it does to the north of my home, all rolling hills and stones and scattered trees.

"Coming?" asks Magda, from the doorway.

Overhead, the clouds have gathered and grown dark.

My foot hovers on the threshold. But why? I have no reason to fear the Thorne sisters or their home.

I take a deep breath and step across.

It still smells like earth, rich and heavy and safe. That hasn't changed. But the room seems darker now than it did when I was here with my father. It might be the gathering clouds and the coming fall, or the fact that he isn't towering beside me, lighting the room with his smile. I fight back a chill as Magda sets her basket down on a long wooden table and lets out a heavy sigh.

"Sit, dearie, sit," she says with a wave to one of the chairs.

I slide into it.

Magda hobbles up to the hearth, where the wood is stacked and waiting. She casts a short glance back over her shoulder at me. And then she brings her fingers up, very slowly, inching through the air. I lean forward, waiting to see if she'll actually let me see her craft, if she'll coax twigs together, or somehow bubble flint up from the dirt hearth floor. The sisters don't make a point of giving demonstrations, so all I have are a few stolen glances when the ground rippled or stones shifted, the strange gravity I feel when I'm close, and the villagers' fear.

Magda's hand rises over the hearth and up to the mantel, where her fingers close around a long thin stick. Just a match. My heart sinks and I sag back into my seat as Magda strikes the match against the stone of the hearth and lights the fire. She turns back to me.

"What's wrong, dearie?" Something shimmers in her eyes. "You look disappointed."

"Nothing," I say, sitting up straighter and intertwining my hands beneath the table. The fire crackles to life under the kettle, and Magda returns to the table and the basket atop it. From it she unpacks several clods of dirt, a few moor flowers, weeds, some seeds, a stone or two she's found. Magda collects her pieces of the world daily. I imagine it's all for charms. Small craft. Now and then a piece of the sisters' work will find its way into a villager's pocket, or around their neck, even if they claim to not believe in it. I swear I've seen a charm stitched into the skirt of Helena's dress, most likely meant to attract Tyler Ward's attention. She can have him.

Aside from the odd collection on the table, the Thorne sisters' house is remarkably normal. If I tell Wren I was here, inside a witch's home, she'll want to know how odd it was. It'll be a shame to disappoint her.

"Magda," I say, "I came here because I wanted to ask you—"

"Tea's not boiled yet, and I'm too old to talk and stand at the same time. Give me a moment."

I bite my lip and wait as patiently as possible as Magda hobbles around, gathering cups. The breeze begins to scratch and hiss against the windowpanes. The congregation of clouds is thickening. The kettle boils.

"Don't mind that, dearie, just the moor chatting away," Magda says, noticing the way my eyes wander to the window. She pours the water through an old wire mesh that does little to catch the leaves, and into heavy cups. Finally, she takes a seat.

"Does the moor really speak?" I ask, watching the tea in the cup grow dark.

"Not in the way we do, you and I. Not with words. But it has its secrets, yes." Secrets. That's how my father used to put it, too.

"What does it sound like? What does it feel like?" I ask, half to myself. "I imagine it must feel like more, rather than less. I wish I could—"

"Lexi Harris, you could eat dirt every day and wear only weeds, and you'd be no closer to any of it than you already are."

The voice belongs to Dreska Thorne. One moment the gathering storm was locked outside, and the next the door had blown open from the force of it and left her on the threshold.

Dreska is just as old as her sister, maybe even older. The fact that the Thorne sisters are still standing, or hobbling, is a sure sign of their craft. They've been around as long as the Council, and not just Tomas and Matthew and Eli, but their ancestors, the *real* Council. As long as the Near Witch. As long as Near itself. Hundreds of years. I imagine I see small pieces crumbling off them, but when I look again, they are still all there.

Dreska is muttering to herself as she leans into the door, and finally succeeds in forcing it shut before turning to us. When her eyes land on me, I wince. Magda is round and Dreska is sharp, one a ball and the other a ball of points. Even Dreska's cane is sharp. She looks as if she's cut from rocks, and when she's angry or annoyed, her corners actually seem to sharpen. Where one of Magda's eyes is dark as rotted wood or stone, both of Dreska's are a fierce green, the color of moss on stones. And they're now leveled at me. I swallow hard.

I sat here in this chair once as my father curled his fingers gently on my shoulder and spoke to the sisters, and Dreska looked at him with something like kindness, like softness. I remember it so clearly because I've never seen her look that way at anyone ever again.

Beyond the house, the rain starts, thick drops tapping on the stones.

"Dreska's right, dearie." Magda cuts through the silence as she spoons three lumps of a brownish sugar into her tea. She doesn't stir, lets it sink to the bottom and form a grainy film. "Born is born. You were born the way you are."

Magda's cracked hands find their way to my chin.

"Just because you can't coax water to run backward, or make trees uproot themselves—"

"A skill most don't look on fondly," Dreska interjects.

"—doesn't mean you aren't a part of this place," finishes Magda. "All moor-born souls have the moor in them." She gazes into the teacup, her good eye unfocusing over the darkening water. "It's what makes the wind stir something in us when it blows. It's what keeps us here, always close to home."

"Speaking of home, why are you in ours?" asks Dreska sternly.

"She was on her way to see us," says Magda, still staring into her tea. "I invited her in."

"Why," asks Dreska, drawing out the word, "would you do that?"

"It seemed a wise idea," says Magda, giving her sister a heavy look.

Neither speaks.

I clear my throat.

Both sisters look to me.

"Well you're here now," says Dreska. "What brought you this way?"

"I want to ask you," I say at last, "about the stranger."

Dreska's keen green eyes narrow, sharp in their nest of wrinkles. The house stones seem to grumble and grate against each other. The rain beats against the windows as the sisters hold a conversation built entirely of nods, glances, and weighted breath. Some people say that siblings have their own language, and I think it's true of Magda and Dreska. I only know English, and they know English and Sister and Moor, and goodness knows what else. A moment later, Magda sighs and pushes to her feet.

"What of it?" asks Dreska, tapping her cane on the wooden floor. Outside, the rain comes down in waves, each one thinner than the last. It will be over soon. "We don't know anything about him."

The rain turns to a drizzle.

"You have not offered him shelter?" I ask.

The sisters stand there, stiff and mute.

"I don't mean any harm," I say quickly. "I just want to see him, to speak to him. I've never met a stranger. I just want to see that he's real and ask him..." How can I explain? "Just tell me if you have him, please."

Nothing.

I force myself straighter in my chair, keeping my head up.

"I saw him last night. Outside my window. Bo Pike claims to have spotted him first, on the western edge, and we're due north. The stranger seemed to know the line that marks the edge of the village. He would have rounded it, to the east." I tap the table with my index finger. "Here."

The sisters would have given him shelter. It had to have been them. But still they say nothing. Their eyes say nothing. Their faces say nothing. It's as if I'm speaking to statues.

"You were the only ones absent this morning," I say.

Magda blinks. "We keep to ourselves."

"But you're the only ones who could have hidden—"

Dreska sparks to life.

"You best be getting home, Lexi," she snaps, "while there's a break in the weather."

I look to the window. The storm has stopped, leaving the sky gray and drained. The air in the room feels heavy, as if the space is shrinking. The sisters' looks are guarded, harder than before. Even Magda's lips are drawn into a narrow line. I push myself to my feet. I haven't touched my cup.

"Thank you for the tea, Magda," I say, heading for the door. "Sorry to bother you both."

The door closes firmly behind me.

Outside, the world is mud and puddles, and I wish I'd been able to trade these silly slippers for my leather boots. I make it two steps before my feet are soaked. Overhead the sky is already beginning to break apart, the clouds retreating.

I look to the west, to the village.

When I was Wren's age, I asked my father why the sisters lived all the way out here. He said that, for the people in Near, something was either all good or all bad. He told me witches were like people, that they came in all shapes and sizes, and they could be good or bad or foolish or clever. But after the Near Witch, the people in the village got it into their heads that all witches were bad.

The sisters stay out here because the villagers are afraid. But the important part is that they *stay*. When I asked my father why, he smiled, one of those soft, private smiles, and said, "This is their home, Lexi. They won't turn their backs on it, even though it turned its back on them."

I cast a last glance back at the sisters' hill, and leave. They're protecting the stranger. I know it.

I head back for the worn path, passing the shed that sits just to the north of the cottage.

If the sisters are hiding him, there must be a reason—

I catch my breath.

There is a dark gray cloak hanging from a nail on the shed, its hems darker than the rest, as if the fabric has been singed. The moor is unnaturally quiet in the post-rain afternoon, and I am suddenly very aware of my steps, of the sound they make on the wet earth as I approach the shed. The structure seems to be losing a very slow war with gravity. It is a cluster of wooden beams stuck into the soil, supporting a messy roof. Between the slats, the moor grows up, weeds taking hold, doing as much to keep the shed up as to tear it down. There is a door beside the cloak, but no handle. The strips of warping wood have gaps between them, and I lean in and press my eye to one of the narrow openings. The dim interior is empty.

I step back, sigh, and bite my lip. And then, from the other side of the shed, I hear it—a soft exhale. I smile and slide silently toward the sound, bending my knees and begging the earth to absorb my steps without giving me away. I round the corner. And there is no one. Not even footprints in the grass.

Letting out an exasperated breath, I stomp back around the shed. I know the sounds that people make just living, and I know that someone was here. I heard him breathing, and I saw the—

But the nail is bare, and the cloak is gone.

4

I quicken my pace as I head home, frustrated and chilled from sloshing through the wet grass. My slippers are ruined. The path splits, one narrow line leading into town, the other arching up around Near to my house. I veer toward home, slipping off the soaked shoes and walking barefoot up the path, succumbing to the mud. It coats my feet, my ankles, climbing up my calves, and I think of Dreska's sharp tongue, telling me I could eat dirt and grow no closer to the moor. I don't suppose covering myself in mud will do much good, either.

Eventually Otto's house comes into sight, and just beyond it, ours. The moor takes over beyond our yard, fluttering out like a cape. A wood stack sits to one side of our house, a small vegetable garden to the other, clumps of green interwoven with orange and red. The garden belongs to Wren more than me. Few things flourish in moor soil, but Wren loves our little plot, and shows an odd streak of gentleness whenever she tends it. Sure enough, that's where she is now, perched on a stone just outside the marked-off patch, gingerly plucking a weed from the dirt.

"You're back," she calls as I draw near.

"Of course. Where is everyone?" My exit from the town square wasn't my most subtle departure, and my uncle will have words for me, I'm sure.

"Wren." My mother's voice wanders like smoke from the house, and a moment later she's standing in the doorway, her fine dark hair curling in wisps around her face. Wren hops down from the stone and skips over to her. My mother's eyes find mine.

"Lexi," she says, "where did you run off to?" Her down-turned mouth confirms it. Otto will indeed want words with me.

"Helena had forgotten something for me at her house," I say, the lie building in my mouth only a moment after I think it. "She was so swamped by her audience, she asked me to go get it myself." I feel around in my dress pockets for proof, but they're empty, so I pray my mother doesn't ask for evidence. She doesn't, only blows out a small breath and floats back inside the house.

I miss my mother. I miss the woman she was before my father died, the one who stood straight and proud and looked out at the world with fierce blue eyes. But there are rare moments when it helps that she's become a shell, a ghost of her former self. Ghosts ask fewer questions.

I turn away from the house. I'm losing my lead. Soon Otto will figure out where the stranger is, if he doesn't know already. If I'm going to find him, I clearly need to catch him off guard. But how? I smooth my hair back and peer up at the sky. The sun is still high and the wood stack by the house is low, and I feel the need to move. I set aside my ruined slippers, take the boots from the side of the house, and trudge off in search of kindling.

*

The ax comes down on the wood with a crack. My dress is dirty and my boots are caked with mud from stomping through the fields after the rain. They were my father's— dark brown leather with old buckles, soft and strong and warm, the insides worn to fit his feet. I have to stuff the toes with socks so they won't fall off, but it's worth it. I feel better wearing them. And they look better this way, freshly stained. I cannot imagine them clean and in the cupboard.

Sitting still is not a skill I have. I never could stop moving, but it's gotten even worse these last three years.

A bead of sweat runs down my face, instantly cooling in the late afternoon air. I put another piece of wood on an old tree stump that sits between Otto's house and ours, lift the ax, and bring it down again.

This feels right.

My father taught me to chop firewood. I asked him once if he wished he had a son, and he said, "Why? I've got a daughter just as strong." And you wouldn't guess it by my narrow frame, but I am.

The ax comes down.

"Lexi!" bellows a deep voice behind me. I set the ax on the stump and begin picking up the split wood.

"Yes, Uncle Otto?"

"What do you think you're doing?"

"Chopping wood," I say, my voice on the narrow line between matter-of-fact and rude.

"You know to leave it. Tyler can come around and do it for you."

"The stack was low, and my mother needs it to bake. I'm only doing what you wanted, Uncle. Helping." I turn and head for the wood stack. Otto follows.

"There are other ways for you to help."

Otto is still wearing his Protector face; his voice stern, edged with power. It may be his face and his voice, but it's not his title. It was my father's first.

"And where are your shoes?" he asks, looking down at the mud-caked boots.

I drop the wood into the middle of the stack, and turn. "You wouldn't want me to ruin them, would you?"

"What I want is for you to listen to me when I tell you to do something. And more importantly, when I tell you *not* to do something."

He crosses his arms, and I resist the urge to mimic him. "I don't know what you mean."

"Lexi, I told you I didn't want you to go off today. Don't try to tell me you didn't."

I test out the lie a moment on my tongue, but it won't get past Otto as easily as it did my mother.

"You're right, Uncle," I say with a patient smile. One of his eyebrows peaks, as if he suspects a trap, but I go on. "I did go in search of the stranger, and look what I came back with." I hold my hands wide. "Nothing."

At the stump, I lift the ax, my fingers sliding into my father's grooves.

"It was a foolish task," I add. "I couldn't find him. He's gone."

The ax drives deep into the stump, sticking with a heavy thud.

"So I came home. And here I am. Relax, Uncle. All is well." I dust my hands off, let one come to rest on Otto's shoulder. "So, what did Helena have to say?"

"Not enough," says Otto, looking down at my father's boots. "Says she saw something, a shadow, maybe our stranger, in the clearing by her house. Claims she doesn't know which way he went. That he just vanished."

"Helena's always loved a good story," I offer. "She can make one out of nothing." It is a lie, of course. She prefers to have me tell the stories to her.

Otto isn't even listening. He's looking over me, and his eyes are even farther away. Dark, lost eyes.

"What happens next?" I ask.

He blinks. "For now, we wait."

I manage to nod calmly before I turn away, the frown creeping across my face. I don't trust for a minute that that's all my uncle has in mind.

*

Tonight there is no moon, and therefore no moonlight playing on the walls. Nothing to entertain those who cannot sleep. I am unbearably awake, but not because of the stranger.

It's the wind.

That same sad note is back again, weaving through the air, and there's something else, a sound that makes me shiver. No matter how I turn away or bury my face in the sheets, I keep hearing something—or someone—calling, just loud enough to pierce the walls. The voice is surely something more than wind, curling and twisting itself into highs and lows, like muffled music. I know that if only I could lean closer, words would become clear, distinct. Words that wouldn't break apart before I can wrap my mind around them.

I push the covers back, careful not to wake Wren, and let my feet slide to the wooden floor. Then I remember my father's words and pull my feet back into bed, hovering awkwardly on the edge, halfway between the motion of standing and slipping back down.

The trees all whisper, leaves gossiping. The stones are heavy thinkers, the sullen silent types. He used to make up stories for everything in nature, giving it all voices, lives. *If the moor wind ever sings, you mustn't listen, not with all of your ears. Use only the edges. Listen the way you'd look out the corners of your eyes. The wind is lonely, love, and always looking for company.*

My father had lessons and he had stories, and it was up to me to learn the difference between the two.

The wind howls and I discard my father's warning, stretching my ears to meet the sound, to unravel it. My head begins to ache dully as I listen, trying to make words where there are none. I give up, slipping back beneath the sheets, folding myself into my cocoon so that the wind song comes through broken.

Just as I'm about to find sleep, Wren shifts beside me. She rouses, and I hear the soft padding of feet as she slides from the bed and crosses the room, slipping out in search of our mother's bed.

But something is off.

There's a slight creak, the sound of footsteps over one of the two warped boards between the bed and the window. I sit up. Wren is standing, framed by glass and wooden borders, her blond hair almost white in the darkness. Without the shell of blankets, I can hear the wind again, the music on it, and the almost-words that hum against my skull.

"Wren?" I whisper, but she doesn't turn around. Am I dreaming?

She reaches one hand up to the clasp pinning the window shut, and turns it. Her small fingers curl around the bottom lip of the window, trying to slide it up, but it weighs too much for her. It has always weighed too much. I realize for the first time that the shutters are open beyond the window glass. I don't remember unlocking them, but there they are, thrown back, exposing the night beyond. Wren presses her fingers against the wooden lip, and somehow the window begins to slide up a fraction.

"Wren!"

I'm out of bed and at her side before she can get any farther, pulling her back into the room and closing the gap where the cool air is seeping in. I look for something out on the moor, something that would have drawn my sister to the window, but there is nothing. Nothing but the usual black-and-white night, the stray trees and rocks and the humming wind. I turn to face Wren, barring her path, and she blinks, the kind of startled blinks of a person waking suddenly. At my back the wind presses against the glass, and then it seems to break, dissolving into the dark.

"Lexi? What's wrong?" she asks, and I must seem crazed, stretching myself across the window frame and looking at my sister as if she's possessed. I peel myself from my post, ushering her back to bed. On my way I light the three candles, and they burst to life and fill the room with yellow light. Wren slides beneath the covers, and I climb in beside her, resting my back against the headboard, facing the candles and the window and the night beyond.

5

Knock. Knock. Knock.

I curl deeper beneath the blankets. I can tell by the smell alone that it's morning. Bread and late-summer air. I don't know when I fell asleep, or if I only slipped into that space between...

Knock. Knock. Knock.

I hear the front door open.

My shoulders and neck are stiff, my head pounding and my thoughts too thick as I pull myself from the bed and lean back against it. I listen, but the voices at the door are too low to be deciphered through the walls. One grumble is distinct enough, and I wonder how long Otto has been here. I pull my clothes on and open my bedroom door, pausing in the doorway.

"Sometimes boys wander off, Jacob," says Otto.

Jacob Drake?

"Think," adds my uncle. "Where might he have gone?"

"No," answers a thin, nervous voice. It is indeed Mr. Drake, Helena and Edgar's father. "He wouldn't. He's afraid of the dark... Afraid of the day, too." He adds a sad, strangled chuckle.

I hear Otto pacing back and forth. "Well don't just stand there," he says finally. "Come in. You too, Bo."

I wait until they've gone into the kitchen before slipping in behind them.

"Could someone have taken him?" asks Otto, accepting a mug of coffee from my mother.

Mr. Drake is slight and unimposing, with hair that must once have been as white-blond as Helena's and Edgar's, but now is flecked with silver. He stands in the middle of the kitchen, crossing his arms and then uncrossing them as he and Otto talk.

"No, no, no," he mumbles. "Who? Who'd have taken him?"

"Did anyone see anything?"

My mother is kneading dough, and shakes her head slowly. Bo limps over to the table and leans against it. The limp is subtle, the relic of a bad fall a few years back, but it makes his steps sound uneven on the floorboards. He chews on a wedge of berry-flecked bread, eyes darting between the other two men.

"What's going on?" I ask.

"Edgar's gone," says Mr. Drake, turning tired eyes toward me.

My stomach drops. "What do you mean, gone?"

There's a knock at the door, and Mother disappears to answer it, Otto still trying to calm Mr. Drake down.

"Let's talk this out," says my uncle. "Walk me through it..."

Mother reappears, an old man on her heels. Not old like the sisters, who seem to crumble and yet never change. Simply *old*. Master Eli. From the Council. His iron-gray hair looks sharp, trailing across his gaunt face. I take a small step back to make room. Mr. Drake and Otto have their heads bowed together, talking, Bo leaning in with one shoulder as if only half interested. They all look up as Master Eli takes a seat.

"What do we know?" he rasps. Something creaks, and I don't know if it's him or the chair. Otto straightens, turning to address the Council member.

"Edgar vanished from his bed last night," he explains. "There's been no sign of him. No sign of struggle. We'll call together a search party. He can't have gone far."

"I just don't understand," mumbles Mr. Drake.

Otto offers a determined frown and sets his mug down. I notice that his hands are red, and he's still wearing his butcher's smock. He clamps his hand on Mr. Drake's slight shoulder and promises that they will find his son. When he lets go, his fingers leave behind a smudge of half-dried blood.

"We don't know any more than that yet, Eli," he says. My uncle is probably the only man in town who can get away with calling the Council members by their names but not their titles. A small benefit of his station, and one he apparently enjoys.

"Poor boy," murmurs my mother, and I turn to see her comforting Wren, who seems perplexed. I can tell my sister thinks our mother is overreacting.

"Stop worrying," Wren says, trying to get free. "He's just playing a game."

"Hush, dear," says my mother, casting a glance at the rest of the room. Master Eli gives her a strange look, and it's hard to tell if it's pity or something harsher. His eyes are dark, set deep beneath his brow. His face crinkles up like paper.

"It's a game," Wren persists. "I'm sure of it."

But I am not so sure. I saw my little sister try to climb out the window last night. I reach for Wren's hand as the men in the kitchen gather their guns and murmur the names of a dozen others they can recruit.

"Otto," Bo chimes in for the first time, "the rest are waiting in town for word. Where will we start looking?"

"We'll meet the others in the square. We can start there and work our way out to all sides."

"That's a waste," I cut in. "You should start at Edgar's house and head out toward the village perimeter, not in toward the center."

"Lexi," warns Otto, casting a glance around the room. Bo wrinkles his nose. Mr. Drake turns away. Master Eli leans back in his chair and looks vaguely amused. Vaguely. Otto turns red.

"Edgar's house is in the west," I press, "so you start there and work away from the village. It doesn't make much sense to spend time heading inward."

"And why is that?" asks Master Eli. His amusement is cool and cutting. His eyes seem to say, *Foolish little girl*.

"If someone did take Edgar," I explain calmly, "they'd never try to hide him in town. There's too many people in too small a space. They'd take him out, away from the houses. Toward the moor."

The old man's smile fades as he turns back to my uncle, waiting. Otto picks up the cue.

"Lexi, I'm sure your mother could use help with the baking. Go be useful." I have to clench my jaw to keep from answering. "Let's go," he says, turning his back on me.

Bo and Mr. Drake follow Otto. Master Eli pushes himself to his feet. I can hear his bones cracking and popping into place. He passes Otto and pauses, resting a skeletal hand on my uncle's shoulder.

"Do you have a plan?" he asks, and I swear his deep-set eyes swivel back in my direction.

Otto looks offended, but he quickly checks himself.

"Yes, of course."

Master Eli gives a short nod and continues past my uncle, who turns on his heel and lifts his gun from the counter.

"Let me go with you, Otto," I say.

"Not today, Lexi," my uncle says, his voice a fraction softer without the other men around. "I can't."

"*All children,*" says Master Eli from the door frame, "are to remain at home until the culprit is caught and the boy found."

"I'm not a child, *Master.*" And I certainly won't be bossed by you, I add silently.

"Close enough." And then he's gone. Otto follows him out. I linger in the doorway, just out of sight, and hear them as they reach the front door and join the two other men, boots scuffing the threshold.

"What about the stranger?" asks Mr. Drake, and my chest tightens. The stranger. I'd almost forgotten about him. Almost.

"He appears here in the village, and the next night a child vanishes," says Bo.

"I knew something like this would happen," grunts Otto. "I should have dealt with him yesterday."

"No one blames you for waiting."

"You know where he is?" asks Mr. Drake.

"Of course we know."

"We are relatively certain," corrects Master Eli in a creaking voice, "that he is with the Thorne sisters. If he's still in town."

"Why would a stranger take Edgar?" asks the boy's father softly.

"More likely a stranger than any of us," says Otto. I hear him shift his gun in his arms.

"Why would *anyone* take him?"

"Start with what we know."

"And what is that?"

"There is a stranger in the town of Near. And now a boy is missing."

That's not much, I think.

"First things first. The boy. We'll deal with the stranger later."

The door swings closed and the men are gone. I wait for the sound of their boots to fade before retreating into the kitchen. My mother goes back to her bread, her mouth settling into a thin line, a faint crease between her eyes as her fingers find their way absently over loaf pans and proofing bowls. Back to work, as if nothing's changed. As if there isn't a growing mass of questions, all tangled up.

I fall into a chair at the table, rapping my fingers on the old scarred wood. Mother slides a scraper across a board and gathers up a few small pieces of clinging dough, too caked with flour to use for bread. Wren happily takes the lump and begins shaping the mass into a heart, a bowl, a person.

Another ritual.

My mother gives Wren these bits of dough each morning, letting her shape them, ruin them, and shape them again until she's happy. Then my mother will bake toys that only last until the end of the day.

It feels wrong to have rituals right now, for things to continue in their carved-out way when something has cut through the routine.

The room fills with heavy quiet. I lean forward. I stand up. I need to give the group of men time to get far enough away that I don't risk crossing paths, but I can't just sit here.

If everyone is looking for Edgar, they won't be looking for the stranger. Now is my chance. I turn to leave, and pause halfway to the hall.

I expect my mother to stop me, to warn or lecture or say anything, anything at all, but she doesn't even look up.

She would have stopped me, once, fixed me with her strong eyes. She would have made me fight for it. Now she just turns to the oven and begins to hum.

I sigh and slip out into the hall.

Halfway to the front door, a shape springs up before me and I nearly run into Wren. How she got from the table to here without a sound, I do not know.

"Where are you going?" she asks.

I kneel, looking at her face-to-face, my hands resting on her shoulders. "I'm going to the sisters, Wren," I say, surprised by how quietly it comes out.

Her eyes widen, blue circles like pieces of sky. "Is it a secret?" she whispers back. In my sister's world, secrets are almost as much fun as games.

"Very much so," I say, my fingers dancing down her arms to her hands, cupping them in mine. I bring our cradled hands up to my lips, whispering into the small place between her palms. "Can you keep it for me?"

Wren smiles and pulls her hands back to her, still cupping the secret as she might a butterfly. And with that, I kiss my sister's hair and hurry out.

*

Half an hour later, I stumble through the grove and up the path to the sisters' cottage. The windows are thrown open, but the house is quiet, and I slow my step, trying to muffle the sound of my approach so I don't attract notice. I have no desire to face the stony expressions of the sisters right now.

I veer left to the shed, and there on the nail is the gray cloak with its blackened edges. As difficult as it is, I slow to a creep and soundlessly approach the shed. People tend to put their weight on the balls of their feet when they don't want to be heard, but in truth, it's better to walk heel to toe, distributing the weight in slow, smooth motions. I circle around the leaning wooden structure. It is the kind with only one opening, the door in front of me. Either he's in there, or he's not. I press my ear to the rotting wood. Nothing.

I chew my lip, weighing my options. I don't want to frighten him off. But I don't want to let him slip away either. I had hoped to catch him off guard, but it seems there's no one here to catch.

"Hello?" I say at last, my ear still pressed against the door. I can hear my own word vibrate through the boards, and I pull back slightly. "I just want to talk," I add, my voice softer, lower, the kind of voice for sharing secrets. It's not a voice I use often, except with Wren. It's the voice my father used to tell me stories. "Please talk to me."

Nothing. I pull the door open, and it groans, but the small space inside is bare. The door swings shut as I step back. Where is he? I wonder, running my fingers over the gray cloak on the nail, the fabric old and worn. All this time lost coming here instead of trailing Otto into town, instead of looking for Edgar.

"What a waste," I murmur into the wooden boards. They groan in reply. My eyes widen as I push off the shed and whip around the corner. The stranger won't slip away again.

And there he is. Almost close enough to touch. He stands there against the moor and looks at me—stares at me—with his large eyes, an even gray like coals or river stones without the slick of water. The wind runs through his dark hair and over clothes that might once have been a color but are now gray, or might once have been black but are now faded. Just like his cloak. He crosses his arms as if he's cold.

"You." That's all I manage to say. There is something startlingly familiar about him. I have never seen anyone so fair-skinned and dark-haired, with such cool, colorless eyes. And yet, the light that dances in them, and that strange pull, like gravity tipped over...

"Who are you?" I ask.

He cocks his head, and I realize for the first time how young he is. He cannot be much older than I am, a few inches taller, and too thin. But flesh and blood, not the phantom on the moor beyond my window who seemed to bleed right into the night.

"Where did you come from?" I ask, examining his features, his clothes, painted in shades of gray. He looks out over my shoulder and says nothing. "Why are you here?"

Still nothing.

"A boy's gone missing today. Did you know?" I ask, searching for some recognition in his eyes, some sign of guilt.

He sets his jaw and strides past me, back toward the shed and the sisters' house. I follow him, but as we reach the shack he still shows no sign of stopping to speak to me. I grab his arm and pull him back. He winces at my touch, withdraws so fast that he stumbles back against the wooden slats. And now he will not even look at me, turning his eyes away and onto the moor.

"Say something!" I cross my arms. He lets his weight sag against the shed. "Did you take Edgar?"

His brow furrows, and his eyes finally return to mine.

"Why would I do that?"

So he *can* speak. Not only that, but his voice is smooth and strangely hollow, echoing. He seems to wish he hadn't spoken, because he closes his eyes and swallows as if he could take the words back.

"Why did you hide from me yesterday?"

"Why were you trying to find me?" he replies.

"I told you. There's a boy missing."

"Today there is. But you tried to find me yesterday." The challenge flickers in his eyes, but it dies away just as fast. And he's right, I wanted to see him yesterday, when Edgar was safe and sound. I wanted to see if he was real.

"There are no strangers in the town of Near," I say, as if that explains everything.

"Nor am I in it." He gestures to the ground at his feet, and I understand. We are officially out of town, on the open moors. He pushes himself off the wall and stands to his full height, looking down at me.

He is not a phantom or a ghost, not a crow-thing or an old man. He's just a boy, as solid and real as I am. My hand did not go through his skin, and his back made a sound as it met the shed. And yet, he is not like me. He is not like anyone I have ever seen. Not just his ghostly skin and dark features, but his voice, his manner.

"I'm Lexi. What's your name?" I ask.

He seems to be mute again.

"Well, if you won't tell me, I'm going to give you one."

He looks up, and I swear I can see a sad smile tease the edges of his lips. But he says nothing, and the smile—if it was one—slides back beneath the pale surface.

"Maybe I'll call you Robert or Nathan," I say, watching his face. His eyes. His hair. "Ah, maybe Cole."

"Cole?" he says quietly. His forehead wrinkles up. "Why?"

"Your hair and your eyes—you look like coal. Like ashes."

He frowns and turns his eyes back to the ground.

"You don't like it?"

"No," he says. "I don't."

"Well, too bad," I say lightly. "Unless you give me your name, I'm going to have to call you Cole."

"I don't have a name," he says, and sighs, as if talking so much is tiresome.

"Everyone has a name."

Silence falls between us. The boy watches the grass, and I watch him. He fidgets, as if being here with me is uncomfortable, as if my gaze is painful.

"What's a waste?" he says suddenly.

"Excuse me?"

"You said that to the shed door, that it was a waste. What did you mean?"

I cross my arms. The wind is picking up.

"Coming all this way to find you, and having you not be here. That would have been a waste."

"Do they have any idea what might have happened to him?" he says after a moment. "The missing boy?"

"No." I turn back toward the sisters' house, hoping *they* have some answers. "No one knows." Myself included. I am no closer to finding Edgar than I was this morning. I don't know why I felt the need to come here instead, to question a boy who hardly has a word to say. I look back one last time. "You should have come into the village and introduced yourself. Now they will suspect you."

"Do you suspect me?"

My feet stop. "I do not know you."

Again my eyes snag on him. There is something in him, distant and sad, this thin boy, his hollow eyes and his singed travel cloak. I cannot stand to blink while looking at him, in case he is not there when I open my eyes. He lifts his chin, as if trying to hear a far-off voice. For a moment he looks unbearably lost, and then he turns and walks away, out into the hills, seeming to put as many weeds and wildflowers between us as possible.

I trudge back toward the sisters' house, checking the angle of the sun in the sky. I'm losing time. How long do I have until Otto returns home? I should have just followed the search party. But I can't fault myself for wanting to talk to the stranger. I needed to see him for myself, to know if he did this, if he's involved.

I kick a stone. Now I have only more questions.

I pass the sisters' house, heading for the path home.

"Lexi," says Magda, calling me back. I spot her kneeling in the plot of dirt just beside the cottage. The patch that Magda calls her garden.

"You lied to me," I say, when I'm close enough, "about the stranger. He's here."

Magda cocks her head at me. "We told you we knew nothing about him. And we don't." She looks past me and out onto the moors. I follow her gaze. Far beyond the house, a thin shape wanders over the hills that dip away from the sisters' house in slow waves. On one of these rises, the boy in gray pauses, looking north, away from Near.

I frown and turn back to Magda, who is hunched over in the small patch of dirt again.

"Why did you call me back?" I ask, scuffing my boot along the patch of barren earth.

Magda doesn't answer, just goes on whispering something to no one at all, and brushing her gnarled fingers back and forth over the empty plot. I squat beside her.

"What are you doing, Magda?"

"Growing flowers, of course." She gestures to the dirt, where not so much as a weedy stem is poking through the soil. "Little rusty, is all."

Normally I'd be intrigued and would want to linger, on the off chance that I could catch a glimpse of Magda's craft. Hoping that she'd forget I was there beside her, and show it. But I don't have time today.

"Did you plant seeds?" I ask.

At this, she gives a dry laugh and whispers a few more things in the direction of the soil.

"No, dearie. I don't need any seeds. And besides, I'm growing moor flowers. Wildflowers."

"I didn't know you could, in this soil."

"You can't, of course. That's the point. Flowers are free-thinking things. They grow where they please. I'd like to see you try and tell a moor flower where to grow." Magda sits back and rubs her hands together.

I look down at the empty plot. I'm more than an hour behind Otto's men, with nothing to show for it. And for all I know, my uncle could be making his way home this minute. Maybe Magda knows something. Anything. Whether she'll *tell* me is another story.

"Magda, there's a boy missing. Edgar. He's five—"

"Little blond thing, yes? What happened?" she asks, turning her good eye up at me.

"No one knows. He vanished from his bed last night. They haven't found any trace yet."

Magda's face changes a fraction, the lines deepening, her bad eye growing darker and her good eye focused on nothing. She looks about to say something, but she changes her mind.

"Do you think someone took him?" I ask. Magda frowns and nods.

"The ground's like skin, it grows in layers," she says, pinching some soil in her crooked fingers. "What's on top peels back. What's underneath can work its way up, eventually."

I sigh, frustrated. Every now and then Magda does this, talking nonsense. In her mind it might very well be a logical train of thought, but it's a pity the rest of the world can't follow. I should have known she couldn't, or wouldn't, help me.

"The wind is lonely..." Magda adds in a voice so soft I almost miss it. The words snag on something, a memory.

"What did you—" I begin.

"Lexi Harris," says Dreska, appearing in the doorway. She motions at me with her cane, and I push myself to my feet and go to her. Taking my hand, she sets a small bundle in my palm. It's a pouch on a string, and it smells like the moor grass and the rain and wet stones.

"Give this to your sister," she says. "Tell her to wear it. For safety."

"So you *did* hear about Edgar."

Dreska gives a grim nod and folds my fingers over the charm. "We've made them for all the children."

"I'll give it to her." I slide the pouch into my pocket and turn to go.

"Lexi," says Magda. "I called you back for the same reason I invited you in yesterday. Because of him. I wondered whether you had heard talk of a stranger in Near." She points a dirt-caked fingernail at the stranger on the moor. I cast a last glance at the boy, his back still to us. He slides to the ground, and suddenly he doesn't look like a person, just a rock or a fallen tree jutting up from the tangled grass.

"Others will be looking for him, too," says Dreska.

I understand her meaning. "I won't tell. I am my father's daughter."

"We do hope you are."

I head back down the path, but turn and add, "You really don't know anything about him? Where he's from?"

"He is safer here," murmurs Magda, cupping dirt.

"He is keeping secrets," I say.

"Aren't we all," says Dreska with a dry laugh. "You do not believe he took Edgar." It is not a question. But she is right.

"No, I don't think he did it," I call, heading home. "But I mean to find out who did."

6

I make it home before Otto, and for that I am thankful. The high sun slides across the afternoon sky, and it's too late now to risk going into town, too great a chance of running into the search party. There's no sign of Wren or my mother, but the house is warm and smells of heated stones and bread. I realize how hungry I am. Half a loaf sits on the counter, along with some cold chicken, left out from lunch. I cut a couple pieces of each and devour them, relishing the freedom of solitude and being able to simply eat, rather than be delicate about it.

Feeling much better, I duck into my room, kicking off my boots and smoothing my hair. I pace the space at the foot of the bed and try to make sense of the day. My father taught me to listen to my gut, and my gut says that this strange, hollow boy did not take Edgar. But that doesn't mean I trust him yet. I do not *understand* him yet. And I do not like the way my chest tightens when my eyes snag on him, as it does for wild things.

Something else tugs at me, and I remember Magda's whispered words: *The wind is lonely.*

I know that line.

I cross to the small table by the window, the one with the leaning candles and the cluster of books, my fingers going straight to the one in the middle. The cover is green and pocked with indents, like the ones my father's fingers made on the knife and the ax. But these are from my fingers, my marks of use as much as his.

The frayed pages of the book smell earthy and rich, as though there is a part of the moor between the covers instead of paper. Whenever my father told a story, I asked him to put it down in here. The book is strangely heavy, like a stone, and I slip onto the bed with it, tracing my fingers over the soft cover before cracking it open and skimming the pages with my thumb. Three years ago, my father's handwriting vanished from this book, and mine took over.

There were so many blank pages left in his wake. I tried, now and then, to remember a snippet he might have forgotten to write down. Out walking, or delivering bread, or chopping wood, a sentence would sneak up on me in his rich voice, and I'd race to my room to write it down.

The wind is lonely.

I know that phrase.

I turn to an entry dated a few months after my hand replaced his:

Clouds seem like such sociable things in the moor sky. Father said they were the most spiritual things on the moors, that they went on pilgrimages every day, setting out as the sun rose, and coming together to pray. The rain, he teased—

The entry stops. Here and there the page ripples, dotted with small wet circles.

I flip back through the book, searching for an earlier entry, one he would have written himself. My thumb catches the corner of a page near the beginning, pinning it back.

Of course. It's from the story I thought of last night.

If the moor wind ever sings, you mustn't listen, not with all of your ears. Use only the edges. Listen the way you'd look out the corners of your eyes. The wind is lonely, and always looking for company.

I run my fingers over the page. Why would Magda quote my father's words?

And then I see it. At the bottom of the page in my father's small script, the letters *M. T.* Magda Thorne. This story doesn't belong to my father—he only copied it. But what does it mean now, coming from Magda's lips in the garden?

The front door opens with a soft groan, and I blink and close the book. How long have I been sitting here, wondering on bedtime poems? Wren's patter of feet reaches me from the hall, her light bouncing steps on the floorboards. I can't hear my mother's, but I know she must be with her. Pushing myself up from the bed, I clutch the book to my chest and head into the kitchen.

Wren is sitting on the table, swinging her legs and playing with one of her baked toys.

I lean against the door frame, holding the book close as my mother wanders like a ghost, setting an empty basket down, picking up an apron, all without a sound. Wren smiles at me and curls her fingers, beckoning me to the table, and when I'm there she reaches up with cupped hands to whisper, "Did you go to the sisters?"

I come close enough to kiss her hair and whisper back, "I did. I'll tell you all about it later."

She bounces happily.

"Wren." My mother doesn't look up, but her voice wafts through the room. "Can you go fetch me some basil from your garden?"

Wren hops down from the table and bounds out. The front door groans shuts. I wait for my mother to speak to me, to ask me where I've been, but she says nothing.

"I went to see the sisters," I offer. "They hadn't heard about Edgar."

Her gaze floats up. Why won't she speak?

"I saw the stranger, too. I spoke to him, and he's not to blame, I don't think. He has the oddest—"

"You shouldn't have gone, Lexi."

"You didn't stop me."

"Your uncle—"

"Is not my father. Or my mother."

She sets a towel down and circles the table. "Otto is only trying to protect you."

"And you?" My fingers tighten on the book. "You could have stopped me."

"You wouldn't have listened," she says.

"You could have tried…" I start, but my words fade as my mother's fingers, ghostly white with flour, come to rest on my back. Her touch is light—not gentle, but thin, ethereal. For a moment I am reminded of the stranger. And then her fingers tighten and her eyes find mine, and something flickers in her, fierce and hot.

"I *am* trying, Lexi," she whispers, "to help you."

The glimpse of the woman my mother used to be catches me off guard. Just a moment, and then it's fading, and her fingers are sliding weightlessly away. I want to speak, but when I open my mouth, another voice breaks through from somewhere outside. Then another joins. And another.

The moment is over. My mother is back at the counter, turning out dough from a proofing pan, looking a hundred miles away.

"I didn't see him," I offer quickly, the sounds of men drawing closer. "I never went." I wait for her to look up and offer a knowing smile or a nod, but she doesn't even seem to hear me.

I swallow, tuck the book under my arm, and slip down the hall. The voices are coming from the west, building on each other like thunder, from where the village sits, hidden by hills. I position myself in the doorway, shivering as the wind cuts through.

What did my mother mean?

I take several long deep breaths, trying to get air past the rocks in my throat.

The book falls open in my hands to Magda's entry, as several members of the search party trudge into sight, looking like shadows cast by the sinking sun. Their faces are long and thin, their brows heavy, shoulders hunched. Their hopes of finding Edgar, at least of finding him alive, must be waning with the light. I watch them from my post, glancing up from the book and trying to give the look of a docile, patient girl.

My thumb traces over the words, *The wind is lonely*.

The men pause at Otto's house and exchange a few low words. Then the group breaks apart, scattering like seeds on a gust of wind.

I step aside as Otto stomps past and into our house, avoiding my gaze. And there, a few strides behind him, a tall boy marches over, his shock of dirty-blond hair glowing in the dusky light. Tyler Ward. His pace slows to a stroll as he sees me, a smile teasing the corners of his mouth, even now. He's trying and failing to look appropriately sober, considering the situation. He slips into the doorway with me, weaving his fingers through mine.

"Pretty sunset," he says, and his imitation of the brooding and forlorn is almost funny.

"No luck?" I ask, pulling my hand away.

He shakes his head, and I can't believe it, but it's almost dismissive. I bite my tongue and force a calm smile.

"Where did you look?"

"Why?" He shoots a blue-eyed glance at me from behind his hair.

"Come on, Tyler," I say. "You're always complaining of not having enough adventure. Regale me. What did you do today? Where did you go?"

"Otto said you'd ask, said you'd try to go off on your own. That would be unsafe, Lexi," he says with a frown. "I'm afraid I cannot risk you getting hurt." His eyes wander down my hands to a small nick, a splinter from chopping wood. He runs his fingertips over it. "I would have done that for you."

"I didn't want to wait," I say, pulling my hand away.

"And I'm more than able." Tyler falls into a strange quiet, and I step closer and brush his jaw with my fingers, guiding his chin up. "The town square? The Drakes' house? That field we used to play in, the one full of heather?"

He offers a slanted grin. "What will you give me for it?"

"This is serious," I say. "It's almost dark, and Edgar's still missing."

He looks away, leaning heavily back against the door frame with a frown. It looks wrong on his face, which is so used to smiling. "I know, Lexi. I'm sorry."

"Have you been to see Helena? Is she all right?"

He interlaces his fingers behind his head and looks away.

I let out an exasperated sigh. The doorway is not big enough for both of us, and I step past him and out into the yard. Tyler trots after me.

"I'll tell you if you answer a question for me."

I stop walking away but don't turn around. I wait for him to reach me, hugging the book to my chest. The wind picks up, the cold air prickling my skin. The world is turning a bruised shade as the light fades. Tyler stops just behind my back. I can almost feel his outstretched hand as he tries to decide whether to touch me or not.

"Why are you doing this to me?" comes his voice, just loud enough to cross the narrow space between us.

"I'm not doing anything, Tyler." But I know it's a lie. And so does he.

"Lexi," he says, and the voice is strange, almost pleading, "you know what I want. Why won't you even—"

"Why won't I give you what you want, Tyler?" I ask, spinning on him. "Is that what you're asking?"

"Lexi, be fair. Give me a chance." He reaches out, brushes a coil of dark hair from my face. "Tell me what you're afraid of. Tell me why I can be your friend your entire life, and yet you won't entertain the thought of—"

"*Because* you're my friend," I interrupt. That's not the whole truth. *Because I loved the little boy you were, and now you're growing up to be something else.*

"I've always been your friend, Lexi. That will never change. Why can't we be more?"

I take a deep breath. The wild grass rolls away from me toward Near.

"Do you remember," I say over the growing wind, "when we were little, and we used to play those games, the spinning games?"

"Of course I remember. I always won."

"You always *let go*. You let go when you thought it would be funny, and the circle broke apart, and everyone fell down except you."

"It was just a game."

"But everything's a game to you, Tyler." I sigh. "All of it. And it's not about skinned knees anymore. You just want to win."

"I want to be with you."

"Then be with me as a friend," I say. "And help me find Edgar."

Tyler looks back at the house, the silhouette of my uncle in the window as he washes his hands. When Tyler turns back to me, he's smiling again, a thinner version of his usual grin.

"No one will ever be good enough for you, Lexi Harris."

I smile back. "Maybe one day—"

"When the moon shines—" he says.

"In the grass-green sky," I finish. A line my father used to say. Tyler walked around for days repeating it. And for a moment we're just two kids again in a spinning game or a field of heather, grinning until our faces hurt.

Then the wind bristles. The last bit of light is bleeding away, replaced by a rich blue darkness. I fight off a shiver, and Tyler slides out of his coat, but I shake my head. He seems caught between actions, so he just lets the coat hang there in his hand, both of us suffering.

"Now it's your turn to talk," I say, trying to keep my teeth from chattering.

"I do love talking," he says, "but Otto's going to have my head for telling you this, Lexi."

"When has that ever stopped you?"

His smile fades as he slides his coat back on, squares his shoulders, and holds his head up in an almost perfect imitation of my uncle. "We went with Edgar's father, Mr. Drake, to his house. Edgar's bedroom was untouched. The window was open, but that was all. Like he just got up and left. Climbed through." My mind flashes to Wren walking in her daze to the window, trying to slide it open.

"His mother said she tucked him in last night. She said she didn't hear anything strange."

"Edgar's afraid of everything. He wouldn't just leave."

Tyler shrugs. "All we know is there was no struggle, and the window was open. We headed west, into those fields by their house, all the way to the edge of the village."

So they took my advice, after all.

"We looked everywhere, Lexi."

Everywhere in Near, I think.

Tyler sighs, and I can't help but think he's almost handsome without the egotistical smile.

"Everywhere. There's not a single trace of him. How does that happen?" He frowns, kicking at a stray pebble. "I mean, everyone leaves marks, right?" He shakes his head, straightening. "Otto thinks it's that stranger. Makes sense, if you think about it."

"Do you have any evidence?" I ask, careful to sound neutral. "Do you even know where he is?"

Tyler nods. "Got a good idea. Only so many places a person can hide in Near, Lexi. If he's still here."

I hope he is. The thought slips in, and I'm suddenly thankful for the thickening dark.

"What happens now?" I ask.

"Lexi!" a heavy voice calls from the door. I turn to see Otto waiting, outlined against the light from inside. Tyler gestures toward the house, his hand coming to rest against my back, urging me toward the door. Otto fades back inside.

"Now," Tyler says quietly, "we get the witches to give up the stranger." His nose wrinkles when he says *witches*.

"Assuming he's still here," I say as we reach the door. "And assuming the sisters have him, and assuming Dreska doesn't curse you for making that face. That's assuming a lot, Tyler."

He shrugs. "Maybe we'll get lucky."

"You need a lot more than luck."

He cocks his head to one side, sending blond hair into his eyes.

"How about a kiss, then," he says, leaning over me with a smirk. "For good measure?"

I smile back, stretching onto my toes. And then I step back and shut the door on Tyler.

I swear I can hear him kiss the wood on the other side.

"Good night, cruel girl," he calls through the door.

"Good night, silly boy," I call back, standing at the door until his footsteps fade into nothing.

7

Wren is skipping up and down the hall in her nightgown, playing games with the wooden floorboards. Her bare feet land with light thuds like rain on stones. Wren knows a thousand games for times between. Between meals and bed. Between people paying attention to her. Games with words and rules, and games without. *Thud, thud, thud* on the wooden floor.

The floorboards in our house seem to have their own tunes, so Wren makes a kind of music by landing on the different planks. She's even found a way to pound out the Witch's Rhyme, a bit clumsily. She is hitting the final bits of the song when I hop into her path, and she just giggles and bounces around me without even missing a note.

I slip into our bedroom and put my father's book back on its shelf beside the three candles. Beyond the window the darkness slides in heavy and tired and thick.

I cannot stop thinking about Tyler's words. *Everyone leaves marks.*

I slide a soft blue apron from the drawer and tie it around my waist, making my way to the kitchen. Otto is sitting at the table, a thick yellow band on each of his arms, talking with my mother. His voice is at the level adults use when they think they're being secretive, but that's loud enough to catch any child's ear. My mother is wiping crumbs and flour from the table, and nodding. I catch the word "sisters" before Otto sees me and changes his tone and his subject.

"You and Tyler have a good chat?" he asks, too interested.

"Good enough," I say.

"And how was your day, Lexi?" I can feel his eyes on me, and there's a challenge in his voice. I swallow and try to pick my lie when—

"She delivered bread with me," offers my mother, almost absently. "A child might be missing, but folks still need to eat." I bite the inside of my mouth to keep the shock from my face at my mother's lie. The image of her and Wren returning home with the empty basket flits into my mind, her sudden stern look as she told me she was trying to help.

I nod, cutting up the last of a loaf and setting it on the table with some cheese. My uncle grunts but says no more. My mother wraps a few extra loaves of bread in cloth, and slides her apron from her dress. It is the last thing she discards each night, when she must put the baking aside.

"And you, Uncle?" I ask. "Any signs of Edgar?"

His eyebrows knit, and he takes a long sip from his mug.

"Not today, no," he says into his cup. "We'll go back out in the morning."

"Perhaps tomorrow I could help."

Otto hesitates, then says, "We'll see." Which almost certainly means no, but he's too tired to argue. He pushes himself up, the chair grating against the floor as it slides back. "I'm on first patrol."

"Patrol?" I ask.

"We've got men all over the village, just to be safe." He taps the yellow bands. "To mark my men. Only a fool would be caught out tonight. I've given them all orders to shoot on sight."

Wonderful.

My uncle excuses himself. I sag into the vacated chair and try to remember if I own any yellow. From the hall come creaks and thuds; Wren is still playing her game. My mother meets my eyes but doesn't say anything, and I wonder if she knows what I plan to do. She yawns and kisses my forehead, her lips barely a breath against my skin, and then goes to tuck Wren in. The *thud, thud, thud* stops in the hall as my sister is led away to bed.

I sit there in the kitchen, waiting as the hearthstones grow cold. I think my mother bakes all day long, until her bones and muscles ache, so that when she collapses into bed each night there is no risk of lying awake, no risk of remembering. My father used to sit up with her, tell her stories until dawn, because he knew she loved the sound of his voice, thick as sleep around her.

I sit until the house is dark and still, until the quiet becomes heavy, as if everything is holding its breath. Then I push myself up and retreat to the bedroom.

The candles are already burning steadily on the shelf, casting pools of dancing light on the walls. I sit on top of the covers, fully clothed, and wait until Wren's breaths are the low and steady ones of deep sleep. She seems so small in her nest of blankets. My chest tightens as I picture Edgar climbing through his window and vanishing onto the moor. I shiver and ball my hands into fists. And then I remember. My palm still smells faintly of wet stones and herbs and earth where Dreska placed the charm and curled my fingers over it. How could I have forgotten it? I search through my pockets and exhale when I feel my fingers brush against the earthy pouch. I pull it out and hold it, and it feels odd in my hands—at once too heavy and too light. A pouch of grass and dirt and pebbles. How much power can it hold? I stifle a yawn and tie it around my sister's wrist. She stirs beneath my fingertips, eyes floating open.

"What's this?" mumbles Wren, looking down at the charm.

"It's a present from the sisters," I whisper.

"What does it do?" Wren asks, squirming into a seated position. She sniffs it. "Do you smell heather?" she asks, lifting it up to me. "And dirt? There shouldn't be dirt inside there."

"It's just a charm," I say, touching my fingertips to it. "I'm sorry I woke you. I forgot to give it to you earlier. Now," I say, holding the covers for her, "go back to sleep."

Wren falls back against the pillow with a nod. I tuck the blankets in around her, and she folds herself into a ball.

I sit on the edge of the bed and wait until Wren's breathing grows even again. Soon enough she is wrapped in sleep, fingers clutching the charm.

It's time to get to work.

I rummage through the low drawers and come up with a pale yellow scarf, a present from Helena two years back. I kiss it, say a silent thank-you to my friend and her love of knitting, and tie the scarf around my arm.

I take my father's knife and my green cloak, and pry the window gently up, holding my breath as it squeaks. Wren does not move. I slip through and hop to the ground beyond, sliding the window shut behind me and latching the shutters.

The lamps are lit in Otto's house, and he must be off patrol rotation, because through the window I can make out his form, leaning over a table. Bo sits near him, his hair hanging down between his eyebrows, and the two men grumble and drink, exchanging a word or two between sips. Uncle Otto has the kind of voice that goes through wood and glass and stone, and I slip near enough to hear him speak.

"As if he disappeared, out of his bed and into"—Otto waves his hand—"nothingness."

That's not possible, though. I'm sure there are marks, even if they're faint. Would Otto know what to look for? Grown men can certainly act like little boys, but can they think like them?

"Strange as strange," says Bo. "What do you think of it?"

"I think I best find the boy, and fast."

"You can't make something appear from nothing," offers Bo with a shrug.

"I have to," says Otto, taking a long drink. "It's my job."

The two men fall into silence, staring down into their cups, and I slip away. I pull the dark green cloak close around my shoulders and leave the men to their drinking, turning my attention toward the village. Edgar's house sits in a cluster of three or four to the west, a flat rim of field between that group of homes and the next. If there's a clue as to who took Edgar, and where, and how, then I'll find it.

I set out, the wind pushing me gently on.

*

In the moonlight the moor is a vast ghost of a place. Thin lines of fog leave the wild grass shimmering, and the breeze blows over the hills in slow waves. As the first cluster of homes comes into sight across the field, I wonder if the search party even bothered to look for the little boy's footprints. They wouldn't have been as deep as deer tracks. But there would have been something, a trace of life and movement. The ground around the house should be disturbed, should give some indication of which way Edgar went. *Everyone leaves a mark.*

In fact, that's what worries me. Everyone leaves a mark, and now a dozen bodies have been stomping through and around the house, crushing clues underfoot. I doubt I will ever be able to uncover them without the light of day, and bringing a candle or a lamp would have been too risky, especially with a night patrol. I can't afford for Otto's men to discover me. Even if they don't shoot me, my own private search will be at an end, and I'll likely find myself under house arrest. *For my own safety, my own good*, I scoff. Lot of good it did Edgar, tucked sleeping in his bed.

No, here darkness must be my ally. My father used to say that the night could tell secrets just as well as the day, and I'll have to hope he's right.

I make my way down the path that winds like a vein toward the heart of town, doing my best to avoid tripping on loose stones.

A crow floats overhead like a smudge on the night sky. The houses sit closer now, small yards separating them, and I slow my pace, making sure to spread my weight out through my stride, trying to make less noise than the wind around me. Someone coughs, and a moment later a man steps forward from one of the houses, a shadow against the dim light within. I freeze on the path, fingers twining around the edges of my cloak to keep it from billowing. The man leans in his doorway, smoking a pipe, a rifle in the crook of his arm just below a yellow band. I remember my uncle's words. *Shoot on sight.* I swallow hard. Another voice murmurs from inside the house, and the man glances back. In that moment, I slip from the path, darting for the darkness between two unlit cottages. Pressing myself against the wall of one, just beside a woodpile, I can see the fourth house, the farthest west. Edgar's house.

There is a light on inside, deep enough within that only a faint glow reaches the windows. I approach and kneel at the base of each one, letting my fingers and eyes linger on the ground beneath, searching for disturbance, for any sign of a foot or a hand landing. I reach Helena's window (I used to be jealous that she had her own room, but it seems impossible to envy her right now) and pause as I consider knocking gently on the glass. Given that a boy just vanished from this house, this seems a very bad idea. I touch my fingers to the pane and hope that my friend is well asleep within, then continue around the house. I linger at the last window, the one I know belongs to Edgar. This would have been the one they say was found open. I crouch at the ground, squinting in the faint light.

It's just as I thought. The surface is a web of prints: adult shoes, boots, slippers, old steps that slide, and younger ones that stomp. A battleground for feet. Still muddy from the rains, the earth has held on to many marks, but none of them small or boyish.

I stand up, fighting back frustration. *Think, think.* Maybe farther out the stomping of men will subside and give way to traces of smaller feet.

I lean back against the house, my head resting on the wall just beside the window frame, and let my eyes follow the line of sight outward from the window. In this direction lies a field, a stretch of wild grass and heather and rocks between this cluster of homes and the next, nested like eggs in the distance. Silvery moonlight spills out over the field, and I walk into it, taking slow steps, my eyes flicking from the tall grass brushing my legs to the hill ahead. The wind picks up enough to make the weeds rustle and sway.

A body exhales behind me.

I spin, but no one's there. The cluster of homes sits quietly half a field away, dark except for one or two dim lights. It might have been the wind, but it is high, and the sound was low. I resume my search when I hear it again. Someone is here, too close.

My eyes strain to make out the deeper shadows near the cut stone cottages, under the thatch eaves where the moonlight cannot reach. I wait, frozen, holding my breath. And then I see it. Something slips across the gap between the houses, caught for a moment by the fractured moonlight. The ghostly form is gone in a blink, vanishing behind a corner.

I sprint across the grass after the shadow, half tripping, and doing a very poor job of keeping the sound of my presence minimal as I run. I can hear my father's scolding voice as the twigs snap beneath my feet, and my shoes kick at stones, but I'm so close. I launch into the space between the homes. I catch sight of the figure just before it turns another corner. It pauses and twists as if seeing me, then cuts between the houses, heading north toward the shadow of a hill, vast and black. If it gets there before me, I know the form will vanish, a shadow inside a shadow.

I run, keeping my eyes leveled on it so that it does not become a part of the night.

It's almost there. My lungs start to burn. The figure moves over the tangled earth with sickening speed. I have always been fast, but I can't make up the ground. The wind whistles in my ears as the figure reaches the base of the hillside and disappears.

I've lost it, whatever it was.

My legs stop churning, and my boot catches on a low stone and launches me forward into the relative darkness at the foot of the hill. The form is here somewhere, so close I feel as if my fingertips might brush it with every outward grasp as I push myself up. But my fingers meet a sharp rock jutting out from the hill, and nothing more. The wind beats in my ears with my pulse.

And then the clouds slip in. They sweep silently across the sky and swallow the moon, and just like a candle snuffed out, the world goes dark.

The entire world vanishes.

I freeze in my tracks to prevent tumbling into another rock, or a tree, or something worse. Fingers still pressed against the rock, I take a deep breath and wait for the clouds to move on the way they should, since the wind carried them in so quickly. But the clouds aren't moving. The wind is blowing hard enough to whistle and whine, and yet the clouds seem impossibly frozen overhead, blotting out the moon. I wait for my eyes to adjust, but they don't. Nothing registers.

My heart is still racing, and it's not only from the rush of the hunt. This is different—a twinge I haven't felt in a long time.

Fear.

Fear as I realize the cluster of houses is out of sight. Everything is out of sight. And still, through it all I can feel the presence, the weight of another body nearby.

The wind changes, twists itself from a simple breeze into something else, something more familiar. It sounds almost like a song. There are no words, but highs and lows, like music, and for a moment I think I might still be in bed, pressed between the sheets. Dreaming. But I'm not. The strange tune makes me dizzy, and I try to block it out, but the world is so dark, there's nothing else to focus on. The music seems to grow clearer and clearer until I can almost tell which way it's coming from. I push off the rock and turn, taking a few cautious steps away from the hill, toward where the form was, when I could still see it.

My fingers reach for my father's knife, and I slip it from the sheath on my calf and hold it loosely, making my way like a blind man, knowing only that the slope is at my back. I remember running past a few low rocks, a tree, before everything went black, so my steps are wary, feeling for sharp edges. The wind keeps humming, a steady rise and fall, and I swear I know this song. A chill runs through me as I realize where I've heard it.

The wind on the moors is a'singing to me
The grass and the stone and the far-off sea

The wind and the sound wrap around me, the rise and fall of the melody growing louder and louder in my ears, and the world begins to spin. I stop walking to keep from falling down. The hair on my neck prickles, and I stifle the urge to scream.

Be patient with it, Lexi, my father's voice intrudes.

I try to calm down, try to slow my pulse, now so loud I can't hear anything over it. Holding my breath, I wait for the wind song to form a layer, a blanket of noise. Wait for my heart to become part of that blanket instead of a pounding drum in my head. A moment after my nerves start to settle, a new noise comes from a few feet away at the bottom of the hill. A weight steps down on the grass.

I spin back toward the sound just as the clouds abandon the moon overhead, shedding slivers of light that seem as bright as beacons after the heavy dark. The light glints off my knife, and the few scattered rocks, and the shadowed form, finally illuminating the outline of a man. I lunge, knocking him back against the slope. My free hand pins his shoulder, my knee on his chest.

The light grazes his throat and his jaw and his cheekbones, just the way it did when I first saw him beyond my window. I am looking into the same dark eyes that refused to meet my own on the hill by the sisters' house.

"What are you doing here?" I ask, the hunting knife against his throat. My heart is racing and my fingers tighten around the handle, and yet he neither flinches nor makes a sound, but simply blinks.

Slowly, the blade slides back to my side, but my knee lingers on his chest, pressing him into the grass.

"Why are you out here?" I ask again, biting back my annoyance, both at the fact he was able to sneak up on me, and the fact that I'm silently grateful he's here. He stares up at me appraisingly, his eyes as black as the night around us, and says nothing.

"*Answer me*, Cole," I warn, raising my blade. His jaw tenses, and he looks away.

"It's not safe out here. Not at night," he says at last. His voice is clear and smooth at once, cutting through the wind in an odd way, more parallel than perpendicular. "And my name isn't Cole."

"So you were following me?" I ask, pushing myself off him, trying not to let him see that I am shaking.

"I saw you out alone." He gets to his feet in an impossibly graceful motion, his gray cloak spilling over his shoulders. "I wanted to make sure you were all right."

"Why wouldn't I be?" I ask, too quickly. I take a deep breath. "Why did you run away?"

I wait, but he doesn't answer, instead studying the ground with an attention that's clearly avoidance. Finally he says, "Easier than trying to explain."

The last of the clouds slide away, and the moonlight illuminates the moor around us.

"You should go back to the sisters' house." I look around at the hill and the cluster of cottages behind us. When he doesn't move or speak, I turn to face him. "I mean it, Cole. If anyone sees you here..."

"*You* saw me here."

"Yes, but I don't think you took Edgar. Someone else might. You do realize you were in the village, by Edgar's house, the night after he went missing. You can see how it would look."

"So were you."

"But I'm from here. And I'm a tracker. My father was too. What are you?" I wince at how harsh my voice sounds.

"Once I realized what you were doing, I thought I could help," he says, and it's barely a whisper. I'm amazed I can hear it over the blustering wind.

"How?"

His dark eyebrows arch up. "I have good eyes. I thought I might find something. A clue or a trace."

"Or cover something up?" I know it sounds mean, but these are the questions my uncle will ask. The accusations he would make if he found the stranger in the western part of town tonight.

"You know it's not like that," he says, and he sounds frustrated. "I haven't done anything wrong."

I sigh. "I'm sorry, Cole." I look up at the moon, amazed at how far it's traveled across the sky. Around us, the night is growing bitter, and my head feels cloudy, tired. I'm losing time. "I've got to go."

I take a step back toward the houses, my hands still trembling faintly from the chase and the penetrating dark. Cole seems torn about what to do, his body turning one way, his head another. The moon casts enough light to make his skin glow. With his pale face, dark eyes, and sad mouth, he seems made of black and white, just like the world at night.

I begin to walk away when he speaks up.

"Lexi, wait," he says, reaching out for my wrist. He seems to reconsider and pulls back, but his fingertips graze my arm. It catches me off guard. "Maybe I can help, if you'll let me."

I turn back to him. "How?"

"I told you I have good eyes. And I think I found something. It's faint, but there. I'm sure of it." He holds his hand out, gesturing back to the cluster of homes across the tangled grass.

I hesitate. When I don't answer, he adds, "Just take a look." I nod. Cole leads me around the cluster of homes and to the west, to the field where I was when I first caught sight of the shadow. Edgar's window stares out at us, the dim light within making it glow faintly. Cole walks with me up to the window, and I swallow as I notice that he seems to make no sound. His feet touch the ground, leaving slight prints, but there's no crunch of leaves or drying grass beneath his shoes. My father would be impressed.

When we've almost reached the house, he turns around, looking out at the field much the way I did before.

"I already looked here," I say, frowning.

"I know," he says, gesturing to the heather and the knee-high grass. "It's faint. Do you see it?"

I squint, trying to find the object, the clue.

"Don't try so hard," he says. "Look at the big picture." He sounds just like my father, quiet, patient. I try to relax my eyes, pull back and take in the field. I draw a small breath in.

"See?"

And I do. It's subtle, and I am so attuned to details that I never would have seen it. The field. It ripples. There are no footsteps, no traces in the dirt, but the grass and heather bend ever so slightly, as if someone walked along the tops of them. As if the wind blew them over and they haven't had enough time to straighten up. A narrow strip of the wild grass leans like a path.

"But how?" I ask, half to myself, finding Cole's eyes. He frowns, giving a slight shake of his head. I look back at the trace. I don't understand it. But it's *something*. The windblown path veers north. I pull away from Edgar's house and begin to follow it out into the field.

"Don't," Cole says. "You shouldn't go alone."

"Why not? Because I'm a girl?"

"No," he says, his expression unreadable. "No one should walk out here alone." And after the strange darkness and the dizzying wind, I half believe he's right.

"Then you'd better come with me," I say, taking a few steps forward.

He hovers behind me, rocking his weight, and for a moment it looks as if he's not going to follow. He seems to change his mind at the last minute, though, and falls into step beside me. We follow the almost invisible path, the windblown road. It seems impossible that it could lead me to Edgar, since there are no signs of his small feet. Then again, it seems impossible that the path could be there at all.

The moon shines down, and the moor doesn't look nearly so frightening now. I chide myself for ever having been scared. The wind dies away, and silence slips over us. Every now and then I punctuate the quiet with a question—*What is it like, where you come from? What brought you to Near? Where is your family?*—but he never answers. I'm growing used to his not talking, but Cole is so unnaturally silent— silent steps, silent motions—that I feel he might fade away, so I tell him about myself, hoping to perhaps coax something more than a look from him.

"My mother is a baker," I say. "She bakes all morning, and I deliver bread around the village. It's why I know the shortest path to any house. It's why I can walk the road at night. I've walked them all a thousand times."

I glance at Cole, who looks back, surprisingly interested in my rambling. I go on. "My little sister, Wren, turned five this spring. She has this garden..." I say whatever comes to mind, the words tumbling out with ease.

The trail fades in and out ahead of us, vanishing altogether where the grass is low or the ground is bare, but always picking up again before we've lost it. It leads us up around the northern edge of Near, and I pause as my uncle's house comes into sight. Cole stops beside me, following my gaze to the darkened house.

"Near is like a circle," I say quietly, scanning for signs of Otto's patrol, or Otto himself. "Or a compass. My family lives at the northern edge, the sisters at the eastern one."

"Why do you live so far from the center?" Cole asks, and I have to bite back a smile at the fact he's speaking again. It's not a whisper, but it blends right in with the easy wind, soft and clear.

"They say only hunters and witches live out this far."

Cole tenses almost imperceptibly beside me. "And which are you?" he asks, flashing a thin attempt at a smile. I wonder if witches are frowned on where he comes from, and almost ask, but don't want to silence him now that he's finally willing to speak.

"My father was a hunter," I say. "And a tracker. There's less need for hunting these days, since a few families keep livestock, but our family always hunted, so we lived on the edge of town. My father's gone now. My uncle lives just beside us, right there," I add, pointing to his cottage, where the windows are finally dark. "He's a butcher. And the sisters, well..." I don't finish the sentence. It seems wrong to call Magda and Dreska witches, if they haven't told him themselves. I don't want to frighten him. And besides, it's not my place. Cole seems content to let the conversation die away.

"That way," he says, gesturing to the place where the grass grows taller and the path appears again, arcing past the houses and down toward the east. East, where through the darkness, beyond the grove, and up the hill, the sisters live. I cast a single glance toward home, the bedroom shutters still closed tight, and we press on.

The wind-brushed path runs parallel to the old dirt one that leans toward the eastern edge and the sisters' house, and I walk along it by muscle memory in the dead of night. The path becomes fainter, though the grass is tall, and we continue in silence.

I pause a moment, leaning against a rock. The world tips dreamily.

"You're tired," he says.

I shrug, but linger another moment.

"I'm fine," I say, straightening. "Tell me a story." I yawn as we continue walking along the narrow dirt lane, the wind-blown path always to our left. "It'll help keep me awake."

I don't want just any story; I want his. I want to know of the world beyond Near and the way they speak and the stories they tell and why he is here, in his singed gray cloak, and why he is keeping his words so close.

"I don't know any," he says. He gazes over the field to the grove in the distance, sitting like a knot of shadows.

"Make one up," I say, glancing back now at the blue-black world that falls away behind us. Cole looks back too, frowning as if he sees something different, more troublesome or alive than the simple landscape, but he says nothing, seems to grow thinner before my eyes.

"All right," I say at last. "I'll start, then. Any requests?"

The silence is so long that I think he hasn't heard me. The wind around us hums. Finally he speaks.

"Tell me about the Near Witch."

My eyebrows rise.

"Where did you hear about that?"

"The sisters," he says. The words don't come out easily, like he's just testing them. I wonder if he's lying.

"Do you believe in witches, Cole?"

His eyes find mine, and for a moment he seems perfectly solid. "Where I came from, witches were real enough," he says. There's a strange bitterness in his voice. *Where I came from.* I cling to those words, the first hints. "But I don't know about here."

"Near knows of witches, too. Or at least we used to."

"What do you mean?"

I start walking again. Cole follows.

"People know, but they try to forget," I say, shaking my head. "They see witches as scary stories, as monsters. When my father was alive, things were better. He believed that witches were blessings. They are closer to nature than any human, because it is a part of them. But most people think witches are cursed."

"The sisters too?" he asks slowly, and I offer a sad smile. So he does know more than he lets on.

"If you ask them if they're witches, they'll just turn away or wink or make some sharp comment. They must have been powerful, once. But they dried up. Or tried to."

I look at Cole.

"Witches are connected to the moor. I think my father wanted to have that connection, too. And he got closer than most, but the fact that he couldn't made him respect witches even more."

Cole seems even paler, if that's possible. The wind is picking up.

"And the Near Witch?"

"She's the reason, I think, that the people here are the way they are. Or so they claim. She's been gone so long. Now it all feels like a story more than history, to be honest. Like a fairy tale."

"But you believe it, don't you?" he asks.

"I do." I realize, only after I've said it, that it's true. "At least the bones of it."

He waits.

"All right," I say, sensing his curiosity, "I'll tell you the story the way my father did."

My voice slips low and soft as I draw out my father's hunting knife. It's nicked along one edge but still dangerously sharp. I let my fingers slide into the impressions on the handle as I picture the writing on the page in my father's book, overlapping in my head with his low, sweet voice. I take a deep breath, let it out the way he always did when he was going to tell a story, and begin.

9

"Long, long ago, the Near Witch lived in a small house on the farthest edge of the village. She was very old and very young, depending on which way she turned her head, for no one knows the age of witches. The moor streams were her blood and the moor grass was her skin, and her smile was kind and sharp at once like the moon on the moors in the black, black night. The Near Witch knew how to speak to the world in its language, and sometimes you didn't know if the sound you heard beneath your door was the howling of the wind or the Near Witch singing the hills to sleep. It all sounded the same..."

My words fade away as we approach the grove. Cole looks up and waits for me to go on.

But something has caught my eye, and I curse under my breath. Just before it reaches the clump of trees, the strange windblown path we've been following disappears. Just like that, the grass resumes its usual chaos, blowing a dozen different ways. Like that, the trail is gone. I pick up speed, hurrying through the canopied dark, tripping over roots and fallen branches, snagging my skirt. At the edge of the grove

I skid to a stop so fast that Cole almost runs into me.

I stare out at the night, my heart sinking as I scan the hill. The wind-made path is nowhere to be found. I wait, focusing and unfocusing my eyes, hoping to catch sight of it. At last I turn to Cole.

"Can you?" I ask, gesturing at the hill ahead. He looks past me, frowns, and shakes his head.

"Maybe at the top of the hill we'll find it. There's too much shadow on this side."

And he's right. The moon is slipping lower, dragging shadows over the world. In front of us the hill curves up. To either side the ground stretches out into fields.

I dig into my pocket for a few seeds and hold them out to the growing breeze.

"What are you doing?" he asks, and I can hear the amusement at the edge of his voice. It's a wonderful sound. He brings his fingers to my outstretched arms, lowering my hands. The way he touches me, it's as if he either thinks I'll break, or that I'll hurt him. As quickly as the touch is there, it's gone, and it leaves me wondering if his fingers ever met my skin, or if they only came close enough for me to imagine they did.

"The wind on the moors is a tricky thing," I whisper, half to myself. "But I'm asking it for help."

Cole stands back, tucks his hands in his cloak, and watches, his eyes vanishing beneath his hair. I'm about to explain that it's a joke, a silly game I've played with myself since I was little and I saw my father doing it, when suddenly the wind steals the seeds and scatters them like bread crumbs down the path ahead of us.

"Aha!" I say triumphantly, following the seed path. "You see?"

"I do," says Cole.

But the breeze I've summoned is growing now. It carries the seeds swirling every direction into the night, and then it begins to bluster and tug at my sleeves. Cole sets his hand on my arm, and the wind settles a bit, dies down.

"Careful what you ask the wind," he cautions.

He turns his head sharply, looking back through the grove, the way we came.

"What's wrong?"

"We should walk." He starts forward up the hill toward the sisters' house.

"Did you see something?" I ask, scanning the dark. I try to look at the world through his eyes, but all I see behind us is the blue-black night.

"I thought so," he says. Halfway up the hill, he veers off the path and heads for the low stone wall that sits just south of the sisters' house. I keep looking back at the way we've come, but I still don't see anything out of place.

"Finish the story," he says, "about the Near Witch. You weren't done, were you?"

I nod and follow him.

"The Near Witch was a moor witch. They say it's the strongest kind, that you have to be born of two witches, rather than a witch and a human, and even then, you never know. She could manipulate any of the elements instead of just one. They say the witch was so strong that the earth itself moved at her command, that the rivers changed course, and the storms bubbled over, and the wind took shape. That the ground and all that grew from it, all that was fed and kept and made by it, the trees and the stones, and even the animals—all of it moved for her. They say she kept a garden and a dozen crows, and that the garden never wilted, and the crows never grew old or flew away. The Near Witch lived on the seam, the one between Near and the moor, the one between humans and the wild world. She was a part of everything and nothing..." My voice trails off, and my eyes widen.

Up at the hilltop, between the sisters' house and the low stone wall, I can just make out a swatch of white. In an instant I break free, forgetting everything but the fabric tangled in a patch of thorny weeds. I stumble to a halt beside a child's sock, scanning the ground for any other signs. Cole comes up beside me.

I kneel before the patch of thorns. The sock has been snagged and upturned so that the sole faces up, as if the wearer stepped over the brambles and snagged the toes, tugging free and leaving the cotton behind. But that's not the strange part. The sole of the sock is a crisp white, perfectly clean. As though the foot never touched the ground.

I frown and pull the sock from the thorns, folding the top part inside out. Stitched around the inside rim are two little letters, *E* and *D*. Edgar Drake. His mother, the seamstress, always marks her clothes this way. I fold the sock carefully, and slip it into my pocket.

Around the patch of brambles, the tangled earth is in its usual messy state, but there are no signs of human shoes. Again, no tracks. I glance up at Cole.

"It doesn't make sense," I murmur. "Where is the rest of him?"

Cole frowns, staring with unfocused eyes at the moor that rolls away from us endlessly. He looks sad but not surprised. I shake my head and push myself to my feet. I scan the ground, hoping to find evidence of the windblown path.

From here atop the hill, I can just make out the strange ripple in the grass, leading up from the grove to the point where we stand. I face forward again, looking past the thorny patch, out at the moonlit moor. The windblown path dips down the hill beyond the sisters' house, but it spreads as it reaches the base, growing wider and wider until it covers the entire slope. And once it covers everything, it's as if there's no path at all, the mass of tangled grass and heather and brambles all bending together. I close my eyes, trying to focus, but my head feels cloudy, slow.

A sharp crack cuts through the night, and I wrench my attention back to Cole and the hillside and the sound of men, remembering in a flash my uncle's threat, his bright yellow patrol bands, the man in the doorway with the gun. From the edge of the grove below come footsteps. Heavy and careless. Boots crush twigs somewhere beneath the trees, and then the men emerge at the base of the hill, looking up toward the sisters' house. I hold my breath as Cole and I slide back over the stone wall, press ourselves into the shadow of the opposite side. Two voices travel over the moor, so much harsher than Cole's against the soft and constant wind. One is older, calloused, but the other is young, smug, and I'd recognize it anywhere. Tyler. The older man must be his father, Mr. Ward. Cole and I crouch silently behind the stone wall as the footsteps come closer, trudging up the hill.

I curse softly beneath my breath. If the patrol catches me out, and doesn't shoot me first, there will be hell to pay. But if they stumble on the stranger here, without the presence and protection of the sisters, what will they do to him? Arrest him? I've never seen them arrest someone, though they've threatened it. But I'd never seen a stranger either. I do know that, whatever they do, if Tyler catches me with Cole, it will be immeasurably worse. I glance to the side, but the shadows here are thick, and I can't see Cole, even though he can only be a foot or two away. I imagine, though, that I can hear his heart, slow and steady and pulsing. Then I realize it's not him, or me. It's the wind.

The wind is beginning to rise and fall, to whip through in short sharp pulses over the moor, tugging the grass in waves and casting a blanket of soft noise over everything. Cole slips a fraction closer, but the darkness against the wall is so thick I can just make out his outline and his eyes. It must be because his skin is so fair that his eyes seem haloed and bright, the way they did that first night on the moor. I rub my own eyes, strained from searching all night with only the moon for light. There's a dip in the wall where stones have slipped free with time, and I peer around the edge of it. Tyler and his father head for the space between the cottage and the wall, as if unwilling to get too close to either. Finally they pause a few yards in front of us, staring out at the moon-soaked moor to the east of Near.

"This is useless," Tyler says. "I can't hear anything over this wind."

"I doubt there's anything to hear or see," says his father.

"But now we can tell Otto we searched as far as the eastern edge."

Tyler kicks a tuft of grass. "Lot of good it did."

My fingers are splayed against the wall, and my hand brushes a group of loose pebbles. They tumble free, clacking against each other until they hit the ground. I hold my breath, but the wind swallows the first half of the sound, and the grass swallows the second. Mr. Ward has already turned and walked away, but Tyler freezes mid-step and looks back over his shoulder.

Impossible. I could barely hear the stones fall. Cole closes his eyes, his breath still careful and even. The beat of the moor wind quickens around us, and I silently pray that Tyler will turn and go. In that moment Cole seems thinner, as if he's fading away. My hand slides across the ground to his, intertwining our fingers, my skin needing assurance that he's still there. I give a short squeeze, and he squeezes back, and for a moment we are like the sisters, speaking without words. It's as if he's praying with me to keep us unseen.

Tyler hesitates a moment longer, eyes lingering on the wall. No, not the wall, I realize, but the air just above it. I look up and see a stroke of pitch black, a flutter of wings. A crow lands atop the wall, peering down at us with a glint in its eye, even in the darkness. Looking back through the hole in the wall, I watch Tyler lift his rifle, train it on the bird.

"Stop fooling around," calls Mr. Ward from the base of the hill. At the sharp sound of the man's voice, the crow takes flight, bleeding back into the darkness. Tyler lowers his weapon, casting one last look at the wall, but Cole and I are hidden behind our stones. Finally Tyler huffs and runs to catch up with his father.

Cole and I exhale together. Slowly the wind around us begins to die down, at last breaking apart into the gentle breeze that it had been before. Cole's hand in mine feels different, strong and solid. But my head is spinning, and I think that the late hour is playing with my senses.

Cole looks down at my hand in his as if it's a foreign object, as though he does not know how the fingers came to be intermingled with his own. He lets go. By the time my eyes meet his, he is distant and closed again. We sit there on the cold ground, backs pressed against the jagged stone wall, half hidden from each other by the shadows. There is a soft light spreading through the sky, a glow so faint that, had it not just been the darkest part of night, I wouldn't have noticed. The morning is a stealthy hunter, my father used to say. It sneaks up quiet and quick on the night and overtakes it.

"I have to get home," I say, brushing leaves from my cloak. "Tomorrow it's your turn."

"For what?" Cole asks, rising beside me, holding his hand palm up, as if it still does not belong to him.

"To tell me a story."

10

I don't remember falling asleep.

I climbed in the window as the dawn was breaking, my mind a nest of questions, and now somehow it is fully morning. I roll over, and Wren is there beside me, her knees drawn up and her head bent down, Dreska's charm still tied around her wrist. She shivers, curls in even farther. I sometimes forget how small she is.

A moment later her eyes flick open, bold and blue. She's not even fully awake when she frowns deeply and sits up. Her gaze goes straight to the window.

"What is it?" I ask, my throat thick from sleep.

My sister begins to pick at a thread on the old quilt, her eyes still staring out the window. Wren is not a quiet thing, so to see her so tight-lipped is strange. She begins to hum that silly rhyme, but only sings little pieces to herself, skipping middles so that the sound is fractured, wandering.

"Are you all right?" I ask, sitting up. I run my hands through my hair, trying to untangle it.

She meets my eyes, but does not stop humming.

"Are you worried about Edgar?" I ask. "They'll find him."

Her fingers keep pulling at the stray thread as the melody finally trails off. Then she says, "I just wish they'd stop playing."

"Playing? You think it's a game?"

She nods very seriously. "They asked me to come play, too, but I said no. I'm not afraid," she adds quickly, "but it was just, they came so late."

"What do you mean, *they*, Wren?"

"Ed and Cece."

"Cecilia?" I ask, the name caught in my throat. Cecilia Porter. The girl who took Wren's hand in the singing circle, a splash of freckles and a cluster of auburn curls.

Wren leans forward, in the exaggerated way children do when confiding a secret.

"I heard them, out there." She points to the world beyond the window, soaked in morning light.

"When did you hear them? Last night?"

She nods, matter-of-fact.

"Are you sure you didn't dream it?"

Wren shakes her head, focusing again on the window.

"Did you see anything out there?"

"No, it was too dark."

I remember the night wind and the way it curled into almost-voices.

"You're sure you heard Cecilia's voice, too?"

Wren nods. "I know I did." Beyond our room, sounds pour through the house. My uncle's gruff tone. Bo's lazy drawl. My mother's slow, steady words. But the voices are all tense, troubled in their own ways. I swallow, knowing the reason before I've heard the child's name. By the time I throw on my clothes and join the group in the kitchen, the conversation is trailing off.

"...again."

"...spoken to Maria or Peter?"

"...Alan saw nothing."

"...would do something like this?"

"What's happened?" I ask, slipping into a wooden chair. But I already know. My heart sinks as my mother says: "Cecilia."

"Been taken," grunts Otto.

"Or walked off," says Bo, leaning an elbow on the counter.

"Disappeared, nonetheless," whispers my mother.

"No one knows."

My chest tightens. Wren knew. Footsteps sound on the threshold, eager and strong, and moments later, Tyler strides into the kitchen.

"Otto," he says, "the men are gathered." I notice he's careful not to say *where*, or what they plan to do. But I'll find out. I have to. My uncle gives him a curt nod, setting his cup on the table.

Tyler's eyes find mine, and his chin tips up. I know he is proud at being considered one of the men. He crosses the room to me, taking my hand from my side and kissing it, knowing I'll endure it in front of my uncle. I can feel the weight of Otto's eyes as Tyler relishes the moment. I stiffen, waiting for him to release me, but his grip lingers.

"I promise, Lexi," he says, his mouth a strong line, his eyebrows appropriately knit, "we'll stop this thief before anyone else comes to harm." Yes, *we* will, I think, keeping my face a mask of calm. But I don't trust myself to speak, so

I only nod and pull my fingers slowly free. I wait for them to go, already carving out a path to Cecilia's in my mind. I'll have to be fast. I can't afford to have them trample what few clues there are to find.

Tyler turns to Otto, waits for his orders. My uncle looks between us.

"Tyler, you'll be staying here, with Lexi."

"What?" We both say at once, frowning. No. I cannot lose this day.

"But, Otto—" starts Tyler.

"You will stay here, Tyler." He turns to me. "As will you. Together."

"If you want us together, then let us both come search," I press.

"Head back to town," my uncle says to Bo. "I'll be right behind you." Bo hoists his gun and disappears.

Tyler slumps back against the table, arms crossed.

Otto's gun is leaning in the corner, and he takes it up without another word. As he passes my mother, he gives her hand a small squeeze. Maybe it's meant to say *Don't worry*, or *I'll fix this*, but my mother only bends her head over her work. As he passes me, I touch my uncle's sleeve.

"Please," I say, trying to keep the anger from rising up in my throat, trying to sound soft, "let me help you search. You said..."

Otto looks at me, and for a moment his mask slips, revealing something tired, tense.

"I said *we'll see*, and I've decided it's not a good idea. You're safer here." I glance at Tyler. That depends on my uncle's definition of safe.

"I want to help." I wonder if the strange, windblown trail will be beside Cecilia's house as well. Where will it lead? "I *can* help you."

His free hand closes on my shoulder.

"If you want to help, then look after your mother and your sister. I can't afford to worry about you or Wren right now. So stay put until we figure out what's going on, all right?" He pulls away, and just like that, the mask goes up again, and his face is all hard lines that are beginning to look more like cracks to me.

"Please, Lexi," he calls as he leaves the room. "Just stay put."

I follow Otto to the front door and watch him sink from sight, swallowed by the hills between us and the village.

"I'm sorry, Uncle," I say to his shrinking shadow. "I can't."

Fingers come to rest on my shoulder. Tyler kisses the back of my hair.

I turn on him, surprised to see him looking as frustrated as I feel.

"Let me ask you," he says, looking out over my head at the path Otto took. "Why do you think he made us stay?"

"How should I know, Tyler? Maybe because I'm a girl, and he thinks me too weak to help, or do anything, for that matter."

"He doesn't think you're weak... and neither do I." He angles his head down until our foreheads almost touch. "Otto thinks you've been to see the stranger. That's why you keep running off."

"Why would he—"

"And I think," he whispers, "he's right."

"And why would I do that?" I push past him and head back down the hall. Tyler follows.

"He's dangerous, Lexi."

"You don't know that," I say too quickly, adding, "and neither do I."

Tyler grabs my arm, pushing me back against the wall. "When did you see him?"

He puts his hands up on either side of my shoulders, caging me.

"This isn't about that stranger," I say slowly. "This is about Cecilia and Edgar."

"How do you know they're not connected?"

"I don't," I say. "And I *was* going to sneak out today—"

"To see him?"

"No!" I push against his chest, but he doesn't budge. "To search for clues, for tracks, for *anything* that might lead us to the children!"

He presses closer, his weight pinning me. "Don't *lie* to me!"

"Tyler Ward." My mother's voice slips through us. She stands in the kitchen doorway, dusted with flour, eyes calm and blue.

Tyler and I stand frozen, my mother's presence dousing us like water.

At last he straightens his shoulders and runs a hand through his hair. "Yes, Mrs. Harris?"

"I need a few more logs for the hearth." She gestures to the front yard. "Would you mind?"

Tyler looks back at me for one long moment, before

smiling thinly. "Not at all." He walks out, shutting the front door firmly behind him.

I slump back against the wall. My mother retreats into the kitchen.

I stare at the closed door for several moments before my head clears, and I realize what my mother has given me. A chance. I take a deep breath and follow her into the kitchen, ready to convince her, and find her adding sticks to the fire, a healthy stack of wood already beside the hearth. Her eyes find mine. And they aren't empty. She wipes her hands on her apron, points to the open kitchen window, and says only one word.

One perfect, sharp word.

"Go."

11

My boots are cinched and I take off, winding a course around the back of the house, behind a small hill and safely out of sight of the chopping block in the front yard. My mind traces over the village, mapping out north, south, east, and west, and all that's in between.

My mother might swear by kneading, but I swear by walking, by running. Moving. I haven't stopped moving in three years.

As my boots pound across the moor, I think of the music that weaves over these hills at night. The adults don't seem to notice, or if they do, they haven't said. But Wren hears it clearly, and I hear *something* that crumbles just before I can make sense of it. Why?

I reach the town square, and the place is cast in a strange quiet. Just a couple of days ago it was brimming with villagers, but now there's no one, just a stretch of cobbled ground and a few low and tapering walls.

Who will be next? I come to a stop and try to think of the spinning game. Edgar was on one side of Wren, Cecilia on the other, and now they're both missing. How many others were playing? I remember a wiry young boy, maybe eight. Riley Thatcher, next to the twin girls, Rose and Lilly; their older brother, Ben. Was Emily Harp there? She's a small girl, Wren's age, with dark braids. Her family lives at the southern edge of Near, so she and Wren don't play together often, but I remember her because their birthdays are only a month apart. I rack my brain but can't seem to reconstruct the circle fully. Rose and Lilly are not yet four years old, and their brother is only a year younger than I am. But Riley and Emily... have they heard the voices of their friends at night?

Who am I missing?

Wren. A small voice in the back of my mind adds my little sister to the list. I wince and shake my head.

First things first. Cecilia.

*

The village is quiet and the doors are closed.

Cecilia's house comes into sight, one of a small cluster just behind the town square. Considering the proximity of the buildings, whoever took the little girl was not afraid of getting caught. I make my way toward the clump of houses, in the hopes that there are clues the men have not found.

I am getting close when a familiar voice pours out from an open door, one of those tones that catches your ear no matter how softly it speaks. Lower than Magda's, it spills out sharp enough to cut. Dreska. My feet catch up on the weedy earth, and I nearly trip. The sisters almost never set foot in the village.

She would sound like she is muttering to herself at something she spilled or misplaced, except that there's another voice picking up when one of her sentences ends, old but less distinct.

"I was there," Dreska snaps, and I wince for the recipient. The stones of the house seem to grind together. "You were not, Tomas. You were not even a thought in your parents' minds, and your parents were not thoughts, and *their* parents were not thoughts. But *I* was there…"

I risk a glance around the half-open door, see Dreska leaning on her cane as she jabs a gnarled finger into Master Tomas's chest. No one ever lifts their voice, let alone their hand, against the Council members, and especially against Master Tomas, the oldest of the three. His hair is a shock of white, his skin as paper-thin as Master Eli's. But his eyes are light, somewhere between green and gray, and always narrowed. Even though he's ancient, he is frighteningly tall and stick straight, not curved with age like the others. He stands just inside the door, looking down at Dreska.

"That may be so." His voice is frail, tired. "But you do not know—"

"Look at the signs." She cuts him off. "Do you see them? I do. You are supposed to be keepers of secrets and forgotten truths. How can you not see…" she trails off. The house trembles.

"I do see, Dreska, but if you were there to see her alive, you were also there to see her die."

"I was. I bore witness to your ancestors' crimes. You have wrought this—" she rasps, when he cuts in again, his nose crinkling as if he's caught scent of something foul.

His voice dips low, and I cannot hear without walking straight into the room. The only word I make out is *witch*. And then Dreska lets out a hiss like water on hot coals.

"Don't test me, Dreska Thorne—" says the old man, louder. "A tree grows, it rots, and new things grow." His pale eyes gleam at her. "A tree does not rot only to come back up from the ground fully formed, bark and all... And you should know..."

But Dreska has had enough, it seems. She throws up her hands, waves them at the man as if he had a few dying flames on his bony shoulders, and storms out. I shove myself as far back from the doorway as possible, and pretend I've just come this way. But it wouldn't have mattered if I'd been standing right there in Dreska's path. She hobbles past me, muttering to herself.

"Fools all," she says to no one, plucking a smooth dark stone from the dirt. She limps away from the three houses that belong to the Council, and turns to the east, where another, larger cluster huddles against the gray day. Dreska uses her cane to unearth a few more rocks and a couple of good twigs before making the effort of stooping down to collect them in her dirty apron. I follow and watch, wondering what on earth she's up to.

"Sticks and stones, Lexi Harris," she says quite suddenly, as if that answers everything.

"Will break my bones?" I finish.

"No, silly girl, *sticks and stones*. For building birds." She half sings in her raspy way as she hobbles along. "Gathered from the village floor, nailed to every village door, watchful eyes turned out at night, keep the evils out of sight." She looks to me, still tottering like a knocked glass before it resettles. She is waiting for some recognition, some reply. When I give her nothing, she shakes her head, bending to fetch another stick from the road. She turns and raps me with it, smiling at its strength. I rub my arm.

"Goodness, I forget how little children know," she says, poking me with the end of the stick. "Long ago, long before the Witch's Rhyme ever became popular, we knew a dozen others. Back when people still had sense. Back when I was a child."

I know that everyone must start out young, but it's impossible for me to imagine Magda and Dreska as anything but what they are now, crooked and old. Or rather, I can conjure something to mind, but the result is a grotesque thing, only a few inches shorter than Dreska and just as wrinkled, with a voice as high as Wren's and a broader smile, but no more teeth.

I close my eyes, trying to unmake the image. When I open them again, Dreska has hobbled down the path that curves south around the village to her home.

"Dreska," I say, closing the distance between us. "Wren said she heard her friends' voices calling her onto the moor. I can't quite hear them, the words fall apart before I can make sense of them, and the adults don't seem to notice anything at all." Her green eyes harden on me, as if seeing me for the first time. "But everyone leaves a mark, and there are none. All I can think is that something else is luring them away, something..." I want to say witches. Craft. But I can't bring myself to say it to her. There are only two witches in Near, and neither of them would do this.

I wait for Dreska to say something, anything, to pick up

where my sentence trailed off, but she just stares at me with her sharp eyes. Finally, she blinks.

"Are you coming?" she asks, turning back toward the path, away from the cluster of homes. When I hesitate, she adds, "You're young and foolish, Lexi Harris, but no more so than the rest of Near. Maybe even a good deal less. Like your father." She frowns when she says it, as if she isn't convinced that my taking after him is a good thing.

I want to go with her, see Cole again, watch her transform the apron full of sticks and stones into something more, and ask her questions that she might finally answer. But I have to finish this first.

"I'll come by soon," I say, looking back in the direction of Cecilia's house. "I promise."

Dreska shrugs, or I think she does; she might just be shifting her weight. She veers off onto the almost invisible path toward her cottage.

At the last moment, I say, "The Near Witch was real," adding a softer, "right?" But when she doesn't turn around, I think she hasn't heard.

I walk on, when I hear her call back. "Of course she was. Stories are always born from something." And then she is gone, swallowed up by the hills.

I turn toward Cecilia's house. Dreska didn't laugh at me, didn't brush my questions off. I feel like I've earned a key to a door that no one else has been allowed, not since my father. "Like your father," she said, and those three words wrap around me like armor. I reach the house, casting a last glance about for signs of my uncle, before knocking quickly on the door. Moments later it falls open, and I'm dragged in.

12

Cecilia's house is a tangle of bodies.

My newfound strength begins to leach away as hands guide me in, and the bodies shift to make room. The last time I saw so many in such a small space, it was for my father's wake. Even the mood is the same. Too much bustling and shifting and chatting, as if it can all cover up the worry and pain. And loss. They act as if Cecilia's already dead. I feel as though I've swallowed rocks.

All around the room the women are whispering, wringing hands and bowing heads together.

"They aren't searching hard enough."

"Why hasn't Otto found them?"

"First Edgar, now Cece. How long can this go on?"

Cecilia's mother, Mrs. Porter, is sitting on the edge of a kitchen chair, her twiggish arms clutching another woman's shoulder as her sobs burst out in spasms. Her friend shushes her. I wind through the room.

"The window, the window," Mrs. Porter says over and over. "It was latched inside and out. How could..." She shakes her head and continues in this way, rambling, repeating herself as the women weave themselves around her. I scan the room in search of my uncle, but he's nowhere to be found. No men are, in fact. They must all be out searching. I draw near, wanting to comfort her but not knowing how. Someone touches my elbow, mutters my name. I press my way through the sea of women until I'm there beside her.

"Mrs. Porter," I say softly, and she looks up. I kneel so that I'm looking up at her. She is back to staring at her clasped hands, muttering of windows.

"Did you notice anything odd?"

She shakes her head harder, her eyes red. She opens her mouth but doesn't speak, and I think for a moment she might scream. The question earns me stern looks from around the room, and a couple of clucking sounds, as if I'm just supposed to sit and sob with everyone else.

"Mrs. Porter," I persist.

"I told them already," she says, her head still swaying side to side. "The window. We keep the window latched. Cece—" She stifles a cry. "She liked to wander, so we put two latches on the window, one inside and one out. I locked them. I know I did. But this morning they were both open."

I frown. "Did Cecilia say anything last night... out of the ordinary?"

"No, nothing," she whispers, her voice hoarse, thin. "She seemed cheerful, humming and playing."

My skin prickles. "Humming? Did you know the song?"

She gives a small shrug. "You know the children, always singing something..."

"Try to remember," I press. Her eyes are still fixed on a piece of wall across the room.

She swallows and begins to hum a quiet tune, full of broken notes and awkward pauses, but I know it. A chill runs through me as her voice trails off. My fingers are digging into my palms, and I wince as I flex my hands, leaving tiny crescents on my skin.

"Is there anything else you can tell me? Anything—"

"That's quite enough, Lexi," warns one of the women, and I realize Mrs. Porter's song has trailed off from the melody and into quiet sobs. Suddenly there are several pairs of eyes narrowing on me. I place my hands over Mrs. Porter's, give a small squeeze, and whisper an apology as I push myself up. My eyes scan the room, trying to pick out something, anything.

A doorway leads into a hall, and suddenly I want nothing more than to get there, into that hollow space and away from these women.

The bent form of Mrs. Porter reminds me too much of my own mother, hunched first over my father's bed, and then over her baking, mourning silently as the village spilled out of our house. A tangle of arms and legs, hugs and kisses and stroked hair, the low murmur of prayers, the gentle grip of fingers.

I slip down the hall toward Cecilia's room, turn the handle, and vanish within.

The covers have been tossed back. There is a rug beyond the bed, one corner flicked up as if a small pair of feet scuffed along the floor, still half asleep.

And there, the window, now shut. I run my fingers over the inside latch. There's a mirroring one on the other side.

The outside latch is still open, but the inside one has been locked again. I push the metal bar to the side, and the latch slides free. I test the frame with my fingers, but the wood is old, stiff. I doubt a child of six could move it up. I pull, and the wood slides up a foot with a loud groan, forcing me to cast a quick glance behind me. Beyond the window, the weedy ground rolls away, and the only signs of trespass are a few trampled patches several yards off, where men's boots have pressed the grass flat. There are no signs of a fall or a jump, no place just outside the window where feet met the ground. No marks at all. I'm about to turn back when I remember Cole, and the wind-swept path.

At first I see nothing, nothing but a few roofs in the distance. And then, slowly, the world shifts, some shapes settling back, others jumping out. A shadow appears, longer than it should be, given how high the sun is. It almost looks as if the tangled grass is bending, arcing away, just the way it did by Edgar's house. I gather my skirt and bring my boot up to the sill, shifting my weight so I can jump through.

"Run him out of town."

I lurch back into the room, pressing myself to the wall beside the window. My breath catches so fast in my throat I almost choke. My uncle and several others have rounded the corner of Cecilia's house, grumbling as they stop just beyond the window.

"And let him get away?"

"Risk him coming back? No." The voice cuts through the fresh air, gruff and low. Otto. My fingers wrap around the thin curtain by the window.

"Eric says he saw him around here in the middle of the

night," joins Mr. Ward. "Says he's sure of it." Eric Porter. Cecilia's father.

"What time?" asks Otto.

"Late. Eric says he couldn't sleep, was standing on the porch, and he swears he saw that boy lurking."

A lie. It has to be. Cole said he saw me and decided to follow. He would never have been over this way. And then we never came by here together. My fingers tighten on the fabric until my knuckles go white. Fear must be making phantoms.

"Is that all the evidence you've got?" counters Bo, with a sickening air of disinterest. I can picture him shrugging as he digs the dirt from under his nails with his hunting knife.

"He's a creep," spits Tyler, and I remember his face in the hall, wounded pride and something worse.

Tyler. If he's here, then Otto knows I'm not at home. I swallow and press myself into the wall beside the window. I had better make the most of today.

"What more do we need?" adds Tyler.

"Sadly, boy," joins an old man, sounding tired but patient, "a bit more than that." I know the voice. Slow and even. The third member of the Council, Master Matthew.

"But that's not all Eric said," Mr. Ward presses. "He said he was watching the stranger, real close, and that one moment he was there, and the next he just broke apart. Vanished."

My heart lurches as I remember that first night I saw Cole. My ears ring with the sound of shutters slamming closed.

"What do you mean?" growls Otto.

"Vanished. Right before his eyes."

"Haven't you noticed there's no clues, Otto? No tracks? Maybe this has something to do with that."

"He's involved."

"We need to get rid of him."

Nothing good grows out of fear, my father said. *It's a poisonous thing.*

"And if he didn't do it?"

"He did it."

"I bet we could get him to talk," says Tyler. I can hear the smirk in his voice. "Tell us where they are, the children."

"You forget the sisters are protecting him," says Master Matthew.

"But who is protecting *them*?"

There's a long silence.

"Now hold on," says another nervously.

"We don't want to—"

"Why? You can't tell me you're actually afraid of those witches. They're all dried up and their craft is too."

"Why shouldn't we march up there and demand the stranger?"

"Why should we wait for more children to vanish?" my uncle growls. "This all started when that boy arrived. How many more children will we lose? Jack, you have a boy. Are you willing to lose Riley because you were afraid of two old witches? My sister-in-law has two girls, and I'll do whatever it takes to protect them.

"Matthew," Otto says in appeal, and I picture the Council member, his face softer than the others, his blue eyes almost sleepy behind the small spectacles on his nose.

The other men murmur approval. Matthew must have nodded. I can make out the sound of metal against the house stones. Guns?

I risk a small step along the wall.

"Let's go, then," my uncle booms, and the others rally. "This ends now." He slams his hand against the side of the house, and I jump, knocking a low shelf. My heart races as the voices fade, their words echoing in my head. They're building a case of lies against him. But right now, with children missing and no one to blame, lies will be enough.

I have to warn Cole.

*

I turn south down the path that Dreska took, the one that curves around the town square, the ground falling away beneath my father's boots. This path is winding, so the men will never take it, and if I hurry, I might make it to the sisters first.

I run along the outskirts of the village. In my mind, Cole bleeds into sight on the dark moor, eyes shining. A gust of wind whips through, and he vanishes, like smoke.

I push the thought away and hurry east.

13

I pull my sleeves down and scold myself for not dressing warmer. The wind is biting as I climb the hill to the low stone wall. When the sisters' house comes into sight, my chest tightens, partly from the exertion of running, and partly from the sudden relief of seeing the cottage untouched. I've beaten my uncle's men here. I hoist myself over the wall and hesitate.

The place is too quiet, too closed.

The edge of the shed peeks out from behind the house, but Cole's gray cloak is absent from its nail.

I reach the sisters' door, and I'm just about to knock when I hear voices within, muffled words, and then my name. It is a strange thing, the way the world goes quiet when we hear our own name, as though the walls grow thin to make way. My fist uncurls and comes to rest, fingers splayed against the door. I slide closer, straining to listen. But the words are muffled again, so I slip around the corner to the next wall, where a window has been cut roughly into the cottage. The glass is old and the wood frame cracking, and through the sliver of space, the voices leak out.

"Lexi found a child's sock nearby."

I glance over the sill and see Cole's narrow frame in the
dim room, his back to me. He's sitting in a chair by the
hearth, staring at the cool dark stones while Dreska fidgets
around him, her long knotted cane scraping the floor as she
goes. Magda unpacks something from her basket, muttering.
Cole looks wrong inside the cottage, without the wind and
the tangled grass. He takes up no more space than the chair.

"Is that all? No other trace?"

"One thing," Cole says, standing. He goes to the mantel,
his long pale fingers moving over it. "A wind-swept path
tracing over the moor. Faint. I showed Lexi."

Magda's eyebrows arch, wrinkles multiplying. "Where
did it lead?" she asks.

"Here."

Dreska lets out a small hiss. "But the villagers have had
no luck."

Dreska's next words are muffled, and I stretch to get a
better look, some scattered rocks shifting beneath my feet.

"And I don't expect they will," says Magda grimly.

"And Lexi?" asks Dreska, turning toward the window as
if she means to ask *me* something. I duck, just before her
gaze finds me.

"She doesn't know what to make of it," he says.

My skin prickles. *Make of what?*

"She will." Dreska's voice is too close this time, just
beyond the glass, and I duck lower, pulse pounding in my
ears so loudly I can barely hear the words.

"If you don't tell her..." Dreska adds before moving
deeper into the cottage, her voice fading out. Cole replies,

but he's moved away too, and it's nothing but muffled sounds by the time it reaches me. I hurry back to the front of the house, hoping to catch more.

But instead the front door swings open, and I'm standing face-to-face with Cole.

I fight the urge to turn and run, even to take a step back. Instead I find his eyes and hold them with mine.

"Tell me what, Cole?" I ask, quiet and angry. His mouth opens and closes just a fraction, his frown deepening. But then his jaw sets, and he says nothing. I let out an exasperated sigh and turn, walking away. Unbelievable. I'm risking my uncle's wrath to help him, and he won't even tell me the truth.

"Lexi, wait." Cole's voice cuts through the wind in my ears, and then he's beside me. He goes to take my arm, to pull me to a stop, but his fingers only hover over my skin.

"Just let me explain," he says, but I walk faster. Too fast. My shoe hits a stone, launching me down the hill. I close my eyes, brace myself, but I never fall. I feel cool arms around my shoulders, and I sense Cole's heart beating through his skin. I pull away, the wind tugging at my hair, my dress.

He folds his arms across his chest.

"Lexi, what you heard—"

I run my hand through my hair. "Cole, I'm trying to help you."

He frowns but doesn't look away. "I know—"

"But I can't possibly do that if you're keeping secrets from me."

"You don't—"

"Everyone in town wants to blame *you* for the missing children. My uncle and the Council are coming for you *right now.*"

I look back down the hill to the grove and the narrow path Otto's men will take, but no one's there. Still, I imagine I can hear the sound of twigs and leaves cracking underfoot, deep in the trees. Cole follows my gaze.

"This way," he says, gesturing past the cottage to the shed. An actual crack, this one unmistakable, comes from the trees below, and I let him lead me past the shed, the grove and the hill and the sisters' house vanishing behind the slouching wooden beams.

Cole turns to the rolling hills. I reach out, bringing my hand to his shoulder, and he tenses but doesn't pull away. I press my fingertips against him, testing him.

"What haven't you told me?" I ask.

And for a moment I think he'll actually tell me. I can see him juggling the words inside his head. Fumbling. I tried to juggle once, with three apples I'd found in the pantry. But I just ended up bruising them all so badly my mother had to make apple bread. The whole time I was trying, I kept getting lost in the movements. I couldn't concentrate on all of them at once.

I wish Cole would give me an apple. And then he looks at me, and there's that same sad, almost-smile, like he's decided to pass me one, but he knows I can't juggle either. Like there's no reason for both of us to bruise things any more than needed.

I hold out my hand.

"Let me help."

He stares at my upturned palm.

"You want to know my story," he says, staring so hard that I think he must be counting the creases in my hand.

"Once, long ago, there was a man and a woman, and a boy, and a village full of people. And then the village burned down. And then there was nothing."

I hold my breath, waiting for him to go on. But Cole turns away, makes his way to the point where Near falls away and the moor takes hold. I have never been to the sea, but Magda told me stories about rolling waves that go on forever. I imagine it would look like this, only blue.

"You're not very good at telling stories," I say, hoping to coax a smile, but he looks so sad, staring out at the moor. The wind around us is whistling, pushing, and pulling.

Then I understand. "Your village burned down?" I ask, staring at his gray clothes, their singed look, and realizing suddenly why he hates the name I've given him.

"Oh God, Cole... I mean..."

"It's fine, Lexi. It's a fine name."

"Just tell me your real one."

He turns away, his jaw tensing. "Cole is fine. It's growing on me."

I hear the door to the cottage swing open, and the sisters hobbling out, Dreska's cane knocking on the ground.

I walk back toward the shed and catch sight of them in the yard. Dreska's hard eyes flick toward us before moving over the path down the hill. I feel Cole come up behind me.

"How did you survive?" I ask, before I can stop myself. He stares at me, weighing his words in his mouth like they are trying to crawl back down his throat.

"The fire was my fault," he whispers.

"How?" I ask. But he begs me with a look, all pain and loss and something worse. He is trying to keep his breath steady, even, his jaw clenching as if he's afraid he might cry. Or scream. I can tell because it's how I felt right after my father's death, like I wanted to shout but all the air had been stolen from my lungs. Like if I opened up one part of me, all of it would pour out. Cole closes his eyes, and his hands wrap around his ribs, as if that will keep him contained.

"Lexi," he says, "I'm not—"

But then the men's voices break through, Otto's above the rest.

As if wakened from a trance, Cole's eyes open wide, dark and gray, his mouth forming a thin line. I push him into the shadow of the shed, pressing him back against the wood.

Peering around the corner, I can just make out the men at the edge of the grove below. They seem to be fighting. Otto gestures up the hill impatiently. Several men gesture back before retreating against the tree line. They don't seem so bold now, with the witches waiting at the top of the hill. Otto huffs, turns, and makes his way up the slope alone.

Dreska casts a warning glance toward the shed, then crosses her arms and sighs, facing the path.

Magda slips down into the patch of dirt, murmuring uselessly to the bare earth and brushing her fingers back and forth in her childlike way. Otto approaches.

Cole and I huddle against the shed. My hand brushes his, and he slips his fingers through mine. My pulse skips at his touch.

"What brings you to the edge of Near?" asks Dreska,

appraising my uncle. I hug the corner of the shed, stealing glances around the edge.

"I need to speak to the stranger," says Otto.

Cole's hand tenses in mine.

Dreska's frown deepens, and overhead the clouds begin to gather. She takes a deep breath.

"Otto Harris. We saw you born."

Magda unfolds herself. "We watched you grow."

When the sisters speak, there is a strange echo to their voices, so that when one stops and the other starts, they blend in to each other.

My uncle just shakes his head impatiently. "The Council has concerns about the stranger's presence," he says. "About his reasons for being here."

"We are older than the Council."

"And we, too, watch over Near."

"The boy has done nothing. We vouch for him."

Otto's gaze hardens. "And what do your words mean?" he barks. His eyes dance with frustration, crease with fatigue. Without the other men, he is not standing as straight, and I remember his hunched form over the table, head in his stained hands. He takes a breath and cools.

"Two children are missing, and that boy you harbor is under suspicion," he says, rubbing his beard.

"Evidence?"

"Witnesses." He ignores a short cough from Magda. "Now, what do you know of it?" His face is settling into its hard lines, burying the fatigue beneath his beard, behind his eyes.

"Now you care for the thoughts of two old hags?" spits Dreska.

"The Council knows who is taking the children," adds Magda with a wave of her dirt-caked fingers.

"Don't waste my time," he growls. "Not with that rubbish."

"All Near knows."

"All Near forgets."

"Or tries."

All Near tries to forget? Before I can make sense of it, the sisters' voices begin to overlap, and the sound is haunting.

"But we remember."

"Stop it," says Otto, shaking his head. He straightens, squaring his shoulders. "I need to speak to him. The stranger."

The sky is darkening, threatening rain.

"He is not here."

Magda's gnarled hand flutters through the air. "Out on the moor."

"Somewhere out there. We do not know."

"It is a very large moor, after all."

Otto frowns. He does not believe a word of it.

"I will ask you one last time—"

"Or *what*, Otto Harris?" growls Dreska. I swear I can feel the earth rumble.

Otto takes a breath before meeting her gaze. When he speaks, his words are slow and measured. "I do not fear you."

"Neither did your brother," says Magda. The ground beneath us begins to shift, just a ripple, but enough to make the house stones groan. "But at least he respected us."

Several stray drops of rain splash down on us. The wind is bristling. I think I feel Cole's hand slip away from mine, but when I look over he's still there, his eyes staring straight ahead but unfocused.

Otto mutters something I cannot hear, and then, louder, "But I will." And with that, I hear his boots scuff the ground as he turns away. Cole shifts his weight beside me, leaning deeper against the shed. The boards creak. His eyes light up with panic, and I catch my breath. My uncle's heavy footsteps grind to a halt. When he speaks again his voice is frighteningly close to the shed.

"He's here now, I know it."

The footsteps grow louder and louder, and Cole casts a troubled glance at me. He seems thinner in the growing wind. I have to do something. If Otto finds me, it will be bad. But if he finds Cole, it will be much worse. I mutter a curse beneath my breath, then release his hand and force my feet to carry me out from my shelter and into my uncle's path. He staggers back to keep from barreling into me.

"Uncle," I say, trying not to wince as his look turns from shock to anger.

"*This* is where you've run off to?" Otto's hand encompasses my arm as he pulls me toward him. I don't have a lie ready, so I opt for silence. Behind me, the boards give another loud groan.

Otto shoves me out of his way as he rounds the corner of the shed, and I bite my tongue to keep from shouting NO! But the look he shoots me when he turns back is enough to tell me Cole isn't there.

Otto says nothing, only grabs me and spins me back past the sisters' house and onto the path home. His sudden silence worries me more than any amount of shouting. He pushes me ahead of him like a prisoner, and it takes all my will to not look back.

*

He doesn't speak. Not when we're down the hill, or through the grove, or when our own homes have come into sight. By then the sun is setting, and my uncle is a black outline against it. The silence is too heavy.

"I was just doing my—"

He doesn't let me finish. "Do you disregard *everything* I say?"

I cannot contain the frustration bubbling up in me. "Only when you treat me like a child."

"I'm only trying to protect you." Our voices climb over one another.

"You should be protecting Wren instead of trying to lock me in the house."

"*Enough*, Lexi."

"You want me to just sit inside and wait, when I could be *searching*." I storm across the threshold.

"Because you *should* be here," he says, following close behind, "with your mother and Wren."

"Because that's what women do?"

"Because it's *dangerous*. The stranger could be dangerous. What if he hurt you? What would I—"

"He's not dangerous." I head down the hall and into my bedroom, Otto on my heels.

"How do you know? Do you know him so well?"

I let out a strangled sigh and run my hands through my hair. "I just want to help, Uncle. However I can. And if that means searching for the stranger, if that means turning to the sisters, then how can I not? I just want to protect my family…" My voice trails off as I catch sight of a small white square tucked under the corner of the window frame, flapping gently in the evening breeze. A note.

"As do I," he says, so low I barely hear it.

I pull my gaze from the note and turn to face him, trying to hold his eyes so they don't wander to the window, where the slip of paper stands out like a splash of paint against the dark glass.

"Lexi, I know I'm not your father," he says. "But I promised him."

The room goes cold, but Otto doesn't seem to notice.

"I promised I'd keep you from harm, remember? I know you were listening that day," he continues. "I'm doing the best I can, Lexi, but it doesn't make my job easier if I'm battling you *and* trying to find the children."

My uncle sighs, the fight bleeding out of him before my eyes, leaving a stiff and tired quiet in its wake.

"I'm trying," he says.

He leans back against the far side of the hall. His dark hair is flecked with gray, and it curls down into his eyes. His face is like my father's, but rougher. When he turns his head certain ways, the resemblance is so striking my stomach hurts, but there's a tension in his eyes, like a trapped animal, that my father's never had.

"Why are you looking for Co—for the stranger?" I ask. My uncle blinks, as if he was lost and is just now coming back to himself.

He holds my eyes but says nothing, then pushes off the wall and heads into the kitchen. I follow. Wren is playing in a corner of the room, making a maze of smooth flat stones on the floor. I am sure she'd rather be outside. My mother slides to my uncle's side, setting a mug within reach. He takes a couple of long sips and shakes his head.

"It has to be him," he says at last. "He shows up here, and then all this." He moves to drain his cup again, finds it empty, and drops it to the table. My mother refills it with something strong and dark. "We have witnesses. He's been seen in the village after dark. Eric Porter says he saw him last night, around the time Cecilia vanished."

"Uncle, fear can make people see strange things," I say, trying to sound reasonable.

"Lexi, I have to do something."

"But—"

"I'm telling you, I intend to see him gone."

"It's not Cole," I say before I can stop myself.

"Cole." My uncle takes a deep drink, swishing it in his mouth along with the word. "Is that his name? And how would you know that?"

Because I named him.

"Dreska called him that," I say with a tight shrug. "When I went there, to speak with them. And to look for him," I admit. A little truth makes a lie stronger. "She said she hadn't seen Cole that day, that he was out on the moor somewhere."

"And why are you so convinced it's *not* him?" Otto's voice, his body, all of it is tense, set.

Because I've been sneaking out at night to search, and he's been helping me.

"Because being a stranger is not a crime."

"Well, it doesn't matter," he mutters, knocking his mug on the old wooden table again for emphasis. "Come morning we will have our answers."

A prickle runs along my spine.

"What do you mean?" I ask slowly.

Otto looks at me long and hard before answering. "If the sisters won't give the boy up freely, then we'll take him." And with that he storms from the kitchen. I follow him into the hall, but he's already out the door, being swallowed up by the dark. A knot is growing in my chest, tangling everything up. I fight the urge to run after him, or better yet to run east until I hit the grove and the hill and the sisters' house and Cole.

"Come morning," my uncle said. I try to slow my breath. Questions buzz around my head, making me dizzy, and I stand in the darkness trying to assure myself that I will find a way to set things right. Fingers settle on my arm, and I feel my mother's touch, firm and welcome, urging me back inside.

My mother floats into the kitchen to clean up after Wren. I turn toward the bedroom, wanting to free the slip of paper from the windowpane. The breeze flicks the note against the dark glass. In a breath I'm there, sliding the window up, begging it not to groan too loudly, and snatching the note before it blows off into the night. The small scrap has only two words, in thin wandering script.

Meet me.

I run my fingers over the hastily written letters. The words make my heart tug strangely in my chest, that same odd gravity that pulls me toward the fresh air. The feeling tells me, as much as the words, that the note is from Cole. When could he have left it? The weight presses the breath out of me, a mixture of excitement and concern. I tuck the slip of paper in my dress.

I realize I'm still wearing my father's boots, and I lean against the bed to pull them off, when I hear soft footsteps.

"Lexi, it's too cold," comes the voice behind me. I glance back with a smile.

"You're right, Wren," I say, pushing the wooden lip of the window down. "Let's keep this one closed tight, all right?"

She gives a twitch of a nod and holds out her hand. I take it and let her lead me into the kitchen.

*

Night cannot fall fast enough.

Cole's note burns in my pocket as I pace the house until my mother's room goes dark. And then I go to Wren, tucked in bed but still awake. I pull the frayed quilt up around her, ruffle her hair playfully. The old house lets out little clicks and thuds as the heat from the day seeps out.

"I hope they don't come back," she says through a yawn. "I'm tired. I don't want to play." She settles in, but her eyes keep flicking to the window. I stroke her hair.

"It will be all right."

"Do you promise?" she asks. She holds out her hands, the sisters' charm still dangling from her wrist, the smell of moss and earth and wildflowers wafting from it. I take her hands in mine and bring them to my lips. I hesitate, trying to choose the right words.

"I promise I will make it right," I whisper into the space between her palms. Wren keeps her hands cupped around the words as she falls back against her pillow.

"And Wren," I add, sitting on the bed beside her, "no matter what happens, do not get out of bed tonight. And if you hear your friends again, ignore them. They can't mean well in the middle of the night."

Wren twists deeper beneath the covers.

"I mean it," I say, as she all but vanishes under the blankets.

I watch the candlelight dance, and wait.

When I'm sure she's asleep, I push myself to my feet and the room tips gently, or maybe I tip, swaying from lack of sleep. The walls and the floor eventually settle, and I tighten my father's knife around my leg. I kiss the top of Wren's head and coax the window open, dropping to the ground beyond. Then I pull the window closed and fasten the shutters before turning my eyes to the waiting night.

14

The moon is bright and the night is still, and the wind is humming in a far-off way.

Gravity pulls me back to him, pulls my feet over a path they know, have always known, with a new urgency. I make my way through the moonlit world, between blue-gray shadows on a blue-gray ground, watching the blue-white circle in the blue-black sky. I remind myself every few steps why I am awake, and Otto's threat helps to keep my eyes wide and my hearing sharp.

Someone is close.

There are footsteps in the dark that I cannot hear. I know they're there, the way one knows when someone else is in a room even if they make no sound. The air around me prickles as I reach the grove. The cluster of trees is so dark it looks like one large shadow. And then a piece of it peels away.

"Cole," I say as he steps forward into a patch of moonlight. The frightened, drawn features of this afternoon are gone. His hands hang at his sides instead of wrapping around his ribs. The exhaustion in his face seems mildly diffused. His eyes are weary but calm.

"Lexi," he says. "You got my note?"

I touch my pocket. "I did. But I would have come anyway. To warn you. My uncle—"

"Wait," he says, his voice louder than I think I've ever heard it. It cuts right through the wind instead of bleeding into it. "About earlier. I asked you to meet me so I could explain. I need to."

"You don't have to explain to me, Cole, if you don't want to."

"No, I don't want to. But I need to." His cloak flutters. "I just don't know where to start."

"The fire? You said that your village burned down. That... *you* burned it down?"

He shakes his head. "It's not that simple."

"Then tell me what happened." The grove behind him looks like a towering shadow. That, or a beast about to swallow him whole. "Cole?"

He hesitates.

"Go ahead. I'm listening," I say.

He casts one last glance up at the night. His eyes slip down again, and by the time they reach mine, there's a kind of abandon in them.

"I'll show you," he says at last.

Cole steps forward, his fingers reaching around my shoulders, and kisses me.

It is sudden and smooth and soft as air against my lips. The wind whips around us, tugging at the fabric of our clothes, but not pulling us apart.

And then it's gone, the cool pressure against my lips, and

my eyes are open and looking into two gray eyes, like river
rocks.

"*That's* what you wanted to show me?"

"No," he says, his fingers slipping down my arms as he
leads me off the path and out, away from Near. "That was
just in case."

*

Just in case *what*? I wonder, as the last signs of Near are
hidden by the hills.

"How far are we going?" I ask.

There's an urgency in Cole's stride; I can almost hear his
footsteps on the ground. Almost. And then he starts talking.
Until now every utterance from him has had to be pried,
coaxed. But now the words spill out.

"My mother had eyes like rain-soaked stone, not so dark
as mine, but close. And long dark hair that she always wore
up, but couldn't contain. It's one of the first things I
remember about her, how pale her face was, framed by the
darkness of her hair. But she was perfect. And strong. You
would have loved her, Lexi. I know it."

"And your father?"

"Gone." The word is so sharp and short. "I never met
him," he adds. "And I know nothing of him. Not his name,
or what he looked like. I only know one thing. One very
important thing."

We reach the top of the slope, and a stretch of flat field
waits before giving way to the next valley. The countryside
beyond this hill seems so vast. It's impossible to tell the
scope of the world beyond Near, actually, because you can

almost never see past more than a hill or two at a time. The world could possibly end, come to a sudden stop, just beyond the next rise. Cole pauses to look out at it, and I can't help but wonder why we've come all the way out here.

"And what is that?" I ask.

And then he holds out his hand. Not to me but to the night.

The air around us seems to shiver, and the wind brushes cool against my skin. I take in a sharp breath as the wind coils around his outstretched hand. It spins faster until it looks like his fingers are bleeding into it. Then they grow thinner until I can see right through them, until there is no difference between the swirling wind and his skin.

"You're a witch," I whisper. I should feel shock, but I must have known in my bones since the moment I saw him, because all I feel is a sweeping sense of calm.

He turns his hand over like he's cradling something. And then his fingers curl in against his palm, and the wind breaks apart, vanishes.

"And so was he." Cole's eyes harden.

"When I was young," he goes on, "I thought it was wonderful. Other children had imaginary friends, but I had something much better. Something vast, powerful—but intimate, too. I was never alone.

"When I felt angry, the wind bristled, blew harder. There were these invisible threads binding me to it. The wind took hold of whatever I felt, and ran away with it. My mother was afraid. Not of me, I don't think, but *for* me. She told me people didn't understand witches, and so they feared them, and she didn't want them to be afraid of me. She was such a strong woman, but I think those worries ate at her."

My chest tightens. She sounds like my father, the mixture of pride and worry in his eyes even as he taught me to hunt, to track, to chop wood.

"But her husband was another matter."

"Her husband? I thought you said—"

"She remarried, before I was even born. But I never saw him as a father. And he, I'm certain, never saw me as a son."

Around us the wind is blustering. "I tried so hard for her, my mother. To stay calm. I thought that if I could be empty, if I could never feel anything too strongly, then it would be all right. And for a short time it was. People even seemed to forget what I was."

Cole does not seem to notice, but the wind around us is growing angry and thick. It tears at the ground, ripping leaves and grass into small circles. His tone is changing, too.

"But not everyone forgot. My mother's husband. He never did." Cole looks up, but his eyes are unfocused, and I wonder where he is, what he sees. He's even paler than usual, and a muscle on the side of his face twitches as he clenches his jaw.

"*The wind on the moors is a tricky thing.* Isn't that how you put it, Lexi?" He lets out a short, joyless laugh. There's a rock nearby and he crosses to it, sliding down onto it as if his legs won't hold. It's such a sad, effortless grace he has. "Well, you were right. The wind is a tricky thing. As is the rain and the sun and the moor itself. These things, they don't always act kindly, or reasonably. The wind can creep into a person's lungs, make itself heard when they breathe out. The rain can leave a chill in a person's bones."

I can see him shaking, but resist the urge to reach out and touch him. I'm afraid he'll stop talking. I'm afraid he'll blink and be that silent stranger again, holding his ribs to keep it all in. He'll melt away, right into the dark.

"She got sick so fast. As fast as the wind sweeps through, and she was gone before she was gone, if that makes sense. All the color left her. She had this fever and she should have been hot, should have been red, but she was gray. Cold." He swallows. "She was dying, her life bleeding out in front of us, and there was nothing we could do. Her husband turned to me. Really looked at me, maybe for the first time."

Cole's hands are balled into fists resting on his knees. He does not see them, does not see anything. I move toward him, but the wind urges me back.

"'You speak to the moor,' her husband said to me. 'Tell it to save her.' He was desperate. 'If you love her, make it save her.' That's what he said."

Cole's stony eyes are glittering, tears cast in blue-white light, gathering in the corners.

"But it doesn't work like that. I cannot control storms, and even if I could, the rain could not take itself back from her lungs, from her bones."

The small circles of wind are growing, and my hands tighten on the lip of a rock for balance. Cole seems to exist in his own space now, where the wind does not even ruffle his hair or tug at his cloak.

"She died." He pauses a moment, swallows. "That was the night the village caught fire."

My breath catches in my throat. I don't know what to say. The wind curves around him like a shell. Yet somehow his voice comes through.

"There was so much wind. I thought it couldn't all be

from me. It was too loud, too strong. Some of the torches got knocked over. I tried to calm down, but the storm just kept growing. A dry storm, just clouds and wind, and the fire kept growing, swallowing everything. I wanted it to swallow me too, but it didn't. The town burned up like a piece of paper, curling in on itself until there was nothing left. But me. I didn't mean to do it, Lexi," he says, finally meeting my eyes. The guilt brims with the tears on his dark lashes.

I reach for him, but he pulls back.

"I couldn't control it."

The wind between us surges up again, but I force my way through it, until I am beside him. I kneel in front of him, put my hands over his. When Cole looks up at me, his face is wet. The pain in his eyes is so familiar it knocks the air from my lungs.

"Then it was over, and all that was left was ashes."

I can't stop seeing him, singed and gray, alone where a village once stood.

"I felt so... *empty*," he says, shaking his head. "Gutted. Hollow. And it hurt. Worse than anything."

"Calm down, it's all right," I say, my voice vanishing in the wind.

He blinks, looking around at whirlwinds tearing up earth and stones. He shakes his head and tries to pull away. "Get back."

My fingers tighten over his, and the wind picks up.

"No."

Small twisters, spirals of leaves and grass and pebbles, draw near to us, pulled to Cole by his strange gravity, the same way I'm drawn to him. They lace together, growing.

"Get back, *please*," he says again, panic in his voice as he pushes himself unsteadily to his feet. I stand with him, refusing to let go. But then the wind wrenches me backward, tangling in my cloak. I tumble away from him as the air coils around me, dragging the loose weeds and dirt up with it. And it keeps growing. The wind howls louder as it spins into a single perfect cyclone, carving a circle in the moor around me.

"Cole!" I shout, but the word is instantly lost in the whirlwind, swallowed as soon as it leaves my lips. I manage to stand. The world beyond the cyclone begins to blur. The moor and the stones and Cole all run together, and then vanish entirely behind the wall of air. The tunnel reaches up and up toward the sky. But here in the center it's so calm, so still, aside from the white noise. The wind tugs gently at my sleeves, the edges of my cloak, the loose tendrils of hair, but it's almost gentle. I picture Cole within his own tunnel that night, his village burning down while the wind kept him safe. Alone. I feel alone here. I hold out my hand, let my fingers brush against the cyclone wall.

And then another set of fingers slices through the wind, touches mine, intertwines with mine. Cole steps through the wall of air and into the circle. The whirlwind parts for him, ruffling his dark hair before closing behind him seamlessly. He pulls me to him, wrapping his arms around me.

"I'm here," I whisper. And his lips move too, but there is no voice but the wind now, as Cole pulls me closer and tips his forehead against mine. There is nothing here but us. Beyond the whirlwind, the world tears itself apart, whistles and blows and pushes and pulls. But just for a moment, impossibly, we two go still.

The whirlwind loses focus, begins to wobble. He pulls me tighter to him as it breaks apart and rushes past us, for one fleeting second strong and violent. And then the whirlwind is gone, and all that's left is a soft wandering breeze as the hills come back into sight and the grass settles. Cole searches my face. He looks as though he is expecting fear, disgust, something strained, but I have never felt so alive. He lets go of me, steps back, shaking.

"Lexi," he exhales, drawing large deep breaths, as if the wind stole the air right from his lungs. The wind has dried the wet streaks on his cheeks and woven soft patterns through his hair. "Now you know. That's what I am. I'm sorry."

He seems to crumble, sliding toward the ground, but I catch his arm. His breath is ragged, and for a moment I think he'll faint.

"Don't be."

"I understand," he says, swaying on his feet, "if you don't want to—"

I cut him off. "Is that what you meant before, when you kissed me, 'just in case'?"

He looks out over my head to the east, eyes shining, but I can see the edge of his mouth quirk.

"Look at me," I say, running my fingers along his jaw and turning his face back to mine. "I'm still here."

Cole kisses me once, a quiet, desperate kiss. I can taste the pain on his lips, the hint of salt. Then he pulls away and looks east again. I follow his gaze. The very corners of the sky are changing. If we do not make our way back toward Near, dawn will sneak in and catch us unprepared.

"Come on."

He lets me lead him, my fingertips pressed against his arm, reassuring my skin with his that he's still there. I walk slowly, not wanting Near to come into view too soon. The cyclone may be gone, but it still feels like we are alone in the world.

It's Cole who breaks the silence as we walk. "I wanted to show you. But not like that. I promised myself," he murmurs, "to never let it happen again, to never lose control."

"But you *can* control it. I just saw you..." My fingers give a small squeeze. "You coiled that wind around your hand before you started to get upset. And when you forgot your anger for a moment it all broke apart. I'm sure if you just—"

"It's too dangerous," he says, his eyes sliding shut as we walk, his feet gliding over the tangled earth. "All it takes is one slip."

"But Cole..."

"Why do you think I led you all the way out here? It's been more than a year since that night, and I have told myself every day, with every breath, to stay calm, to be empty." He meets my gaze. "Why do you think I stay out of the village? Why do you think I tried not to get close to you?" I remember the way he pulled away, avoided even brushing his hand against mine. The strange expression, concern and something else, when he found my fingers intertwined with his.

"I never intended to stop here," he says. "I was just passing through."

"Where were you going?"

He shakes his head, and the effort of it seems exhausting. "I don't know. Ever since that night, I couldn't sit still. I couldn't bear to stop moving."

"But you stopped here. Why?"

He stops walking, and I turn back toward him.

"I heard something," he says, his hands coming to rest, weightless, on my shoulders. "Something terrible is happening in Near, Lexi. This place, it's as if it's possessed. The wind is possessed. By songs. And voices."

I frown.

"My sister, Wren," I say. "She said the strangest thing this morning. She said the missing children came to her window, asked her to play. She said she heard them."

Cole tenses down to his fingertips. "The voices I've heard couldn't have belonged to those children. Not exactly. It was a woman's voice. She wasn't shaping the wind. Not the way I shape it. It was as if her voice *was* the wind. And it wasn't just the wind, either. It felt like everything was moving under a spell. At first I just stopped to listen, to see if there was another witch here."

His hands begin to slip from my shoulders, but I bring mine up and keep them there.

"So is there a witch? Luring the children from their beds?"

He nods. "The voice had this singsong quality to it. I was circling the village when I heard it. I didn't understand what was happening, but I knew something was wrong."

"What do you mean, *wrong*?"

"I've never met another witch before coming here," he says. "But what I do, I can only do it with the wind, and only the surface, the shape. This witch was using the wind in a way I never knew possible. That's what I mean. Wrong."

"And you stayed?"

"The next night the children started disappearing. I knew it had to be connected. Nothing can make up for what happened in my village, but I thought if I could do something to help, then I needed to."

"That's why you were out on the moors last night, near Edgar's home."

He nods again, his breath slowing, coming easier. We start moving again, over the hills toward the sisters' house. "Then I met you. The sisters didn't want to talk to me about what was happening. But they said I should ask you about the story."

The pieces click into place. The way the wind sings the Witch's Rhyme. The lack of clues, the eerie path running on top of the heather and tall grass. Dreska's fight with Master Tomas. "You think it's the Near Witch?"

"You sound so disbelieving," he says as we crest a small hill and the grove comes back into sight. We make our way to the nest of trees.

"It *is* hard to believe."

"Why?"

"Because she *died*, Cole. Calling rain or flowers forth is one thing. Rising up from the dead is another."

Cole frowns, the crease between his eyes deepening. We reach the far side of the grove, not the place where he pulled me from the path and onto the moor, but the side that looks up at the sisters' house. My eyes sweep up the hill to the old stone cottage. Beside it the low stone wall shimmers like a slice of moon, or water, and all I can think is how badly I want to reach it and lie down. That's how tired I am: I could sleep happily on rocks. My head is cottony thick with questions as I step from the grove, and that's when three things happen.

Cole's hand tightens around my wrist.

The wind picks up, burying our breaths.

The metal barrel of a gun glints in the moonlight.

15

Cole pulls me back into the shadow of the grove just as Otto and Bo climb into sight on the moonlit moor. They're by the shed; my uncle hoists his gun and disappears around the corner of the slanting structure while Bo limps back and forth, hands in his pockets, and looks out at the moor. Otto appears again from the other side of the shed, and I can hear his muttered curses from here.

"Where *is* he?" My uncle's voice rumbles down the hill toward us.

"Are you sure he's here?" asks Bo, toeing a patch of dirt with his boot. He gestures to the sprawling countryside. "Come on, Otto. Let's head back," he says, yawning. "I haven't seen my bed in days."

"He's got to be here. I know they're hiding him." He sounds tense, tired. "Dammit." He looks out past the shed at the night-soaked world. I can imagine him squinting, hoping something comes to life.

"I thought you said we were doing this in the morning, anyway. Now you're pulling me out here in the middle of the night."

"I changed my mind. I thought we'd have a better shot now. Before the village is up."

He means before I'm up, before I can get here to warn Cole. He knows. Or at least suspects.

Behind Otto, Bo sighs and pulls a few things from his pockets. He strides over to the shed and kneels as best he can with his bad leg, dropping a small object to the ground. Then he shoves a swatch of cloth beneath the edge of one of the rotting boards of the shed, when my uncle finally turns and notices him.

"What are you doing?"

"Speeding things up," says Bo, kicking some dirt over the piece of cloth. "What's *your* plan? Pull up a chair and wait for the boy to show? Or wait around for the sisters to find you and throw you in the hearth?"

I swear beneath my breath as I realize what's going on. He's planting evidence.

"I don't like this at all, Bo," my uncle says, his tone a mixture of shock and anger.

"Look, Otto, something has to be done." Bo brings a hand down hard on my uncle's shoulder. "We know it's him. This way we can help the others realize it too."

"The Council put you up to this, didn't they?"

Bo pauses, seems to weigh his words. "Master Eli says it's for the best."

"He told you and not me?"

A grim smile creeps over Bo's face. "You've been pre-occupied. But this needs to be taken care of."

"And what about the *children*?" growls Otto. "How does this get us any closer to finding them?"

"Once we have the stranger," he says, gesturing back toward the shed, "we can get him to tell us where they are. Until then…"

My uncle's shoulders have crept up to his ears. I'm leaning forward, hoping he'll say, *No, enough, this is wrong.*

But he doesn't.

He just runs his fingers through his hair, tugs his beard, and follows Bo down the hill. I shrink back against Cole. Bo and Otto are coming along the path toward the grove.

Toward *us.*

My pulse quickens, and Cole must sense it, because he tightens his arms around me and breathes into my hair, something between a kiss and a shushing sound.

Then he slips backward through the trees, impossibly silent over twigs and dead leaves, taking me with him. Inch by inch we slide back from the path, into the shelter of the thicker trunks. The wind picks up just enough to make the branches and the clinging leaves hum as the two men enter the grove.

My uncle passes, inches from my face.

But he doesn't see me. His eyes never leave the back of Bo's head.

And then they're gone, out of the grove and back toward Near. And there we are, Cole and me pressed against a tree in the thickening night. He lets out a long breath. It wanders down the back of my neck, and I shiver.

"That was close," Cole whispers. I peel myself away, and we slip back onto the path.

"Cole, they're going to *frame* you."

"Then I'll remove the evidence."

"Don't you see? That's not the point." I lean back against a tree. "They don't care if you did it or not. How can we prove you're innocent?"

"We can't. They don't care about innocence."

"We've got to find the one who's really doing this," I say. "If it *is* the Near Witch, if she's somehow come back, then how do we find her? How do we *stop* her?" My head is pounding. I feel ragged.

"Lexi," he says, with a strange calm that might just be exhaustion, "you said yourself the children's voices weren't made by children. And that wind path wasn't made by feet. This is craft. How many witches in the town of Near?"

"The sisters, and the Near Witch—who's dead, last time I checked—and you."

"Do you trust the sisters?"

"I do."

"And do you trust me?" he asks.

I take a step toward him. "I do."

"Then it has to be the Near Witch."

I nod, warily. My gut tells me that it's true, or at least possible, and my father taught me to trust my gut. But what is it that she's doing, exactly, and how do you stop a witch who is supposed to be dead? My head spins. *Sleep, just a little*, my body pleads.

"We'll figure this out, Lexi." He closes the gap between us, and his fingers wander down my jaw. "What happens to the Near Witch in the story?"

"She was banished. Cast out of Near. She died alone among the weeds hundreds of years ago."

"How did your father tell it? Maybe there are clues."

I lean my head against his chest and close my eyes. My thoughts drag, but I try to pick up where I left off, try to remember my father's ending. The thing about reciting a story is that it's hard to start again when you stop in the middle. I remember things in wholes, not pieces.

"Let's see," I whisper, feeling as though I could float away. "The Near Witch was a part of everything and nothing. And she loved the village, and the children, very much. Some days, when she was feeling patient, she would do tricks for them. Only small ones, like making the flowers bloom in a blink, or making the wind whisper things that were almost words. The children were starved for craft of any kind and eager to see it everywhere, and they loved her for it."

I pause, because my father always paused at this point. My father only told me the next part once or twice, and it's hard for me to find the words. "Until one day. One day a boy died in the garden, and the world changed. The three hunters who protected the village banished the witch. The night she was cast out, her cottage sank into the grass, and her garden grew back into the soil. And she was never seen again. But she was heard, out on the moor, singing her hills to sleep. Over the years and years the singing softened, until it was little more than the wind. And then it died away entirely. And that was the last of the Near Witch." I sigh. "Not terribly useful, but that's how my father told it, anyway."

Cole leans back a little to look at me. "You say that like there's another version."

"I think so." I shake my head, dazed. "Magda has never told it, but I know she doesn't believe this ending. I told it to her once and she scrunched up her face and shook her head."

"Well, that's a start. If there's another ending, one the sisters aren't sharing, then maybe it's because there's truth in it. We'll ask them in the morning."

"They don't trust me," I say.

"They don't trust anyone. But they'll tell us. Now go home. Sleep." He plants a light kiss on top of my head and turns to leave the grove.

"Wait," I say, pulling him back. "What about Otto? He'll come back."

"I'll be all right."

"How?" I ask, the tightness working back into my chest. "Where are you going to hide?"

As if in response, the wind around us picks up, whipping leaves into small swirls, and right before my eyes, Cole begins to blur, his edges fading into the night around us. He offers a faint smile. "There's plenty of space."

My grip tightens on his arm, afraid he'll melt away entirely. But the wind dies down and he's there, flesh and blood again.

"How long can you hide?" I ask, hopelessness creeping in with fatigue.

"Just until we find the real one responsible. Just until we find the children. Then I won't have to."

It's not as specific an answer as I was hoping for, but I suppose it will do. I lean in to kiss him good night.

"Just in case," I whisper.

His hands wrap around my waist, but he hesitates.

"What is it?" I say, taking a step back.

"I'm tired. I don't have as much control."

"Then stay calm." I lean forward, as smooth and slow as

if he were a deer. When my lips are inches from his, I pause, wait for him to pull back again, but he doesn't. My breath presses against his.

"Stay calm," I repeat, and my lips brush his. The clouds suddenly stop moving, as if they want to pause the moment as much as I do. When I pull away, there is something new on his face, something faint, a trace of a smile. Tired, but there.

And then he's the one pulling me closer, his cool hand against the curve of my back as he lets kisses fall on my shoulder, my neck. A small laugh escapes me as his hair tickles my skin. It feels good—both to laugh and to be held like this. The wind around us begins to ripple, to rise and fall. Cole works his way up until his eyes meet mine. Overhead, the sky grows darker, almost black, and I know that that's not right. We have passed the darkest part of night, and the light should be spreading. I lean my head back, peering up through the tree's canopy at the sky. The clouds are still there, blotting out the moon.

"Cole," I whisper as the wavering wind turns into something stronger. "Cole, stay *calm*."

His eyes lock onto mine again, and this time he frowns. "It's not me," he says as the wind grows and grows, curling itself into a familiar melody that makes my heart sink. "It's her."

And just then the world goes black and the song gets louder. There beneath the melody, I hear it, those almost-words. The ones the adults do not hear and the children hear too clearly, calling them from their beds.

Wren. My chest constricts again as I realize what's happening. The song and the unnatural darkness come each night, and in the morning beds are empty. I have to get home. I pull away from him, turning back through the grove, when the world sways violently beneath my feet. Cole's fingers tighten around mine, and he says something, but I cannot hear. The music overtakes everything, and the night is thick as ink. The moor beneath me falls away. His fingers fall away. The night falls away. And all goes dark and still.

16

Sunlight, sudden and warm, pours across the bed.

I sit up with a start. My mother's soft steps sound in the kitchen. Wren's skipping ones thump in the hall. Wren. Home and safe. A shuddering breath escapes. I feel numb, dazed. How did I get here? The light filtering in is crisp and clean.

A memory ripples, as thin as a dream, of being half carried, half guided home, a low voice whispering as my boots slid over the tangled grass. I cast off the sheets. My cloak is sitting by the dresser. I cross to the window and push it open, looking down. My boots are waiting neatly beneath the sill. Everything is in its place.

When I bump into Wren in the hall, I kneel and throw my arms around her, ignoring her attempts to wriggle free.

"They're all playing without me," she pouts.

"Who is?" If Wren is here and safe, then whose bed was found empty this morning?

But the answer greets me soon enough.

"And Mrs. Harp says the same thing," a voice says.

It's Tyler, of all people, eagerly relaying the details to my mother.

And he's talking about Mrs. Harp. *Emily's* mother. The girl takes shape in my mind, doing a tiny, playful twirl, two dark braids trailing behind her like kite tails.

"No clues at all?" asks my mother softly.

I linger there in the hall a moment, still hugging Wren and listening for more fractured bits of conversation.

No evidence. I am no longer surprised. The wind came in and stole Emily from her small bed. I can picture it. A quilt peeled back neatly, exposing the pale sheets, cool and empty. Maybe they found her charm on the bedside table, cast off like blankets on a warm night.

Wren wiggles out of my arms, her own pouch still around her wrist, smelling sweet and earthy. I bring my fingers up to it as a breeze weaves through.

I shiver and see that the front door is open.

That's when I realize how late it is, the sun already too high. As if on cue, I hear my uncle's heavy tread across the threshold, and my breath catches in my throat.

Cole.

The planted evidence.

Wren escapes, flitting down the hall to Otto. She nearly runs into him, throwing her arms out at the last minute for a hug. He catches her, lifting her up and wrapping his heavy arms around her.

"Morning, Wren," he says into her hair before setting her down.

His eyes meet mine for a moment, and then, to my surprise, he smiles.

"Good morning, Lexi," he says, his voice even.

I try not to let the shock make its way into my face. "How are you, Uncle?"

Then I notice his sleeves, pushed up and dirty, a long scratch down one forearm.

"What did you *do*?" I ask, eyes narrowing.

Otto rolls down his sleeves carefully. "I did what had to be done."

I try to rush past him, but his hands are too fast, grabbing my wrist.

"Did you go to him? Try to warn him?" he asks.

"What are you talking about?" I pull back.

His fingers tighten and I wince, trying to break free as Tyler spills into the hallway.

"So help me, Lexi, I told you not to disobey me." Otto's voice is choked. "Don't you see what you're doing? What you've already done?"

"*Otto*," says my mother behind him, her voice stronger than I have heard it in months. "Let her go."

My uncle abandons his grip at once, as if he did not notice he was hurting me, and I stumble back into Tyler, who seems all too eager to catch me.

I swallow all the curses rising in my throat as I push past him out of the house.

"I cannot save her now," Otto mutters as I go.

There are red finger-shaped lines on my wrist, but I can't feel anything but anger and frustration and most of all fear for Cole and the sisters. I take my boots from beneath my window, abandoning my father's knife and my cloak, ignoring the brisk late summer air. I can't go back inside. I don't have time.

Otto's threats rise in the air behind me, but I don't look back.

*

The first thing I see is smoke.

But as the cottage comes into sight, I realize it's coming from the chimney; the air has gone from cool to cold in a matter of days. The front door hangs open, and even from the path I can see the table overturned within, the floor littered with cups and bowls and leaves and other things that blew in. One of the kitchen chairs is sitting in the front yard, and in it, Magda. At her feet is a basket of sticks and stones, and she hums to herself as she works, as if nothing is amiss. Her tune mixes with the wind, so entangled that I cannot pick the two melodies apart. As I get closer, I can make out a few of the words of her song. They slip between her wrinkled lips with almost no consonants.

"...village door, watchful eyes turned out at night, keep the evils out of sight..."

She is building birds. Her gnarled fingers peel thread-fine strips from short straight sticks, and wrap the string around and between stones and scraps of wood. I hurry toward the house, scanning the moor for a swatch of dark gray between the pale green world and the pale blue sky. But all I see are rolling waves of grass. A fog has settled over everything. The backs of the hills bristle up from it like sleeping beasts.

"Magda!" I call as I draw near. "What happened? Where's Cole? Is he—"

From the corner of my eye, I catch a glimpse, a shadow. And then he's there, in the doorway, waiting for me.

I run up the path and throw my arms around him. He staggers back a step but doesn't push me away. His arms encircle me gently.

"You're here," I say, breathless with relief. "I thought... I don't know what I thought. Otto came home and was saying these things... about doing what had to be done. He accused me of warning you."

"I'm here," he says. "It's all right."

"What happened, Cole? Last night... and then this? I thought..." I fumble my words and tighten my grip, inhaling the scent of his gray cloak, fresh air with a hint of smoke.

He bends his head, kissing the curve of my neck gently. I look past him into the house. "I warned Magda and Dreska," he says into my shoulder, "but they refused to leave."

"Of course we did," snaps Dreska, sweeping up a few broken plates, using the broom at once as a crutch and a tool. She stoops to grab the leg of an overturned stool and rights it by the fire.

"What happened?" I ask, bending to pick up a basket.

"What do you think happened?" says Dreska. "Your uncle and his men came up here looking for our guest, and when they didn't find him, they made a mess of things." She picks up a bowl. "As if he could be hiding under dishes."

"They came to the shed," Cole adds, shaking his head. "I shouldn't have removed their evidence."

"All the things they knocked around have been knocked around a hundred times before," Dreska grumbles. "Put the basket on the table," she adds, "once Cole has set the table right."

Cole slips away and turns the wooden table on its feet. Its surface is a web of scars and burns, but aside from the groan it gives at being set upright, it seems fine.

"That's why he asked me if I'd warned you," I say, rubbing my arms for warmth. Cole notices and pulls his cloak off, settling it around my shoulders. It's surprisingly soft and warm.

Dreska hauls the kettle over the hot fire.

A few moments later, Magda toddles in with her basket of finished stick-and-stone birds. She lets it fall to the ground beside the door with a rattle. "Their eyes were full of dark things. That man is the worst," she says.

I feel the unexpected need to defend my uncle, even though he's letting this happen. Even though there are still red marks on my wrist from his heavy fingers.

"Otto doesn't—" I begin.

"No, not Otto," says Magda, waving a hand. "The other one. The tall, bored-looking one."

"Bo," I say, and the word comes out like a curse. "Bo Pike." Behind my eyes I see him kneeling, planting the scraps of children's clothes, his nose and his hair both pointing down at it.

"This can't go on." I turn to Cole. " You can't keep hiding from them. If Otto's men manage to turn everyone against you, there will be nowhere to hide."

"I'm not leaving, Lexi." His stubborn expression leaves me no room for argument.

"Magda," I say, meaning to change the subject. "Dreska." The sisters do not look at me or stop their bustling, but I know they are listening, waiting for me to go on.

"The Near Witch didn't just fade away on the moor, did she?" I ask, my voice shrinking. "Something must have happened. Something bad."

Magda takes a deep breath and blows the air out. "Yes, dearie," she says, slipping into a chair. Her body cracks like dead branches as she bends. "Something bad happened." She casts a glance out the window at the rolling hills to the east, as though she's afraid someone might be listening.

"What happened?" I ask.

Dreska stops sweeping, but only for a moment, and then redoubles her effort, the *swoosh swoosh* of the broom filling the room like static. The metal top of the kettle whistles as the water boils. Magda grabs a towel and, with both hands, hoists the kettle from the fire.

"Tell me the end of the story." I hesitate, then add, "The real ending."

The cups clank against each other as they're put on the table with the kettle and the sliced bread.

Magda looks at me as if I've gone mad. Or I've grown up. It's kind of the same thing. She opens her mouth, revealing the gaps where teeth are missing, but before she speaks, Dreska shakes her head.

"No, no, no reason for that, dearie," Magda says, fidgeting with a wooden stick she's found on the floor.

"I need to know," I press, glancing at Cole. He's taken up a place beside the open window. I wonder if it's hard for him to be confined, if he needs fresh air. "If the Near Witch is stealing the children—"

"Who said she was?" cuts in Dreska.

"How could she?" adds Magda. "She's dead and gone."

But the way they say it, it's so guarded. They don't believe a word of it. Cole gives me a small nod of encouragement.

"I know you think it's her, Dreska," I say, trying not to crack under her stony glare. Neither sister speaks, but they exchange a series of glances. "I heard you with Tomas, in the village. You tried to tell him, and you both tried to tell Otto. They don't believe it, but I do."

All the sound has gone out of the room.

"And if we don't find the culprit and the children soon..." My eyes flick to Cole beside the open window. Then to Magda, busying herself with tea, and Dreska, staring straight at me, almost through me, with those sharp eyes. This is my chance to persuade them.

"Things are going to get worse. No one can figure out who's taking the children. They'll blame Cole, but it won't fix anything. The children are going to keep disappearing. Wren is going to disappear, and I can't sit by and wait for that to happen while they look for someone to blame!" I stare up at the ceiling, trying to compose myself among the wooden eaves. "We have to give them proof. We have to put things right."

Dreska gives me a heavy look, as if she can't decide whether to tell me to go home, or confide in me.

"Magda. Dreska. My father spent his life trying to make Near trust you. Now please trust *me*. Let me help."

"Lexi is the one who warned me, warned us about Otto's men," Cole finally adds.

"And why are you so convinced it's the Near Witch, Lexi Harris?" Dreska asks.

"She could control all the elements, right? Even move the earth. She could cover tracks. And there's this strange path, like a trail, on the tops of the grass."

Dreska's eyes narrow a fraction, but she doesn't interrupt.

"So the only thing I don't know is how she came back, and why she would want to steal the children in the first place. Will you tell me or not?" The words come out louder than I expected. They echo off the stone walls.

Dreska's face wrinkles, all the cracks working in toward the center, between her eyes. Magda hums the Witch's Rhyme as she pours hot liquid over the old wire mesh strainers and into the cups. Steam winds up through the air, curling around her.

Dreska casts one last glance at Cole, leaning up against the wall by the window, and shakes her head. But when she speaks, it's to say, "Very well, Lexi."

"Might as well sit down," adds Magda. "Tea's ready."

17

"The Near Witch lived on the edge of the village," Magda begins, "on the seam where Near met the wild world. This was many, many years ago. Perhaps before Near was even Near. And yes, it is true that she did have a garden, and it is true that the children liked to go and see her. The villagers did not bother her, but they did not befriend her either. One day, so it goes, a little boy went to see the Near Witch, and didn't come home." Magda stares into a corner of the room.

Dreska is shifting around the space, clearly uncomfortable. She pulls the windows closed, and Cole winces, but she continues on, fiddling with the kettle and looking out through the glass at the darkening moor. The rain breaks at last, comes down hard and heavy against the house. Magda continues.

"As the sun sank, and the day wound down, the boy's mother went to find him. She reached that little cottage on the edge of Near, just over there." And now Magda points over her sister's shoulder, out past the house. "But the witch wasn't home. The boy was there, though, in the garden, among the red and yellow flowers." Her fingers grip her teacup.

"He was dead. Dead as if he'd fallen asleep in those flowers and never thought to get up again. The mother's screams could be heard, they say, even over the moor wind.

"Later, the Near Witch returned home with her arms full of tall grass and berries, and other things that witches like to gather. Her house was engulfed in flames, and her precious garden stomped and scorched. A group of hunters was waiting.

"'Murder,' they cried, 'murder!'" Magda's voice cracks as she says it, and I wince. "And the hunters swooped down like ravens on the Near Witch. She cried out to the trees, but they were rooted and could not save her. She cried out to the grass, but it was small and flimsy, and could not save her."

The rain pounds against the stones of the house, and Dreska seems to be listening to her sister's story with one ear, and the storm with the other. Cole stands in the corner and says nothing, but his jaw is tense and his eyes unfocused.

"At last, the Near Witch called out to the earth itself. But it was too late, and even the earth couldn't save her then." She takes a long sip of tea. "Or so they say, dearie." I can see it just the way she says, only it's not the witch behind my eyes, begging the moor for help. It's Cole. I shiver.

"Goodness, Magda, the stories you tell," Dreska says from her place at the windowsill. She turns away then, continues to busy her hands, moving a pot, pushing away a few stray leaves with her cane.

Magda eyes me. "They killed the witch, the three hunters did."

"The three hunters?" I say. "The men who formed the original Council? They were given their title for *protecting* the village."

Dreska gives a short nod. "Weren't the Council then, just young hunters, but yes. Men like your uncle, like that Bo. The hunters took the witch's body out onto the moors, far, far out, and buried it very deep."

"But the earth's like the skin, it grows in layers," I murmur, remembering Magda's nonsensical words in the garden. The old woman nods.

"What's on top peels back. What's underneath works its way up, eventually," she says, this time adding, "If it's angry enough."

"And strong enough."

"It was a very wrong death for such a powerful witch."

"Over the years the body grew up and up until at last it reached the surface and broke through," says Dreska, darkly. "And now at last the moor has been able to save its witch." After a long pause, she adds humorlessly, "Or so *we* believe."

Again the sisters speak in their intertwining way.

"She climbed up and out onto the moor," says Dreska.

"Now her skin really is made of moor grass," adds Magda.

"Now her blood is made of moor rain."

"Now her voice is made of moor wind."

"Now the Near Witch is made of moor."

"And she is furious."

The sisters' words echo through the cottage, winding like steam around us. I suddenly wish the windows were open, even if the rain poured in. It's hard to breathe in here. The dirt floor of the cottage seems to ripple as Magda speaks. The stone walls jostle.

"That's the reason that the children are disappearing now," I say quietly. "The Near Witch is taking them to punish the village…"

Magda is still nodding, as steady as a water drip.

The words from my father's book, Magda's words, slip back to me: *The wind is lonely, and always looking for company.* That's exactly what the witch is doing, drawing them from their beds. I shudder.

"But why only at night?"

"Powerful though she is, she is still dead," says Dreska.

"Dead things are bound to their beds until dark," says Magda.

But there's something in their tones, something I've been trying to pinpoint this entire time. A softness when the sisters speak of the Near Witch.

"You liked her," I say, only realizing it as the words leave my lips.

Something almost like a smile flickers on Dreska's face. "We were children too, once."

"We played in her garden," says Magda, stirring her tea.

"We respected her."

I press my fingertips against my teacup until the heat radiates up my hands. All this time Cole has stood like a shadow on the wall, silent, unreadable. I wonder if he sees himself in the story, his own house burning to the ground. Or if he is witnessing darker things behind his eyes. But when he looks up from his corner, and meets my eyes, a sad almost-smile passes across his face. It's thin, more for me than for him, but I mimic it, and pull my eyes back to the sisters.

"She didn't do it, did she? Kill that boy?"

Dreska shakes her head. "Sometimes a life gets cut short."

"And we need someone to blame."

"The boy, he had a very bad heart."

"He lay down in that garden and went to sleep."

"And they killed her for it," I whisper, teacup pressed to my lips. "You knew? All along you knew? Why didn't you tell me? Why haven't you done anything?"

"Believing and knowing are different things," says Dreska, returning to the table.

"Knowing and proving are different things," says Magda.

The sisters are wearing matching frowns, deep and creased. In the corner, Cole's face is cast in shadows again. And beyond the window, the rain is ebbing, but the sky is still dark.

"We don't know where the witch is buried," says Dreska, with a long sweeping motion of her hand.

"And we tried to tell them," says Magda, tipping her head back toward the village. "Tried to tell the searchers right from the start, but they wouldn't listen."

"Stubborn," says Dreska. "Just as they were back then."

"As you said yourself, Lexi." Magda turns her cup in small circles on the table. "The villagers will never believe it. Otto's men will never believe it."

I look out through the gray day, light leaking back into the corners.

"What do we need to do," I ask, "to make things right?"

"Well, first," says Magda, finishing her tea and pushing herself to her feet. "First, you've got to find the witch's body. You've got to find the bones."

"And put them to rest," murmurs Dreska, almost with reverence.

"Properly buried."

"Properly kept."

"That is the way with witches."

"And with all things."

"Where?" I ask, standing.

"Where she lived," they answer.

The sisters lead us from the house. Outside, the air is cool, not bitter, but enough to make my skin prickle.

"Yes, I know it's around here somewhere," says Magda, scratching her wrinkled cheek with a dirt-caked nail. "Ah yes, right there." She points to the second patch between the cottage and the low stone wall, the one beyond her garden. The patch that's always seemed scraped clean, strangely bare in a place overrun with grass and weedy flowers. I lean down and realize that the ground, close up, is burned. Barren, devoid of grass. I run my fingers over it, the whole patch turned to mud from the storm. It doesn't make sense. The fire would have been centuries ago. The grass should have recovered. And yet, I can almost see the scorch marks. As if the ground's been freshly ruined.

"This was her house," I murmur.

"And the garden's almost ready," says Dreska, gesturing down at the soil bed between the stone cottage and the scorched spot of land. Magda's garden. It was the Near Witch's first.

"The witch deserved respect, in life and death," says Magda, so quietly that Dreska shouldn't be able to hear. And yet they nod beside each other, heads bobbing at slightly different paces. "Instead what she got was fear, and then fire and murder."

"But how will we find the bones?" I ask. "They could be anywhere."

Dreska lifts a tired hand to the east, to the open moor.

"That is the way they took her body. That is the way you'll find the bones. How far out, I do not know."

A hand comes to rest against my shoulder, and Cole is there, behind me.

"We'll find them," he promises. Magda and Dreska turn back to the house, and we are alone at the edge of Near.

"It seems impossible," I say, my back still to him. "Where do we even start?"

I look out at the moor, and my heart sinks. The world rolls away. Endless. Hill after hill after hill, flecked with trees. The moor always seems to be eating things. Half-digested rocks and logs jut out from the sloping hillsides. And somewhere out there, it has swallowed the Near Witch, too.

18

I look out at the unending hills, and all I feel is hopeless.

Cole takes a step forward, but I pull him back. "Not yet," I say, shaking my head. "We can't just walk out onto the moor. We need a plan. And they're going to come for you, Cole. Otto and his men will follow us."

He just looks at me.

"There are people I need to visit. I can be as persuasive as my uncle when I need to be." I won't need long.

Cole still says nothing, and I realize how quiet he's been since the sisters told their story. I turn in his arms, and his gray eyes are still strangely dead, looking in instead of out. When he finally speaks, his voice is hollow, almost angry.

"That's a waste of time, Lexi."

"What do you mean?"

"It doesn't matter. What they think of me doesn't matter." The wind around us thickens, like a weight on my chest.

"It matters to *me*. And if Otto and his men catch you, and you're put on trial, what people think will matter a great deal."

He closes his eyes. I bring my hands up to his face, his skin cool against my fingers.

"What's wrong?"

The crease between his brows lessens a fraction at my touch, but he keeps his eyes closed. I can hear his breath filling his chest in short, uneven gasps, as if being torn from his lungs the moment he draws it in. I keep my hands there, on his face, until his skin grows used to my touch, until his breathing grows easy, and the wind around us settles back into a gentle breeze. I could stay right here forever.

"I sometimes wonder what I would do," he says at last, without opening his eyes, "if anyone had survived the fire. Would I have confessed and let them punish me? Would that have eased anyone's pain?"

"Why would you talk like that?" I am surprised at the anger in me. "How would that have made anything better?"

His eyes float open, the lashes black against his pale skin.

"You heard the sisters. Sometimes people need something— someone—to blame. It gives them peace until they can find the real answers."

"But they don't need to blame you. They can blame the Near Witch, and we can prove it, as soon as we find the children." I try to fill my voice with enough determination for the both of us. So this is what he was thinking in the sisters' cottage, when he offered me his sad smile. Was he wishing there had been hunters alive to catch him, to punish him, so he couldn't punish himself?

He softens, but it doesn't go beneath his skin. He shakes his head a fraction, and then he's there again, seeing me.

"I'm sorry," he says quietly. "I didn't mean to upset you." His voice is bare, honest.

"Cole, you're not a rock," I say. "You're not a tree, or a bunch of grass, or a cloud. And you're not just something to cast aside, or burn down, or walk over. Please tell me you understand that." He holds my gaze. "And you're not just the wind, either. You're here, and real, and it may be in you, but it isn't all of you. It doesn't make you less than human."

He gives a soft nod. I slide my arms around his waist, his cloak wrapping around us both.

To every side, the moor is calm, the light is crisp, and the air feels warmer. Right now it does not seem as if any evil could pass through such a place.

In this small moment of peace, my uncle's words creep in: *I cannot save her now.* What did he mean? I tighten my grip on Cole. He bends his head against mine.

"You have a gift," I whisper. He smells like ash still, but also wind, the way clothes smell when left to dry in sun and morning air. "And I need your help. I need you."

I reach up and brush the hair from his face, and his eyes fall shut as he exhales, the tension in his body ebbing.

"When do we start?" he asks.

"We'll find the bones tonight."

"I thought you needed a plan first."

I flash him a smile. "By then, I'll have one."

I give him one last kiss, and I cannot hide the small pleasure I feel when the wind rustles around us.

"I'll see you tonight, then," he says.

I nod and let my arms slide away from him, unfastening the clasp of his cloak. Then I slip it back around his shoulders and make my way down the path. The wind around me weaves through my hair, which I've forgotten to tie up today.

It plays with the dark waves, brushes against the back of my neck. When I cast a last glance back, he is not watching the clouds or the rolling moor. He's watching me, and he smiles.

Smiling back, I head down the hill, eager for night to come.

But there's work to do first.

19

I reach a nest of homes just south of the sisters' cottage and the center of town. Houses are sparse on the eastern side, as if the villagers lean, like grass, away from Magda and Dreska.

I'm cutting through the cluster of houses, thinking over my plan, when a small boy darts out, followed by the muffled protests of his mother. Riley Thatcher.

Eight years old and as sharp as a bundle of sticks, Riley sprints across the yard, stumbles in the dirt, and is up again in a blink. But in that moment something is different. Missing. He's already heading for another house when I catch sight of the small thing left in the weedy grass. I kneel and lift the sisters' charm, the pouch of moss and sweet earth, its cord now broken.

"Riley," I call after him, and the boy turns back. I catch up and return the pouch to him. He nods, smiles, and shoves it in his pocket just as a woman's hand clamps down on the back of his shirt.

"Riley Thatcher, you march yourself inside; I told you not to come out."

Mrs. Thatcher turns him about-face with one hand and gives him a firm shove back through the doorway. I suppress a laugh as she sighs.

"He's so restless. They all are. Not used to being shut inside while the sun's still up," she says.

My laugh dies away. "I know. Wren's allowed to run errands with our mother, but she still misses her freedom. Thankfully it's been damp. If the sun comes out for too long, we'll have to tie her to a chair."

Mrs. Thatcher nods sympathetically. "But with all that's happening, what else can we do? And that stranger, nowhere to be found."

"What are people saying?"

She rubs her forehead with the back of her hand. "Don't you know? They're scared. It doesn't look good for a stranger to show up here, the day before all of this…" She waves her hand, gesturing to the cottages, to the footprints Riley made in the dirt, to everything.

"That doesn't mean he's responsible."

She looks me over, and sighs.

"Come inside, dear," she says. "No reason to talk in the open air. Especially with the weather fickle as it is."

I cast a nervous glance back at the sky, but the sun is still high enough, so I follow her in.

Mrs. Thatcher is a strong woman. She has a way with her hands, like my mother, and she makes most of the village's pots and bowls. Where Riley and his father look like sticks connected with rough twine, she is shaped like one of her pots. But round as her sides might be, her eyes are ever sharp. She does not treat me like a child. She and my mother have always been close. Even closer before my mother became a ghost.

"The stranger, what did you say his name was?" She wipes her hands on a towel that always rests on her shoulder.

"I didn't. It's Cole."

"Well, he hasn't said a word to anyone in the village. And now they go to question him, and he disappears. And I gather it's not the first time they tried to find him. I say good riddance if he's gone, and fair hunting if he's not."

"But it's *not* Cole."

She turns back to the table, preparing a tray.

"Really, now? And how are you so sure, Lexi Harris?"

I swallow. She won't believe it's the Near Witch. "Mrs. Thatcher," I whisper confidingly, leaning forward like Wren does, "I've been searching, too, at night. And that boy Cole has been *helping* me. He's smart. He's a good tracker. I'm a lot closer to finding the real thief because of him."

Her back is to me, but I know she's listening.

"Otto and his men have no idea who's taking the children, and they don't want to look like fools, so they picked Cole. They could have picked anyone. And if they run him from the village, we might never find out who's really taking the children."

"He'll be lucky if that's all they do."

My throat tightens. "What are they going to do?"

Mrs. Thatcher sets a plate of cookies on the table between us, circular disks that look as hard and set as her pottery. Within moments, Riley is there, snatching two or three in a single swipe. Mrs. Thatcher's large hand catches his arm before the cookies can make their way into his pocket. Riley has a wicked grin that reminds me of Tyler when he was that age. I watch as his free hand slips two more cookies into his back pocket.

"Off with you, Riley," she says, and the boy takes one more swipe at the tray and cheerfully departs, having gathered half a dozen cookies between his pockets and palms. I lift one, biting into it politely. The cookie resists. I bite down until my teeth ache, but it's no use, so I lower it into my lap.

She gnaws on a cookie, her eyes narrowed.

"I don't know, Lexi. Everyone is growing restless. They want to see someone pay. Do you really think the stranger is innocent?"

"I do. I'm sure of it. Do you believe me?"

"Oh, I'm inclined to," she says with a sigh. "But unless you and your friend find those children soon, it won't matter what I'm inclined to think."

And I know she's right. I push myself up and thank Mrs. Thatcher for the cookies, and for listening. She smiles, tight but genuine. As I step outside, the cold air bites at my cheeks and hands. The sun slips lower. I turn back and find her waiting in the doorway to see me off. But when I go to thank her again, she is looking past me, her mouth a thin line and her hands crossed over her broad stomach. I turn to see a crow circling overhead, a black smudge against the pale sky.

"You need to convince those who've lost," she says, still staring at the bird. "Those with missing children. The Harps, the Porters, the Drakes. I've heard Master Matthew has taken this hard."

Master Matthew. And then my mind lurches. Matthew

Drake. The third member of the Council. And Edgar and Helena's *grandfather*.

"If you can find the children, do it fast," Mrs. Thatcher says beneath her breath. And with that she slips back inside the house. But I'm already moving as fast as I can. My mind is racing and my heart is racing and my feet are catching up. I'm off toward Helena's house.

*

Three people once knew where the witch was buried. That much I know.

The sun is slipping slowly down the edge of the sky as I head for the Drake house.

Three people. The members of the Council. When Dreska was fighting with Master Tomas, she called him a keeper of secrets and forgotten truths. Is the witch's grave a secret that would have been passed down from Council to Council? I have to hope the knowledge has lasted this long. My only chance of finding the grave is to coax the answer from one of them.

Master Tomas fought with Dreska, and I can tell by his tone that he won't budge.

Master Eli supposedly ordered Bo to plant the evidence, so he's of no use either.

But Master Matthew *Drake*. He has been strangely absent during all of this. And the loss of a grandchild might be enough to sway any foundation. If there's a chance of learning where the witch was buried, it lies with him.

I catch sight of Helena a field's length before their home, and my feet drag to a halt. The guilt sits like stones in the pockets of my dress, like a bad taste in the back of my throat.

She looks wasted away, even from here. I urge my feet forward. I should have come sooner. Not to interrogate her, but to see how she was faring. My cheeks are burning from the run and the cold air, and when I reach Helena I see that her face is red, too, but in different ways. Red-rimmed eyes and splotchy cheeks. Her cool blond hair is tied back against the wind, and she's washing clothes in a stream.

Helena has been transformed. Cheerful Helena, my Helena—who craved the eyes and ears of the village when she announced she'd seen the stranger, when she joked about how attractive he was—now looks gaunt, exhausted. She hums to herself, wandering through melodies like a ghost through rooms. Every now and then the melody strays into the Witch's Rhyme. As I draw closer I can see her hands, red from the cold of the water. When she catches sight of me she tries to smile, a tug of her lips that is closer to a grimace. I slide down beside her in the grass, and wait. She continues rinsing something dark and blue. A boy's shirt. I wrap my arms around her shoulders.

"I want everything to be ready for when Edgar comes back," she says, wringing her brother's little blue shirt out over the water. "That way he'll know we haven't forgotten him." Her fingers keep twisting the fabric. "I hope they find that stranger," she says, and her voice doesn't sound like her own. "I hope they kill him."

The words hurt, but I don't let her see.

"I'm so sorry," I whisper against her cheek. It takes several moments before her hands stop making their small desperate motions over the clothing. I pull back enough to look at her, surprised at the sudden heat in her eyes. "We'll find Edgar. I've been looking, too, every night."

"Where have you been?" Her voice is so low and strained, I can feel my own throat closing. "All the others have come to see us," she says, her voice sliding even lower as she adds, "to see *me*." She breaks the look, letting her gaze escape out over the river. I start to say I'm sorry again—such a useless phrase, but I have to say something—when Helena cuts me off.

"Have you been tracking the stranger? That's how you'll find Edgar."

I shake my head. "The search party is spreading lies, Helena. They do not know who, or what, is taking the children, and they are accusing this poor stranger because they have no suspect. But it's not him. I know it." I take her hands from the water, where they are still working furiously, and pull them out, trying to warm them with my own.

"What do you know?" she says, wrenching her hands from mine. "Would you be so sure if Wren was missing?" She doesn't wait for an answer, doesn't seem to care. "I just want my brother back." Her voice is quiet again. "He must be so scared."

"I'm going to find Edgar," I say. "But please don't blame Cole."

She looks shocked that I know the stranger's name.

"He's been helping me, Helena," I whisper. "We're getting closer to finding the real culprit. We all want answers," I say, tucking a strand of stray blond hair behind her ear, and turning her face to mine. "But it's not him."

"What am I supposed to think, Lexi? Mr. Porter swore he saw him near Cecilia's the night before last, when she vanished. And now Mr. Ward, he says he saw him outside our house the night Edgar disappeared."

The breeze picks up, and I fight back a shiver as the sun seems to slip lower before my eyes. Helena puts her hands back in the icy water, and doesn't flinch.

"It was the middle of the night," I press. "How could they swear they saw anything besides darkness? I don't want to argue with you, but think about it—why didn't that other witness come forward sooner? Yesterday they claim someone saw him near Cecilia's house, but no one said he was by yours. Today they suddenly add another, earlier sighting? And what was Tyler's father even doing out this way at night? Any minute now someone will jump up and say they saw him by Emily's window, too, when really they were all sleeping in their beds."

I wait for her to agree, to flick her hair or make a comment on the Council, on the strangeness of it, on *anything*.

She just pushes another piece of clothing beneath the water.

I stand and brush a few leaves from my skirt. This is a waste. Wherever Helena is, *my* Helena, she's not here.

"Where's your grandfather?"

She waves a raw hand in the direction of her house.

"I'll come back soon. I promise." With that I turn and leave my friend by the icy stream.

*

There's a porch on the house that wraps around three sides. At the corner, just before the narrow wood columns and the simple rail vanish, a shadow of a man stands, looking out.

I approach the porch, trying to stand straighter, make my shoulders somehow broader, hold my head high. It's odd to see Master Matthew so far from the action, tucked away in his old house, the one he has lived in since before he was named to the Council. I hear the flutter of pages and realize he has a book braced against the wooden rail, a dark shawl wrapped around his shoulders.

"Lexi Harris," he says, without turning. His voice is deep and strong for such an old man. "Your uncle seems to think you've taken up your own search at night. What brings you here in daylight? Some wasted hope for clues? I assure you we've looked... I've looked." He keeps his back to me, turning a thin page. "Or are you here to clear that boy's name, to convince me that it isn't him? I fear that will not go well for you."

My legs weaken a fraction, but I only swallow and hold my head high.

"I'm here to speak to *you*, sir."

At last he turns to look at me. Master Matthew's eyes have a softness to them, a feature I don't readily attribute to the Council. It must be from having a family, children, grandchildren. Those things that shape us, round our edges.

He tips his face down and takes in the sight of me over his spectacles, standing there without a coat, trying not to shiver from cold and things that have nothing to do with weather.

"You look just like your father, standing that way. Like you can challenge the world and the way of it if only you can hold your head high enough." When I don't answer, he adds, "Stop holding your breath, Lexi. It doesn't matter how straight you stand." He raises a hand, gesturing me to the porch beside him. I join him. The western sky is plunging into reds and oranges, and all I can think of is fire.

"I need your help, Master Ma—"

"Just Matthew."

"Matthew," I whisper, "I need you to tell me a story."

He turns his head toward me, eyebrows arching. The setting sun lines his face with red-lit wrinkles. I can't help but wonder how old he is. He must be at least eighty, but when he turns his head some ways he looks years younger.

"I need you to tell me the story of the Near Witch. Just the ending."

In a heartbeat, his eyes change from curious to wary. I try not to fidget beneath his cold pale gaze.

"The part where the Council dragged her out onto the moor and buried her." What am I saying? "I really just need to know that part..."

The frustration painted on his face has shifted back into surprise, but I don't know whether it's the question or my boldness. My father would smile. My uncle, on the other hand, would slaughter me if he heard me speaking this way.

"I know nothing more than an old legend, child." There's no malice in his voice, but no kindness either. Each word is careful and measured.

"I think the Near Witch is back, and she's the one taking the children. If I can find where she was buried, then I think I can find them. How can you not help, if there's any way, any way at all to find your grandson? Blaming the stranger won't bring Edgar back. What happens when they get rid of him and the children keep disappearing? Even if you don't believe it's the witch's doing, it's a possibility, and that's more than my uncle and his men have."

I feel like I've used all the air in my lungs.

After a painful silence, he says, "The Near Witch is dead. Chasing ghosts does no one any good."

"But what if—"

"Child, she's *dead*." He slams the book to the porch floor. "Hundreds of years dead." He looks down at his hands, fingers white from gripping the railing. "She's long gone. Long enough to be a story. Long enough that some days I doubt she ever lived."

"But if there's any chance," I say in a small voice. "Even if it's just a silly theory. A theory is better than nothing." I place my hands over his, both of ours cold as the last light bleeds out of the sky. He just stares at my fingers. "My sister, Wren, is friends with Edgar. They're almost the same age. I can't..." I tighten my hands over his. "I can't sit and wait for her to disappear. Please, Matthew." I don't realize I'm near tears until my voice hitches in my throat.

Master Matthew won't meet my eyes. He's looking at the dregs of light, which have lost their color, casting the world in shades of gray.

"Five hills due east, in a small forest." The words spill out of him in an exhale, barely above a whisper.

"The founding Council took her east, out past the house, what was left of it, out five hills until they reached a group of trees. According to the stories, it was barely a grove, but that was a long time ago, and things grow fast out on the moor, if they choose to grow at all."

Funny how when we start to tell a secret, we can't stop. Something falls open in us, and the sheer momentum of letting go pushes us on.

"I choose to believe, Miss Harris, that the Council did what they thought was—not right; right is the wrong word. What they thought was necessary."

"She didn't kill the boy."

He finally looks at me. "I doubt it mattered." And in that moment, I realize how much danger Cole is in. My hands slide off of Master Matthew's.

"Thank you."

He gives a small tired nod. "You really are like him, your father."

"I can't tell whether you think that's good or bad."

"What does it matter? It's simply true."

I step off the porch when he adds, almost too quietly to hear, "Good luck."

I smile and press north, toward home, to wait for night.

*

There is a wooden crow nailed to our door.

The center stick is almost as gnarled and knobbed as Magda's fingers. Two long nails have been driven through, one pinning the stick to the door, and the other splitting the wood as it breaks through the front, like a rusted beak. A few black feathers dangle to the sides, bound to the stick with rope, and they flutter in the evening air. And there, just above the sharp nail of a beak, two river rocks, as smooth and polished as mirrors, glisten for eyes. I push the door open, and the wooden crow rattles against it. What was it Magda said?

Watchful eyes turned out at night, keep the evils out of sight.

20

Inside, the house is too quiet.

I wait for Otto's grumbling to pour out of the kitchen, for the sound of his cup hitting the table, but there's nothing. Wren is sitting cross-legged in one of the kitchen chairs, spinning a makeshift top on the old wooden table and looking painfully bored, while my mother clumsily mends the hem of a dress. Even the sounds of the fabric and the top are dulled, as though the air has been sucked out of the room. I hover in the doorway, my earlier argument with my uncle replaying in my head.

"Where's Otto?" I ask, and my voice breaks the strange quiet, sends the moment crashing down. The wooden top falters and bounces off the table with a harsh *tap tap tap tap*. Wren hops down and hurries after it. My mother looks up from her work.

"The men were meeting. In town."

"Why?"

"You know why, Lexi," she says.

I want to scream from frustration. Instead I clench my fist until my nails dig into my palm, and say only, "Cole is *innocent*."

Her eyes sharpen. "The sisters trust him, don't they?"

I nod.

Her brow knits ever so slightly, and she says, "Then he can be trusted."

She reaches out, and her fingers come to rest on my arm. "Near might not look after the sisters, Lexi, but they look after Near." She offers a sad smile. "You know that."

They are my father's words coming from her lips. I want to throw my arms around her.

At that moment, Wren bobs back into the kitchen, Otto in tow. His dark gaze immediately falls on me.

I remember Matthew's words. *Your uncle seems to think you've taken up your own search at night.*

"Otto..."

I brace myself for another fight, but none comes. No loud accusations or threats.

"Don't you see, Lexi?" he says, his voice barely above a whisper. "You've betrayed me and my wishes. That I can forgive. But you've betrayed Near by helping that boy. The Council, they are not forced to forgive. They can banish you, if they see fit."

"Banish?" I ask. The word feels odd in my mouth.

"There would be nothing I could do to protect you from it."

Otto slides into his chair, and my mother peels away from me, fetching him a mug. My uncle puts his head in his hands. The image of the wild moor, rippling to every side, flickers in my mind. No signs of Near. Only space. Freedom. Would it be so bad? As if reading my mind, Otto says, "No home. No family. No Wren. Ever again." The image in my mind begins to darken and transform until the endless space feels too small. Terrifying. I swallow and shake my head. It will not come to that. I cannot let it.

It will be over soon. I will fix things.

I don't know how the town meeting went. I don't know the Council's plans, or those of Otto and his men. But I do know this: They might have a plan for the morning, but I intend to settle this tonight.

*

Deep in the house my mother is humming.

It's something old and slow and sweet, and the sheer fact that it is not the Witch's Rhyme makes my shoulders loosen and my body sigh against the dresser by the window. The candles are already lit. The pouch still dangles from Wren's wrist. Outside the light is gone and the moon is low. My mother's song fades away, and moments later I see her through the weathered glass, leading Otto home. She brushes the tension from his shoulders and ushers him toward his cottage, waiting by the door until he vanishes within. Moments later a dull glow fills the space inside, and she turns back home.

Behind me, Wren fidgets with the bracelet, legs swinging back and forth from the edge of the bed.

"Listen, Wren," I say, turning to her. "Do you remember the way Father used to tell the Near Witch stories? What he said about the way she would sing the hills to sleep at night?"

She shakes her head. "I don't remember him," she says, and my heart sinks.

"Father was…" How will I ever recreate our father for her? Not just his stories, but the way he smelled like firewood and fresh air, and his smiles, impossibly warm and gentle for such a large man. They'd be just images, pretty pictures with no weight.

"Well," I say, clearing my throat, "Father used to say that the Near Witch loved children very much. And, well, she..." I cannot find the words, cannot seem to reconcile these stories with the idea that the witch is real and somehow back and stealing children from their beds instead of singing to them in her garden. It is all knotted, like the time between sleep and waking, where dreams and real life get tangled, confused. I try to mimic my father's stories.

"What if it's not your friends calling, Wren? What if it's the Near Witch coming to call you out onto the moors?"

"Because children taste better in moonlight," Wren recites, clearly not amused. "Don't try to scare me," she adds, wriggling beneath the covers.

"I'm not," I insist. "I'm very serious." But she's right. I cannot make it sound real. These are the stories we grew up with. I smooth the covers over her small form, and touch the charm around her wrist. "Magda and Dreska are witches, Wren, that much is true. And they made this to keep you safe. No matter what happens, you've got to keep it on."

"More and more are going to play," she pouts, "and I haven't gone yet. They all try to call me out." Wren lets out a heavy sigh and curls up beneath the covers.

"They'll all stop playing this game soon." I stroke her hair and whisper stories, the soft, sweet kind my father told. Not of witches or wind songs, but hills that rolled and rolled until they slipped right into the sea. Of clouds that grew tired and sank from the sky, and stretched out on the moor in tendrils of fog. Of a little girl's shadow that grew and grew until it covered the sky and became the night, and under it, all things slept, safe beneath their covers.

21

Five hills due east, in a small forest.

I repeat the words over and over in my head as I slip barefoot from the window to the ground beneath, and slide on my boots. I look back at Wren fast asleep, and say a silent prayer that her charm continues to work. I tighten my boots and latch the shutters, checking twice that they won't open, before I turn to face the moor and make my way to the sisters' house.

When I get there, the windows are dark and the roof blots out the moonlight so that the space hugging the house is a ring of black.

"Cole," I whisper, and then I catch the faint movement as my eyes adjust to the shadowed house and the glaring moon beyond. He's leaning back against the cottage stones, arms crossed and chin tucked against his chest as if he's fallen asleep while standing. But as I draw near, he looks up.

"Well, Lexi," he says, coming to meet me. "Have you got a plan now?"

I smile in the dark. "I said I would."

Cole gives a silent nod and takes my hand, and we hurry
to the edge of the sisters' hill. I tell him about the afternoon,
about Matthew, about the five hills and the forest separating
us from the Near Witch. We pass the small scorched plot
where the witch lived, reaching the place where the sisters'
hill gives way to the moor. We pause, as if we are standing at
the edge of a cliff, looking out to sea. And for a moment I
am utterly terrified by how vast the world is. For a moment
the five hills seem like five mountains, and then like five
worlds. Doubt begins to creep in. What if we're wrong?
What if Matthew lied?

But then the wind begins to blow, just enough against my
back to urge me forward. Cole's hand tightens around mine,
and with that, we set out for the first hill.

*

The sisters' house is quickly lost from sight. We keep the
rising moon in front of us, and under its silvery light I scan
the untouched earth for any signs of trespass. But the land is
messy and wild, and it's hard to tell what's untouched, really,
in a place where everything looks tousled. Now and then I
kneel, sure I've caught sight of a step, or a trace, but it's only
the moor playing tricks.

I notice a few sticks snapped cleanly by the weight of a
foot. Up close it is clearly the work of a deer's hoof, not a
child's foot, and an old break at that, nearly swallowed by
rain and dirt and change.

We make our way up the second hill.

"Where did you learn to hunt and track?" Cole asks.

I stop and kneel, my fingers tracing a stone embedded in

the weeds, smooth and dark like the ones the sisters used for eyes on the wooden crows. I lift it, rubbing the dirt away with my thumb.

"My father taught me."

Cole kneels next to me. "What happened to him?"

I let the smooth stone fall back to the earth with a small thud.

I know my father's story. I know it as well as the ones he told me, but I cannot tell it in the same practiced way. It's written in my blood and bones and memory instead of on pieces of paper. I wish I could tell it as a tale and not his life and my loss. But I don't know how yet. A small broken piece of me hopes I never know how, because my father wasn't just a bedtime story.

"If you don't want to…" he says.

I take a deep breath and begin to descend the second hill.

"My father was a tracker. The best," I say as Cole falls in step behind me. "He was a big man, but he could make himself as small and silent as a field mouse. And he had this laugh that shook the leaves from the trees.

"You can ask anyone in Near, and they'll tell you about his strength or his skill, but I will always remember him for that laugh, and for the way he could make his booming voice soft and warm when he told me stories.

"People loved him so much they gave him a title, right beneath the Council. They called him their Protector. He watched over the village, and even the moor seemed to trust him. As if he knew how to be both, to walk the line between person and witch. That's how I always thought of him, growing up. I wanted to learn to walk that line, too."

"Is that why you keep calling this"—he gestures to himself and the breeze tousling his hair and his cloak—"a gift?"

"I can't help but think that if... if I were like you, I'd never feel alone. My father had this way with the moor," I explain. "Like he knew what it wanted, like it confided in him. I know witches are born, not made, but I honestly thought he'd found some way to speak to the moor, to make the land and the weather answer to him. I thought that it was the ultimate gift, to be connected to something so vast."

"It is the loneliest feeling in the world," says Cole. "I don't feel like a person. I want to feel pain, and joy, and love. Those are the things that connect humans to each other. They're much stronger threads than those connecting me to the wind."

I frown. I'd never thought of it that way. "So, you don't feel those things?"

He hesitates. "I do. But it's easy to forget. To lose yourself."

And I want to say that I understand, that I too have felt that lost, but I just nod.

We climb the third hill, and Cole says nothing, so I go on.

"Whenever my father went out, he began by first thanking the moor," I say. "He would look up to the clouds, and down to the grass, and then out to the hills, and whisper a prayer."

We crest the third hill. The world dips away around us, and I focus on the fourth hill ahead, instead of the sickening lightness that floods my head and chest when I speak about my father, stealing all the space for air.

"'I entrust myself to you, the moor,' he'd whisper. 'I am

born of the moor, as is my family. I take from the moor. I give back to the moor.' Every time he set foot on the hills he would pray, and for a very long time the moor kept him safe."

We make our way down an uneven slope, and I glance over at Cole, who is keeping his eyes leveled on the wind as it weaves through blades of wild grass, listening.

"He was always drawn to the sisters. I think it was the same feeling that drew me to you..." Cole's eyes find mine, and I feel my words trying to crawl back down my throat. I continue.

"Anyway, things were even worse then. Near was a place made stubborn by time, and the people had turned away from the moor. They were afraid of it. Ever since the Near Witch and the Council, ages ago."

We climb the fourth hill.

"The Council has always led Near through fear. Fear of what *had* happened. What might happen again.

"As my father got older, he grew closer to the sisters, watching what they could do, moving the earth and making things grow in a way that nothing in town would. They only do charms now, but he said they used to be so strong they could make plants grow up from barren earth with a single touch. They could draw houses of stone up from nothing. My father asked the Council why they clung to such old fears—why they didn't embrace the sisters and their gifts. The Near Witch had been gone for centuries. Near had named him its Protector, and he was watching the town wither because of old fears. But the Council did not want things to change."

"What happened?"

"They tried to silence him," I say. "They called him foolish, and when that didn't stop him, they took away his title as Protector and gave it to Otto. Nothing was the same after that. Otto publicly denounced him. They didn't speak for two years."

We reach the top of the fourth hill.

"Even after Otto's betrayal, my father didn't give up. He tried to change their minds, tried to show them how the village could thrive with the sisters' help."

"Did it work?"

"Little by little," I say with a thin smile. "Some people began to listen to him. At first only a few were willing to trust the sisters, and then more, and more. Magda and Dreska began to come into town, began to speak to the people and teach them ways to build gardens and coax things to grow. And it looked like the villagers would finally begin to soften."

I take a long breath, trying to keep it from wavering.

"Until one day."

The valley below us is cast in shadow. Looking down, it seems like an abyss. With every step I take, I feel as though the darkness will swallow me, will creep up over my boots and my cloak.

Something cracks behind us. We both spin, scanning the night and the way we came, but all is empty.

I sigh.

Probably just deer.

"One day," I go on, my throat and my chest and my eyes burning as we descend, "he was out on the hills to the south. It had been a rainy autumn and then a very dry winter, and the earth was cracked, not on top, but deep down, where you can't see. He was halfway up the hill, when there was a landslide. The slope crumbled, and he was pinned underneath... It took hours for them to find him. They brought him home, but his body was broken. It took three days for him to..."

I swallow, but some words won't come out. Instead I say, "It's amazing how much can change in one day, let alone three. In those three days, I watched my uncle stiffen. I watched my mother become a ghost. I watched my father die. I tried to take in every word he said, tried to commit them to memory, tried not to break inside.

"Otto came and sat by the bed. They spoke for the first time in two years. Most of the things they said were too quiet for anyone to hear. But once I heard Otto raise his voice.

"'Flesh and blood and foolishness.' That's what he said. Over and over.

"My uncle sat with his head bent for three days. But he never left. He didn't sound angry. He sounded sad. Lost. I think Otto blamed himself somehow.

"But my father never blamed him. And he never blamed the moor. On the third day, he said good-bye. His voice always carried through our house, no matter how soft he spoke. The walls just made way for him. He asked the moor to watch over his family, his town. The last thing he said, after he had made his peace with everyone and everything, was, 'I entrust myself to you, the moor.'" I close my eyes.

When I open them, the fifth hill looms ahead of us, and we make our trek up, everything in me aching. I falter, but Cole is there and catches my arm. His touch is cool even through my sleeve, and he looks as though he wants to say something, but there's nothing to say.

His hands are soft and strong at once, and his fingers tell me he is there.

I burrow against his cloak, still half lost in the words. I squeeze my eyes shut. The words have scraped my throat raw. Maybe one day the words will pour out like so many others, easy and smooth and on their own. Right now they take pieces of me with them. I regain myself and pull away, and know that we must keep moving. The cracking sound comes again behind us, but we press on.

We are almost to the top of the fifth hill.

Overhead, a single crow wanders like a black cloud.

It comes into sight as it nears the moon, the blue-white light dancing on its black feathers. But once it glides past, back into the thicker dark, it vanishes. Still, I can hear its wings on the wind, and it makes me shiver. I think of the Near Witch and her dozen crows. We must be close. The crow crosses into the light again before heading farther east, dipping below the line of the fifth hill.

Cole and I make our way up the hill, but after several feet he pauses, frowning as he tilts his head, as if listening to some far-off sound.

That's when I realize that the wind around us has been growing thicker, building so gradually I didn't notice, not until now when it begins to ripple, not with Cole's low tones, but higher, almost musical ones. Cole winces beside me, but we press on toward the hilltop. The wind seems to be spilling over the hill, pushing us back, and we have to lean forward hard to keep from falling.

"We're almost there," I say.

The wind surges around us, pushing and pulling. One

gust shoves us back from the lip of the hill, the wavering tone so strong that I can almost hear the words of the rhyme on it. The next nearly flattens us against the matted grass. It vibrates through my bones.

A gust draws back, as if for breath, and in that moment we push to the top of the hill. The world beyond unfolds. Five hills due east and... I see it.

The forest.

22

"Cole, look!" I shout, pointing to the shadow of the trees in the valley below.

But he doesn't answer. I turn back just as he staggers and collapses to the grass, holding his head.

"What? What is it?" I ask, dropping to my knees beside him.

"The music. It's like crossing two tones," he says, wincing. "It hurts to hear it."

The wind picks up and Cole bows his head, taking deep breaths. I can see him struggling to stay calm, to stay in control. The wind is fighting with itself, ripping the air from his lungs.

The clouds above slide toward the bright moon, and I don't know what to do. I reach down to help Cole, but he shakes his head and pushes himself up slowly, the wind whipping his cloak back behind him. It ripples and snaps in the air. He points down to the forest in the valley below.

"It's her," he shouts, breathless, over the wind. "She's controlling... all of it at once... pulling it in toward her."

And then the light goes out, and all is black.

No longer blue-grays and blue-whites and blue-blacks.

Just black.

The wind around us has changed, too; all the noise and force condensed into one crisp melody.

Then the night itself begins to shift.

A strange glow not overhead, but below us, in the valley. The forest.

It is as if the moon and the trees have switched places. The sky is plunged into the heavy cloud-lidded darkness that seems to come every night, but in the valley below, the trees—or the places between the trees, it is impossible to tell the source—are fully lit, glowing. The woods are alight like an ember, bluish white and cradled by the rolling hills. It's like a beacon, I think with a chill. So this is what happens when the world goes black. The forest steals the light from the sky. Cole straightens beside me, taking ragged breaths. I cannot stop staring at the glowing trees. It is strange and magical. Almost lovely. The wind song has become simply a song, clear and articulate, as if made by an instrument instead of the air. It is all a perfect dream.

The music continues, clearer than ever, and it's hard to listen with only the edges of my ears, because I never noticed how beautiful it is. It's still on the wind, made by the wind itself, but it is wafting toward us like the scent of my mother's bread, oddly filling.

A gust blows through, so strong and sudden it nearly tears the melody apart. The same low, sad strain I'd heard that first night, like a second layer. Cole. But the music persists, pulling itself together on the other side.

My feet carry me forward, drawn toward the trees of

their own accord, and I can't help but feel like a moth, a fluttering insect blind to everything except the impossible glowing forest. I take a few silent steps down the hill before Cole's fingers tighten around my wrist.

"Wait," he urges, but even he seems dazed by the light.

"What is that place?" I ask. I feel him beside me. I do not see him there, because I cannot seem to tear my eyes from the glow.

And then, one hill over, a dark shape moves. A small silhouette, like a child, cloaked in a deeper darkness, as if wrapped up in night itself. The shape flits over the moor toward the tree line with unnatural lightness and speed, as if propelled, half carried by the wind and the grass. As if its feet do not touch the ground.

It dances down into the valley and up to the forest.

"No," I say, calling out to the form as it nears the moonlit grove. Cole does not let go.

"Can't you see?" I ask him, wrenching free. "It's a child. We have to save her."

I break away from Cole and into a sprint, stumbling down the hill, and I can feel him right beside me. He is speaking, asking me to slow down, to wait, and something else, but the wind is up against my ears, and I can't tear my eyes from the figure cast in silhouette against the glowing trees. Maybe it's a small girl with blond hair that won't mess, and a chirpy voice. The *maybe* seems to transform the shape before my eyes into my bubbly little sister.

I hit the base of the hill too hard and fast, and stumble to my hands and knees. The tangled earth cuts into my fingers and shins, but the burn of it is lost as Cole helps me to my feet. I'm amazed at how close the forest is. It looked farther away, but now that we're standing in the valley with it, the thin branches and slips of leaves are visible in the blue-white light.

"Wren?" I shout, but the small child does not turn to us, does not even cast a glance over her shoulder. She walks straight into the forest and is instantly lost from view.

I shout her name again, rushing toward the tree line, but Cole's grip is no longer gentle, his voice no longer a suggestion.

"No, Lexi. It's not her. Something's wrong." The wind is still growing, but the music is gone, and now it's just howling and angry. Cole winces, turning his head away from the source of the sound, the forest. I twist free and make it several feet, almost close enough to touch a half-broken branch that juts into the clearing, when it happens. A dozen crows erupt from the canopy of the forest, bursting from the jagged line of trees, blacker than the night and screaming in their raspy tones. The wind rises and falls with the words in my head.

A dozen crows perched on the low stone wall.

Cole and I step back together. Cold comes over me, nerve-bristling. I hear branches cracking. Dead branches on the forest floor, snapping beneath the weight of something. Someone. I manage to take another step back and so does Cole, and we are caught somewhere between the need to flee and a horrible curiosity that digs into our bones and slows them down. My sister might be in that forest. I cannot run. I cannot leave her. But something else is in the forest, too. Something is making the branches crack, the shape of it drawing closer and closer through the trees. And then I see it.

Five white lines curl around a thin tree near the front of the forest. I gasp. Finger bones. Fear wins a little, and I slide back a few feet. Two glistening circles hover just behind the narrow tree, like river rocks. The finger bones release their hold on the tree and reach forward, out toward me. And as they do, as they graze the open air of the small valley, they grow moss. Dirt and weeds coil around the bones like muscle and flesh, sinewy and slick. Cole reaches me, putting himself between me and the woods. The shimmering circles slip forward, and they are indeed river rocks, set like lifeless eyes into a face of moss. A woman's face. Just beneath the eyes, the earthy skin tugs itself apart, and the woman hisses. She opens her mouth, and what comes out at first aren't words at all but wind, and a raspy hint of voice, as if her throat is clogged with dirt.

The branches snap beneath her bare moss feet as she steps forward from the glowing woods. She breathes out and the wind picks up hard enough to bend everything down, to make the world bow. The grass presses flat to the earth, and even the forest seems to lean. I can't hear anything but the white noise of it and the witch's voice.

"Don't you dare," she hisses. I shrink back, but Cole is standing straight. His eyes are as dark as the witch's, swallowing the light from the forest.

"We have to get the child!" I shout to him over the wind. We step forward, and another gust of wind rushes against our backs, but it breaks uselessly like water on rocks when it meets the forest and the witch. She inhales, and the wind howls around her, amplifying her words so that they surround us, seeming to come from everywhere.

"DON'T YOU DARE DISTURB MY GARDEN," she booms. The sound echoes through the world, and then falls apart, breaking into hisses and howls.

Cole tightens one arm around me, never letting his eyes stray from the moor-made thing that is the Near Witch, and he looks paralyzed; but then his eyes narrow, and the wind surges at our backs again. His free hand flies up, and the air behind us pours over our heads and fills the space between the Near Witch and us like a wall. It blows so hard that the world beyond the wind is distorted, rippling. Then the Near Witch lets out a sound between a growl and a laugh, and just like that, the wall breaks and slams into us, throwing us back onto the grass.

In that moment the trees go black again, and the moon reclaims the sky, and we are left in the valley by the darkened forest, with the moon full and bright overhead. Cole breathes heavily beside me.

"What just happened?" I whisper, pushing myself to my knees and helping him up. His arm wraps tightly around me, but now I worry it's as much to hold himself up as to keep me close. His eyes meet mine, and then he kisses me, and it isn't cool and smooth, but warm and desperate, and afraid. Not just afraid of the witch, but of what he's done. He presses his mouth to mine, as if he can force normalcy and humanity and flesh and blood back into himself, and erase the image of the Near Witch's eyes, which were the mirror image of his own.

And that's when we hear the cracking sound again, the one that followed us over the hills. Footsteps. Heavy boots at the top of the hill. Cole tears his lips from mine, and we both look up. I see the glint of the rifles before I meet my uncle's eyes. Otto. Bo. And Tyler. We are all as frozen as the trees and the rocks around us, staring at each other. I see my uncle's grip on his gun tighten as his eyes make their way from me to Cole. Tyler curses, the sound spilling down the valley. I have never seen so much hatred in his eyes. His blond hair glows white in the moonlight, but his blue eyes look black from here. I can feel his gaze as it winds around the contours of my body, taking in the way it fits with Cole's. Five people, all waiting for one to move. The three men on the hill stare down at us as if we are deer. It happens all at once.

Otto's gun catches the moonlight as he lifts it.

Bo cocks his head.

Tyler steps forward.

Cole's arms tighten around my waist as he brings the side of his face to mine and whispers, "Don't let go."

Before I can ask what he means, the wind picks up around us, whipping so fiercely that the world once again begins to bleed away. The grass flattens as the gust tears up the hill toward the men with such force that I find myself waiting for the sound of impact, the crash, but there's only the whistling wind filling my ears and Cole's voice weaving effortlessly through it.

"Run."

And then we're plunging into the forest.

*

Branches tear at our cloaks and sleeves and skin as we weave through the trees, trying to skirt the edge of the forest. Half-rotten roots curl up from the ground. I keep my fingers on Cole's arm, running as much by feel as anything, letting his motions ripple through me, my feet finding the spaces left by his.

We keep the clearing to our left, and the deeper forest to our right. The center of the forest is black and cold and quiet. Every time I begin to veer toward it, remembering the little-girl-shaped shadow and the five bone fingers, Cole forces me back to the rim of the trees.

"I haven't bought us much time," he calls back. "Who knows how long... the wind will hold." He sounds breathless, and I feel him begin to thin beneath my fingers, turning to something more like mist than skin.

"Cole," I say, tightening my grip. He slows enough to look back at me, eyes shining.

"I'll be all right," he says, reading the worry in my eyes. His arm feels solid again beneath my touch. "But we have to hurry." We set off, my lungs burning, skin buzzing from fear and cold.

"Matthew must have told them!" I say.

Behind us, branches snap underfoot.

The men are in the forest. I glance back, but all I can see are black branches, the moonlight slanting in on our left. I stumble and fall back a step, my hand sliding down Cole's arm, his wrist, until our fingers are knotted. Men's voices echo in the dark. Growing softer. They have taken a path deeper into the woods.

Cole turns suddenly left, and we break through the trees at the edge of the forest. The moon is high and bright again, showering the moor in light, exposing everything. Including us.

We make a break for it, up the hill, everything in me burning, desperate for air and rest. When I think my lungs and legs won't make it, the wind picks up, presses against my back, urging me on. I reach the top of the hill, Cole's fingers still twisted in mine, and risk a glance back at the forest below, at the three men just surfacing again. Before they look up at the hill, we're gone.

*

The wind is at our backs, all the way home.

We don't stop at the sisters' house, don't talk, only run, needing every ounce of strength to make it. Only when my home comes into sight do we stagger to a stop, the wind dissolving into a frightening quiet. I sink to the ground, gasping, and close my eyes as a kind of world-tipping dizziness takes over. When I open them, Cole is kneeling beside me. He bows his head, trying to regain his balance. When he looks up, he is ghostly pale.

"You've got to get away from here," I say. "They saw you. They'll think we're hiding something."

"Check on Wren," he says, and only then do I remember the small dark shape as it slipped into the forest. I turn to the house. The bedroom window is open, and my heart plummets through my stomach. I can see the curtains billowing in the room I share with my sister, can see clear through to the back wall where the moon is casting shapes. I am there, at the windowsill, faster than Cole, fighting the urge to cry out to Wren in the darkness. I bite back tears and panic as I launch myself over the sill and into the room, clumsy and loud.

And there she is.

Tucked deep within her nest of blankets. I cross to her and my eyes catch on the charm at her wrist, still smelling of earth and something sweet. I say a silent prayer to Magda and Dreska. Cole reaches the window breathlessly, and I lean out. Concern flickers in his eyes, but I meet them with a small nod and an exhale. He glances back, over his shoulder.

"How many children are there in the town of Near?" he asks, leaning against the window.

"At least a dozen," I whisper. "Why?"

"One of them was not as lucky."

23

Wren's chest rises and falls.

I watch her sleeping form and think of the silhouette at the edge of the forest, and of the haunting wind song. I imagine it coaxing a child's eyelids up, drawing small legs from beneath the covers. Urging the half-sleeping form out into the pitch-black night.

I turn back to the window, where Cole is waiting. In the distance, a bird takes flight, disturbed.

"You have to—"

"I know. I'm going." And the way he says it is so final, and the panic in my eyes must be clear, because he brushes his thumb over my fingers on the sill.

"Wait for me. I'll come back," he says, tired and pale. He looks numb, lost. His hand falls away from mine. "We'll make everything right in the morning."

There are footsteps somewhere in the dark, and I peer out past him.

"Cole, go," I warn, but when I look down, he's already gone.

I retreat into the room, pulling the traveling cloak from

my shoulders, the boots from my feet. I peel the covers back beside Wren, and as I curl up in the warmth of the bed, I feel the cold seep from my skin for the first time all night.

"Tomorrow," I whisper to the moonlight and my sister's form, as sleep slips beneath the covers with me. "Tomorrow we'll make everything right. Tomorrow we'll go back to the forest and find the witch's bones while she sleeps. Tomorrow I'll find the children. Tomorrow..."

I fold myself deeper into the blankets as the wind picks up, and beg for sleep to bring the morning faster.

*

The thing about bad news is this:

All bad news might spread like fire, but when it takes you by surprise it's sharp and hot, gobbling everything up so fast you never have a chance. When you're waiting for it, it's even worse. It's the smoke, filling the room so slow you can watch it steal the air from you.

In the morning. Words I cling to, waiting for dawn to come. I blink, and time passes in strange, awkward jumps, but the sun won't seem to rise.

I find myself watching as the dregs of moonlight make circles on the ceiling. I stare up at them, up past them, waiting for the night to pass, trying to make sense of everything, unable to hold on to anything as my mind slips in and out.

My eyes flick to the window.

One of them was not as lucky.

But who?

Dawn is just reaching the edges of the sky. I give up on the idea of sleep, pull myself from the bed, and wander down the hall. A candle burns in the kitchen. My mother is there, pouring tea.

My heart sinks when I see a familiar round woman sitting in a kitchen chair, wringing her large hands.

Mrs. Thatcher reaches for the tea my mother offers. She herself made the cup; you can tell by the way her fingers fit perfectly into the ripples. She does not cry, like the others, but sits and drinks and curses. She hardly notices the burned edges of the roll she eats, or how hot it is. I make myself silent against the wall, as my mother stops her baking and comes to sit with Riley's mother, cradling her own mug.

"Fool, fool," Mrs. Thatcher mutters, and she reminds me of Dreska when she says it, only younger and much larger. "I told him to just put it up, to be safe. But he'd have none of it."

"Put what up?"

"That damned crow. Jack wouldn't have it. Said it was a silly thing for silly people with silly fears. And look now!" The cup hits the table with almost as much force as my uncle's when he rants.

"We could have used all the luck we were given. To guard against who"—her eyes flit to me—"or what, is taking these children. I'm not saying it'd fix things. Not saying the crows could keep that boy safe, but now..." She finishes the tea, but this time sets the cup down silently, the anger bleeding into sadness at last. "Now we won't know."

My mother reaches across the table and takes her hand. "It's not too late," she murmurs. "We'll find him. Lexi will help find him."

Mrs. Thatcher gives a heaving sigh and pushes away from the table.

"I've got to get back," she mutters, and the chair groans as she stands up. "Jack's been in a fury for an hour, raving and causing a storm. Out for blood." Her eyes find mine. "I warned you. Where is your friend now?" She shakes her head. "If he's got any brains, he's long gone from Near."

"Come," says my mother. "I'll walk you home." And with that my mother leads Mrs. Thatcher out into the chilly morning.

Where is Cole? His promise echoes back to me. *Wait for me. I'll come back.* My hands begin to tremble, so I clench them into fists. I should go before Otto has the chance to come and stop me. I should go and find Cole so we can get to the forest. I don't want to go back alone, even in daylight. Where is he? What if he's hiding? What if he needs me?

Wren wanders sleepily into the kitchen, her hair already smooth. I pat her head—a simple, thankful motion. She looks at me as if I've lost my mind. It's not a child's look. It's sympathetic. *Poor old sister*, I can picture her thinking. Old is old to a child. I might as well be Magda or Dreska. *Poor Lexi, losing her mind. Thinks the boy speaks wind and burns down villages. Thinks the Near Witch is stealing children. Thinks she can stop any of it.*

"Wren, where do you think your friends are?"

She studies me. "I don't know, but they're together." She sighs, crossing her arms. "And *they* don't have to stay inside."

I bend to kiss her forehead. "It's turning cold out anyway."

Out in the yard, sounds are rising, climbing on top of one another. The tense quiet in the house is suddenly replaced by a clamor of voices and shuffling feet. Otto's and Mr. Drake's and Mr. Thatcher's and Tyler's and a handful of others' who have gathered. But one of the voices is soft and smooth and airy, and it doesn't fit with the dry, rough anger in the others.

Cole.

I push myself from the chair and hurry out into the yard just in time to see Otto thrust the butt of his rifle into Cole's chest, sending him to his knees.

The wind picks up right then, not so much that anyone else can tell. But to me, it's like he's gasping. I feel the war of pain and temper in the air, and I can see in his jaw the desperate attempt to keep a level head. He tries to stand, but Otto's fist connects, and he stumbles back to the tangled ground. The wind erupts.

"Cole," I cry out, and shoot my uncle a deathly glare. I run toward them, but a form appears in front of me, and I collide with flesh and bone and blond hair and a sharp smile.

Tyler wraps his arms around me, pinning my body against his. The wind howls.

"Now, now, Lexi," he says, squeezing me. "Don't be like this."

I try to push back. He's strong. I remember when he was a wisp of a thing, no taller than me. Now his arms encircle my chest, press their own lines into my skin.

"It's your fault it's come to this," my uncle adds. "You should have listened."

"Come on, let's go inside," Tyler says, casting a backward glance at Cole's bent form on the weedy ground. He's pushing himself up unsteadily, and Tyler tugs me, practically carries me backward, toward the house.

"Let go," I warn, but he only smiles that sickening grin. And there's something in his eyes, something worse than that cocky smile. Anger. Hate. He's always thought my resistance was a game. But he saw me, last night, in Cole's arms. He understands it's not that I wouldn't pick anybody. I wouldn't pick *him*. His grip tightens, and I try not to wince.

I warned him, I remind myself, as my knee connects, making a satisfying crack. Tyler gasps and staggers back. Cole is on his feet again, holding his chest. I run toward him, but then arms come from behind, wrap themselves around my neck, and I can barely breathe. I fight Tyler's hold, but the angle is awkward, and instead of freeing myself, I only make it worse.

"Lexi, stop," coughs Cole, straightening. He rubs his chest, looking not at my uncle or even at me, but at the dirt at my feet. The wind is dying back, little by little.

"Don't be ridiculous, girl," growls my uncle, his hand landing heavily on Cole's shoulder. Cole looks as if he might collapse beneath the weight of that hand, but his eyes don't move from the patch of dirt.

There's a strange, weary resignation in my uncle's eyes, and all I can think of is Matthew shaking his head and saying that the Council did what they thought was necessary.

"We just need to talk to him," Otto says.

"The hell you do," I spit.

"He should have stayed away," Tyler whispers to me, his breath against my cheek. "He should have run when he had a chance. But Otto knew he wouldn't. Otto knew he'd come back."

And then, to the gathered group of men, Tyler speaks,

loud and clear. "Last night I witnessed this stranger leading a child into a forest on the eastern moor." It's a bold-faced lie, and everyone there knows it.

"You see, Lexi," says Otto, cold and even, "Tyler says he saw him. And so did I."

"He led the child into the darkness, and came out alone."

They're all lying, so bald and open.

"This is absurd. You know that's not what you saw. Let him go."

Cole's eyes level on me. He forces a thin smile.

"I'll be fine. The bones, Lexi."

"Don't you say her name," growls Tyler, but Cole seems to see only me.

"Set things right," he says.

There's something off in his eyes. He's trying to look strong, trying to assure me that it will all be okay. Even now, that's what he's *trying* to say. But there's a fleck of sadness in his eyes, a hint of *good-bye*, or *I'm sorry*. I don't know what, exactly, but I know I don't want to decode it. The wind sinks back beneath the moor, as weary as Cole. Something he said comes back to me.

I sometimes wonder what I would do if anyone had survived the fire. Would I have confessed and let them punish me? Would that have eased anyone's pain?

No. I can't let him. And he wouldn't. Would he? He promised me we would fix this. Together. I want to believe him. I lunge forward, catching Tyler off guard, but before I can break free, his hands are there again, pulling me against him.

"Come on," orders my uncle. He turns Cole away from me, away from the house, away from Near. Out toward the north and the open moor.

"Keep her here," Otto calls back.

Everyone except Tyler and Bo follows Otto and Cole. In moments, they are lost behind a rolling hill. Where are they going? Where are they taking him?

"Won't spill a stranger's blood on Near soil," mutters Bo, his voice slow as honey. He sounds almost amused.

"But he didn't—" I try to wrench free, but Tyler is a wall.

"Dammit, Tyler, let me *go*," I growl.

"Otto warned you, Lexi," Tyler says. "*I* should have warned you. You're in enough trouble as it is. But I'm sorry it had to end like this." *End. End.* That's the word that thuds in my chest with my pulse. I can't get enough air.

"Now, come on," he soothes. "Let's go inside." I let my posture slacken, and rest the back of my head against his chest. Sure enough, his hands slip from my wrists. I turn slowly toward him, look up into his cool blue eyes. He smiles cautiously at me. And I punch him in the face.

24

My hand hurts, but I'm sure his face hurts worse, and none of it compares to the sickening feeling in the pit of my stomach. I should have run after Cole the minute Tyler hit the grass, but I hesitated only a moment, and Bo was there, pinning my arms down, trying to drag me into the house.

"What's going on?" calls my mother, coming up the path.

"Lexi isn't herself," says Bo.

Tyler pushes himself up, a trail of blood in the corner of his mouth. My mother reaches us, and her eyes pass from Bo to Tyler to me. I beg her with a look, but she just watches. She lets them usher me into the house, an odd expression on her face, like she's holding her breath, all of her quiet and still except her eyes, which flick feverishly between us.

I pace my room, making sure my steps echo because the silence of this place is choking me. I can hear her in the kitchen with Bo, the latter calmly unfolding the same lies about Cole. Tyler is sitting outside the front door because my mother will not let him in. I am sure he would like to guard me in my room, from my bed. But my mother gave him only a glance and a few harsh words, and Tyler set one of the kitchen chairs up beside the front door, beneath the gathering clouds. I can picture him, still holding a dishrag to his nose, leaning his head against the door.

They cannot keep me captive in my own home. I know how to slip away, to make myself small and silent. I fasten my father's knife around my waist, and my green cloak over my shoulders. Tyler might be by the door, but the wind uses the window, and so do I. But when I go to push it open, I cannot. Two heavy rusted nails have been driven into the wood, pinning the pane down. I kick the wall beneath, and feel several warm tears escape, frustration and fatigue and fear.

"Lexi," my mother's voice wafts from the doorway. She's gripping a basket and looking more awake than I have seen her in a year. I wipe the tears away with the back of my hand, but she is here now, beside me.

"Come on," she says, taking my hand and tugging me into the hall. In the kitchen, Bo is leaning against the table, his back to us. Wren is playing with a few fresh dolls, but even she does not seem enthused. Tyler is still on his perch by the door, humming a tune that is half obscured by the dishrag at his face. My mother leads me into her bedroom and slides the door shut. She sets the basket on the floor and pulls out my boots, still caked with mud. I throw my arms around her and then crouch down and slip them on, while my mother eases her window up with silent fingers. She gives me a tight hug before she turns and glides away. I step through the open window and drop silently, my legs bending and my boots sinking into the tangled earth. And then I run.

*

I want to run north.

Away from Near, where the hills ripple out, hiding dozens of valleys. Where Otto and his men have taken Cole. Everything in me wants to run that way. But I force myself east. East toward the forest and the bones. This is my only chance. Cole knew it, too. The sun creeps up the side of the sky, slipping into late morning.

I'll be fine. Cole's promise echoes on the wind as I run. *The bones, Lexi. Set things right.*

Cole will be all right.

Cole has to be all right.

Another voice intrudes: Bo's voice, slow and vaguely amused: *Won't spill a stranger's blood on Near soil.*

I force myself over the eastern hills.

As I run, my uncle's face flickers in my mind, and then his rifle, glinting in the moonlight. I wish Cole had fought back in the yard, but I could see in his eyes that he knew it would not help. Now in every gust of wind I am looking for a sign of him. It blows past my cheek, brushes the hair from my neck. But it's only the wind. Cole's promise that we would fix everything overlaps with the almost good-bye in his eyes, and I imagine I can hear a gunshot, far off and high. I wonder for a moment if the rain will wash any red from the ground, make small dark puddles the way it does after a hunt, cleaning the stained earth. No. Not now. I realize my chest has been growing tighter, and I focus on taking long wavering breaths as my legs churn.

Stay calm. My father's voice seeps in. *Pay attention. Don't let your mind wander, or your prey will too.* I shake my head and climb the fifth and final hill, knowing what waits beyond. The trees come into sight like low clouds left in the valley, so heavy they've sunk to the ground. I descend the hill.

The forest is a different thing in the dappled light of day, but not a better thing, not a less frightening thing. It does not glow blue-white from within, but dull gray-white from without, diffused by the dead branches of the trees. The trees themselves make jagged lines, thin poles jutting up from the ground. There is something violent about the way they've been stuck in the soil like pins. Careless and sharp. And everything feels deadened by a stifling quiet.

I inch forward to the edge of the forest, and the ground crackles beneath my feet, a blanket of dead leaves and brittle sticks. As my fingers brush the outermost trees, the bone hand springs to mind, curled and white against the dark trunk. I recoil. I do not want to touch this place. I do not want to leave a mark. I am as afraid of finding answers as I am of finding none, and that fear makes me angrier than anything else. I find the spot where the Near Witch stood when she peered out, and with a deep breath and a quick touch of my father's knife, I force my feet to carry me through, over the threshold and into the witch's woods.

25

I hold my breath, but nothing happens, nothing comes.

The wind doesn't pick up, the world doesn't change, so I start moving. Instead of skirting the tree line, clinging to the edges of the forest, I head straight in, toward the center, the way the witch must have vanished. I swallow and remind myself that dead things are bound to their beds so long as the sun is up. I look up through the canopy, but it's impossible to gauge the time. The forest swallows the world beyond, gnaws at the light and the warmth so that only pieces find their way through. It seems endless.

I look for any signs of the child-shaped shadow, but all I can find are dead leaves—this forest is thick but hollow, drained, the bark brittle, the limbs snapping off.

Most forests harbor a range of animals. Some creep across the floor, others inch up trees. They fly or perch or skitter. Every kind of thing makes noise. But here, there is nothing.

And then, a sharp caw breaks the quiet. A crow. Overhead a single black bird weaves between the trees. And then another. And a third. All making their way deeper into the woods. I follow the trail of caws and black feathers, winding my way through the trees, brambles and branches snagging my cloak, grasping at my legs. I pick up speed until something catches my boot, flinging me to the damp earth. Pain shoots up my leg, and I try to twist free, but the grip only tightens. A long gnarled root has caught the buckle on my boot. I struggle with it, freeing the leather strap, and am halfway to my feet when I see it.

Half erased by my fall, among the moss and dirt, is a footprint. Five small toes. A ball. A heel. And another. I scramble to my feet.

And another.

And another.

There are no prints between here and the village, but the forest itself is brimming with them. Multiple pairs of child-size feet.

Footprints but no children. And none of the sounds children make. I think of how loud Edgar and Cecilia are when they play their games, of the way Emily dances and laughs, of how much noise Riley makes knocking into things. Now I hear only the occasional caw of crows circling overhead.

I try to follow the footprints, but they go a dozen different ways.

A smaller pair, maybe Edgar's, trudge sleepily off to the right, dragging over the earth and smudging the other marks.

A light-footed girl with small dancing steps, almost all ball and toes, no heel, curls to the left.

Another pair wanders back and forth in even waves, as if walking an invisible winding line.

And a fourth walks deliberately, proud, the way a small boy does when he is trying to pretend he is a man.

I follow each set and discover that though they take different paths, they all go the same way, eventually. They make their way to a spot up ahead where the trees edge aside to form a kind of clearing. When I reach it, a nervous flutter of wings draws my eyes up. Gaunt blackbirds wait on almost every half-dead tree, black eyes unblinking. Issuing caws as sharp as the woods.

My eyes flick down to the ground where the forest has made just enough space to allow a kind of mound. A dense mass of tangled branches and leaves sits in the middle of the space. Here in the clearing, the footprints vanish.

"What is that?" I ask aloud, because sometimes it's better to pretend there's someone else with you. I imagine my father's soothing response, since I don't have one.

Let the moor tell you, comes a rather thin version of his default.

"Well?" I ask the moor again. A crow overhead lets out a single sharp caw. I edge closer, and several of the birds flutter their wings menacingly, but don't release their clawed hold on their perches. The nestlike cluster of branches is actually several trees, their limbs bending down awkwardly to guard the space between them.

It's like a home, I realize. Like a cocoon. I build my cocoons of sheets and blankets. But this one is all sharp sticks and half-rotted wood. The branches are close together, in some places side by side, but in other spots they bow out, leaving gaps large enough for me to fit through. I already have one leg into the cocoon when a gust of wind lifts the air inside to meet me. It's damp and thick, and smells like natural rot.

Overhead a crow clicks its black beak over something white and smooth. It reminds me more than anything of a knucklebone. The bird plays with it, but the pale shape slips free and falls down through the cocoon, bouncing off a branch before plunging into the cold, dark hollow. I can see it sitting on the earthy mound, a glint of white. And then I see that there are other pieces down there, all half buried and white.

Bones.

They glint in the slivers of light that slip through the forest and the nest of trees. A forearm juts up from a mass of tangled weeds.

This is the Near Witch, or what remains of her.

Again I remember the five white finger bones curled around the tree, the way the moss and dirt crawled over them like muscle and tissue in the night; and then I look down and feel ill. All is rot. I swallow hard and am just about to lower myself into the mossy pit, to dig through the decay for the witch's bones, when I hear it.

A crack, sharp enough to send one of the crows into flight.

The branches snap beyond my line of sight, and my father's knife is out and molded to my hand before I've even turned to find the source. I've pulled my leg free of the cocoon, and I hop down to the ground and step back, putting the nest of bending trees between the sounds of approaching feet and myself. There are two people, two different strides, one heavier than the other. I recognize Mr. Ward's voice, a thicker version of Tyler's, as he speaks to someone who mumbles a reply. I can tell by the latter's tone that he's the more uncomfortable of the two, the more superstitious. It's Mr. Drake, Edgar's father, a nervous twig of a man whose eyes move too much, twitching from sight to sight so fast it's a wonder they don't just leap out altogether.

What are they doing back here? What did they do with Cole?

"Yeah, this is where they saw them last night," Mr. Ward says, his voice growing louder. He must be entering the clearing. "Outside the forest."

I take a slow step back, the nest still between us.

Mr. Drake comments on the smell, but I'm holding my breath entirely as I scan the forest and attempt to orchestrate my retreat without a sound.

"Lexi and that stranger?" he asks nervously. Mr. Ward must nod, because Mr. Drake continues. "You really think he took Edgar?"

"Doesn't matter," mutters Mr. Ward. I take another step back as the voices grow nearer, and I can picture him on the other side of the cocoon, running a hand over it. "At least he's gone now."

The air catches in my throat.

No.

I close my eyes, sure that they can hear my pulse pounding.

No.

"You don't think he did it," says Mr. Drake, and it's not quite a question.

"Like I said," says Mr. Ward. "Doesn't matter. It doesn't bring your boy back."

No. No. No, I say to myself, taking a silent step back. I shake my head, try to focus. They're wrong. They're wrong, and Cole said I had to find the bones, and he would find me. So where is he? And where are the children? I focus on this last question because it seems like the only one I might be able to answer.

"Then why?"

I saw a child walk into this forest, when the moonlight went into the trees and the music swept through. I saw a child. They must be nearby, but *where*?

"To make sure, I guess," says Mr. Ward.

I scan the trees, the ground, the dirt and moss and dead twigs, and—

My foot comes down hard on a brittle branch, creating a deafening snap, and even without seeing the men, I know they've heard it. Overhead, all twelve crows alight and begin to caw, sharp terrible sounds. I can't wait. This is my only chance. I turn and sprint as fast as I can, abandoning the bones, through the forest and out onto the moor, my knees wobbling with every stride, my body beyond exhaustion now. I look up, shocked to see that the sun has fully crossed the sky and is now sinking in a haze of color. I run, over the five hills and back toward the sisters' house. My lungs cry, and my legs cry. But I cannot cry. I will not cry.

The look in Cole's eyes, the strange almost-good-bye, the apology.

Would I have confessed, and let them punish me?

I will not cry.

Would that have eased anyone's pain?

I will not. He promised. He said he would be fine. He—

My knees buckle beneath me as I reach the top of the last hill, and the sisters' house comes into sight. I tumble to the grass, gasping for breath, and bury my fingers in the weedy earth.

"What are you doing there on the ground, dearie?"

I look up to see Magda leaning over me the way she does. Her voice is thin, tired. Everyone seems so tired. She urges me up and leads me toward the cottage in silence. There is no gray cloak on the nail of the shed. Dreska is standing in the yard, arms crossed, staring at the scorched spot on the ground. Her green eyes flick up at me, but she doesn't move. The earth beneath us seems to hum. Magda urges me past her and into the house.

"You haven't seen Cole, have you?" I ask, my voice raw, as if I've been screaming.

"No, no, no..." She says it like a sigh, wandering off with the word as she pours water into the kettle. I slide into a chair. I feel the tears stream down my face as the images of red puddles streak before my eyes. I wipe them away.

"They took him," I say, because I have to.

Magda gives that sad, knowing nod, and wraps her gnarled fingers around my shoulder.

"They saw us last night. They came this morning and took him, took him out onto the moor. And Bo said they wouldn't spill a stranger's blood on Near soil, and I don't know what they've done, but he promised me he'd come find me if I found the bones, and I did, but he wasn't there. He wasn't there, and the hunters are saying he's—"

I gasp for breath, hands wrapped around my ribs. Gone. I should say *Cole is gone*, but that is not right. If I said it that way, one might think he just left, wandered off the way he came. But Cole was pulled away by men of flesh and blood. Men looking for someone to blame.

I should say *Cole is dead*, but I don't think I can speak those words without breaking, and I cannot break right now. I do not have the bones, and I have not found the children, and there are too many things to do before I am allowed to break.

"So, you found them," Dreska says, from the doorway. I didn't even hear her come in.

"Aren't you listening?" I say, pushing back from the table. The chair topples over. "Cole's *gone*."

"And so are four children."

"How can you not care that they've taken him? That they've probably…"

"He knew what he was doing."

"No! He didn't. He didn't know. He promised me!"

Everything in me hurts. The room tips. The kettle hisses.

"Then trust him," Magda says at last. She pulls the water from the fire. A strange numbness is settling over me, a kind of cottony padding in my head. I cling to it.

"Things are about to get much worse," murmurs Dreska, but I don't think her words are meant for my ears.

"I have to go back," I say. "I have to get the bones. Cole said… and I didn't find the children. I couldn't find them."

"You will go home, Lexi Harris," Dreska says.

"What? But we need those bones now! She'll come back tonight."

"Go home, dearie," Magda says, her gnarled hand closing over mine. I realize I've been gripping the table.

"Do not leave your sister's side," says Dreska.

"And in the morning," adds Magda, "you come straight here, dearie, and we will put things right." She gives my hand a pat and slips away.

"You just come back in the morning, Lexi," Dreska chimes. "Everything will be all right." There's that stupid phrase again. People are always saying it, and it's never true. I give her a look that says as much.

"Go home, Lexi," she says in a different voice, softer, like the one she used with my father. Dreska ushers me to the door. Her long bony fingers graze my shoulders. "We'll put things in their proper place." I step outside. The sky is red.

"Everything will be all right," she repeats, and this time I don't fight it. I don't disagree.

How? asks a voice inside me, but it's sinking, slipping beneath something warm like blankets.

*

Somehow I make my way home. My feet must take me, clever things, since I don't find the path with my eyes.

My house comes into sight, and with it, Otto, Tyler, and Bo. They are standing in the doorway, bathed in the red light. Bo cocks his head to the side. Tyler's back is to me. Otto catches sight of me, and even in my daze I expect him to go into a rage. But there's only grim fatigue. It's not a victorious look. It's one that says *I might not have won yet, but you've lost.*

I push past them, past my mother, who knew I would come back. She casts me a glance, a look exchanged between prisoners of sorts, before turning to the oven. I shrug the cloak off, free my feet from the boots, and go to drop them out the window. But the window is still locked from the outside, the wood still freshly splintered from the nails. I rub my eyes and let the boots fall to the floor with a thud, before slipping out of my dress and into my nightgown.

Every inch of me aches for sleep. How long has it been since I slept? There is still an hour until dark. I can rest, just a little, and be wide awake to guard Wren tonight. I peel the covers back, slide beneath them, and sleep folds over me, welcome and warm, and complete.

26

The first thing I realize is that the room is dark.

I've slept too long, and panic floods me, but then I see that Wren is fast asleep and safe, tucked beneath the blankets. The night has settled in around us, the wind humming through the window cracks and the floorboards and the space beneath the door.

My thoughts come to me thick and slow. That cottony numbness is still here, filling my chest. I drag myself from the bed, meaning to light the candles, when the room tilts, my body and mind still caught in the dregs of sleep. I pause against the bed, waiting for the dizziness to pass. And then I hear the voice. One soft, simple name, faded at the edges.

My name. *Lexi.* The wind is playing tricks on me again. My eyes wander sleepily to the window, to the moor beyond, expecting to see nothing.

But there is a person standing there in the darkness. Waiting in the field, just beyond the village line, a foot or so across the seam where Near meets the northern moor, someone tall and thin and crowlike.

"Cole?" I ask. When he doesn't vanish, I drift in my

lovely haze, my almost-sleep, to the window, forgetting the
nails that pin it shut. I press my hands against the surface
and look through, heat fogging the glass around my
fingertips. Outside, the wind picks up, and the windowpane
quivers. Cole tips his head to the side, and the nails tremble,
then begin to slide up and loose and away, falling to the
grass. I push the window open; it creaks once and then
glides up silently beneath my fingers. The sound beyond the
glass is stronger. The wind whistles past me into the room,
rippling any surface that can peel away.

I hesitate, glancing back at my sister's sleeping form
beneath the blankets, but she is sound asleep, the bracelet
fastened around her wrist.

Outside, the moor is cool and dark, and I climb through
the window, nearly tripping over my own feet. I latch the
shutters hastily. I want to see Cole, his face and his river-
stone eyes, and know why he has left me, and how he has
come back, and what has happened. He wavers once, and I
want to feel his skin and know that he is there. I cross the
small stretch of land in only my nightgown, numb to the
rough and tangled earth beneath my bare feet and the cold
night against my arms.

"Cole," I call again, and this time he makes a motion
toward me, holding out his hand. As I draw near, I see that
it *is* him. I close my eyes, find it difficult to open them again
as he takes my hand, his fingers oddly cool as they intertwine
with mine. He is not hesitant, not flinching. On the contrary,
his grip is firm, pulling me toward him. It makes my heart
leap in a strange way, not unlike when I am tracking and
catch sight of my prey, and all my nerves bristle beneath my

skin, alert. He embraces me in silence, and the wind curves playfully around us.

"Are you all right?" I ask, running my fingertips over him. "You're alive. Cole, they said... I heard them..." He says nothing, only pulls me along, out onto the moor, and I follow, delirious with relief.

"Where have you been? What happened?" I am angry that he left, that he let them take him away. I tug back.

"Cole, say something." I try to turn toward my home, toward Near, when he pulls me to him again, pressing me against his cool, wind-touched form. His cheek brushes mine. I feel like I'm forgetting something, but then his lips find my lips and his kiss knocks the air out of me.

"Follow me," he whispers in my ear, his breath cold against my face. I feel my legs bend beneath me, and I will them to keep me up as I let him lead me, and he adds, "I'll tell you everything."

"What happened? Where did Otto take you?" The questions pour out. "Where did you go?"

"I'll show you," he says, so low and hushed that the sounds barely seem like words at all.

"I found the bones," I say. Cole's grip on me tightens for only a moment, and his face darkens, but the shadow passes and his eyes grow calm. The wind picks up around us, and he holds me tightly, his arm wrapped around my waist as he guides me across the moor. Whenever I resist or ask him to explain, he pauses and turns to me, his eyes looking down into mine, and brings his hand to my chin. I feel my face grow hot beneath his palm. When he kisses my forehead, it's like a raindrop on my skin.

"Cole," I whisper, confused and relieved at once, but then he kisses me again, really kisses me, cool and ghostly smooth. There is no fear in his kiss, no uncertainty. He kisses me and brushes the back of his hand against my flushed cheek and leads me away, out onto the hills. I barely even notice the village disappearing behind us. I yawn and lean on him in the darkness, sure that this is a dream, that perhaps I have slipped to the wooden floor in the bedroom of my mother's home. And here, in this dream, Cole is alive and we are walking. I can feel and see him beside me, but the rest of the world seems to have fallen away.

"Where are we going?" I ask. Cole's grip on me is strange, at once light and tightening, and I resist momentarily, focus on the motion of pushing. Pushing him back from me. Pushing with my fingertips. It takes effort. Cole stops again and turns to me.

"Lexi," he says in his whispering way, tracing the curves of my face with his fingertips.

As gentle as his fingers seem, I can't loosen their grip. I blink, the cold air and the panic gnawing its way through my chest. I'm not supposed to be here. I'm supposed to be home. "Let go, Cole, and tell me what's going on. Tell me what happened." And then, when that still elicits nothing but more kisses, I growl, "Cole, let go!" But he doesn't. He holds me tight with one hand, while the other, which had been on my cheek, wanders down my jaw to my neck. His fingers close around my throat. I gasp, mostly in shock, and fight his hands, but my own go through them, straight through his like they are nothing but... air.

"I did it," he whispers in my ear, his wind fingers

tightening around my throat. I can't breathe.

"Did what?" I gasp, as Cole's stone eyes meet mine. Strange how much they look like real stones now.

"I took the children." The words break into hisses. "I took them all."

I try desperately to break free, to fight back, but nothing touches this Cole made of wind and stone. The dream dispels, and the world is taking shape around us again, the night thick and the hills rolling away in every direction. How have we gotten so far from the village? Even if I could scream, would the sound reach Near? Would it just melt into the wind?

"What's wrong, Lexi?" he asks as he chokes me. "You look upset. Hush now. Everything will be all right." Cole begins to hum that awful tune as my pulse pounds in my ears and the wind whips around us.

How could I have forgotten my father's knife? I'm not even wearing shoes, I finally realize, looking down at my scratched and bleeding feet. I don't feel it. Fear has overtaken all other feelings. I push into him with all my force, and not all of him is wind, because I connect, meet with something solid, and he steps back, lets go. I stumble to the tangled grass and wince as a stray and broken branch tears through my nightgown, scratching my leg deeply. Warmth runs over my knee.

"Why are you doing this?" I ask, gasping for air.

"You got in my way," hisses Cole, and his voice is no longer his, but angrier, older. My fingers close around the branch, still tinged with my own blood, as I push myself to my feet and swing it at Cole, hard. I miss, and the wind picks up and rips it from my hands. I stumble forward. Cole, made of stone, sticks, wind, and something horrible and dark, is leaning over me.

The wind tugs at my limbs, whistling white noise in my ears as it pulls me to my feet. And around the boy I named Cole, several sharp branches rouse themselves from the ground, floating up like leaves in the wind.

"Good night, Lexi," he whispers, and the branches turn their points toward me and sail through the air. Just then, something takes hold of me from behind, firm and flesh and bone. Arms close around my chest and force me down, down to the matted earth of the moor as the branches soar through the air and smash into shards against the rocks behind me.

The angry moor-made Cole lunges forward, but the form pinning me down lets out a kind of growl, and the wind cuts through from a different side. When it touches Cole, he crumbles midstride to the ground in a heap of stones and twigs and grass. I close my eyes and fight the body on mine, trying to free myself from the warm weight of it. I throw a punch and feel it connect.

"Dammit, Lexi," comes a familiar voice. "It's me."

I blink and find myself looking into Cole's dark eyes, like some nightmarish duplicate of the face that just disintegrated.

"Get away!" I cry, throwing him off and stumbling back against the rocks. "Don't come near me." Cole looks hurt, but I am aching, too, and confused.

"What are you talking about?" he asks quietly, and the edges of his words are clear and crisp. He looks from me to the pile of moor things that had moments before been a frightening likeness of him.

"It wasn't me," he says, approaching slowly, as if I am a deer and he's afraid of startling me. "It wasn't me. It's okay." He takes another step. His face is as pale as the moon overhead. "It's okay." My breaths are coming heavily, and I clutch my arms to myself but do not run.

"I'm sorry, Lexi." Now his fingertips graze my cheek, and they are warm and not made of wind. "It's okay." He slides his arms around me. "It wasn't me."

I stare past him at the pile of stones. "Then who was it?"

But by the time the question leaves my lips, I know. I step back and slide down onto one of the shorter rocks, trying to catch my breath, the shards of wood scattered around my feet. The world is not swaying as it was, though I still feel ill. The cut on my leg isn't too deep. In fact, I don't feel any pain. I shiver, partly from shock, and Cole peels off his cloak and wraps it around me. The shirt he has on beneath is worn and thin, and I take him in for the first time. Alive. And hurt.

In the moonlight I see it, the stain, even darker than his shirt, that's spread across part of his chest. I touch my fingertips to it. They come away wet.

My uncle. My uncle did this. Or Bo. Cole takes my bloodstained hand as I pull it away, instead drawing me closer, wincing even as he does so.

"I got away," he says. His hand is warm in mine, and I want to throw my arms around him because he's there and real, but the stain on his clothes, and the pain in his eyes, warn me not to. I still cannot pull my eyes from the darkness covering his shirt, and part of me is thankful it's night and the blood is cast in black and gray instead of red.

"I'm fine," he says, but his jaw clenches as my fingers wander over the stain.

"If by 'fine' you mean 'bleeding,' then yes, you are," I snap, trying to examine the wound. I start to lift his shirt, but his hands catch mine.

"I'll *be* fine," he corrects, easing the shirt back down and pushing my fingers gently away.

"Let's get you home," he says, helping me to my feet.

"I don't think so, Cole. You're the one who needs help. We need to get you to the sisters." He's shaking his head in that slow way Magda does. An amused smile tugs at his mouth.

"Lexi, I left you alone for one night, and you got yourself abducted and nearly killed by the Near Witch. There's no way I'm letting you walk home alone." He gestures to the shards of wood at my feet, at my generally bedraggled state.

"To be fair, it looked like you," I say, suddenly tired. "And when you didn't come today, I was so..." My voice trails off, finds another path. "When I saw that thing"—I point to the pile of twigs and moss and stone—"I was just so relieved..."

"I'm sorry," he whispers, taking my hand. "I'm sorry I couldn't be there."

My eyes wander to the dark stain.

"What happened?" I can't stop shaking my head. I feel like all my cottony padding is being pulled out, and the blood and the feeling are coming back.

"They took me out," he whispers, "onto the moor..." His fingers drift up to his shoulder. "It doesn't matter. I'm here."

"It *does* matter."

Cole slips back, and I gasp as he tugs the collar of his shirt aside enough to reveal strips of gray fabric, the lining of his worn cloak, wrapped around his shoulder, just above his heart. The gray has turned almost black where the bullet struck.

I don't have words for the anger bubbling up in me. "*Who?*" I manage to growl at last.

"Not your uncle, if that's what you're thinking." He lets go of the shirt with a wince. "He couldn't do it. Another man took the gun."

"Bo," I say. "Are you going to be all right?"

"Better already." The pain bites into the corners of his eyes, but he tightens his grip on my hand. He leads me back across the moor, tucking me gingerly in beside him. Despite his injuries, he seems to feel what I feel: We are each anxious that the other will blow away. And he shares the same desperate need to remind his skin of my own, to prove that he is still here and I am still here.

"How did you survive?" I ask.

"Not as well as I'd have liked," he says, taking a shallow breath. "Things are going to get harder."

"What do you mean?"

"I had no choice. Staying in control wasn't a high priority at that moment." He almost laughs, but stops in pain.

"You showed yourself to them, as a witch?"

"The only thought in my head was surviving."

"What did you do?"

Cole's arm falls away in response, and by the time I turn to face him, all of him is fading, rippling like heat. The wind picks up and blows *through* him, and he just bleeds away before my eyes. I turn in a circle, but he's gone. Panic flashes through me as the wind grows, tugging at Cole's cloak, curling itself around me; and moments later it's his arms again, holding me close, eyes looking down into mine.

"Lexi, when they led me out on the moor, for the first time in a very long while, I didn't want to suffer. I didn't want to lose... everything for someone else's crimes. Would that I had realized it a little sooner," he says, with a small pained laugh. "The only thing I could think of when he raised the gun, when he pulled the trigger, was you. Wanting to hear your voice. Wanting to feel your skin against mine. I feel connected to you, and I couldn't bear the thought of that being severed. Lost."

He kisses my forehead. Mouths the words *thank you* against my skin.

"Luckily for me," he says, "the hunting party didn't expect me to do what I did. You should have seen them. Even rabbits don't scurry off so fast."

I laugh with him now because we need to laugh. I laugh as his kisses find their way down my cheek, to my lips. They leave tracks across my face, cool and smooth enough to make me pause, to make me remember the Cole of sticks and stones that kissed me with moor wind. He winces as he leans in to me, and I'm still laughing as his mouth finds mine, warm and alive. There is no cyclone around us, but the world is falling away again. Everything beyond our skin is falling away. His kisses push the moor-made Cole, the Near Witch's Cole, from my mind. They push the fear of failing, the fear of banishment, away. His kisses push everything away.

The darkest part of the night passes, and we keep walking. We are almost to my house. And then he stops. I realize that there's probably a hunter, almost certainly Otto, waiting on the other side of the last hill. Cole brings his hand to his chest defensively, eyeing the slope. I take off his cloak and slip it back around him.

"Cole," I say, remembering. "I found her bones. The witch's." I don't know why I'm suddenly excited, but I haven't had a chance to tell him. I try to keep the smile on my face for him. He needs it. "I went back to the forest and I found them."

"I knew you would. What do we do now?"

"We go back first thing in the morning," I say.

And then I remember. I'm not supposed to be out here. I'm supposed to be with Wren. Watching Wren. Guarding the window that the ghostly replica of Cole drew open.

"First thing."

I'm already pulling away.

"Good night, Lexi."

"I'll see you in a few hours," I promise. Our hands slip apart, and he's gone.

My cottage comes into sight, and Otto is there, propped against the door in the chair my mother set out for Tyler, and fast asleep. His chin is to his chest, and he makes a sound like a rumbling stomach. The sun is just out of sight now, the haloed light at the edges of the moor announcing its approach.

Soon the morning will come, it says as it brushes the grass. *Soon the day will dawn*, it says as it reflects on the dew. *First thing*, I add, as I creep back through the window and latch it shut. I see the familiar nest of blankets still piled on the bed, and slip in beside it with a swell of relief. *First thing, we will set things right.*

27

In my dreams, someone is screaming.

The voice cries out and gets caught in the wind. It's tangled, faltering. And then it changes, stretches long and thin, pulled taut before it breaks, and all is quiet. Silent as the sisters' stone house, where even the wind can't go. Stifling. I wake with a start, the blankets wrapped too tight around me, too hot. The only sound in the room is my heartbeat in my ears, but it is so loud I'm sure it will wake my sister. By some strange workings, I slept. Not only until dawn, as I had planned, but much longer. Too long. The sun is cutting through in slivers of gray light as I wrest myself free, one limb at a time, from the sheets wound up around me. I stop as my eyes take in the room, registering the subtle changes.

There are two wooden tables beside the bed, one on either side. On mine, my father's hunting knife rests in its leather sheath, nicks and indents and all. But on Wren's side, her charm is sitting, cast off, still smelling faintly of earth and sweetness. The window is open and the sun is bright, and the blankets are piled in the same way they were last night, like a nest. But my sister is not beneath them.

The air snags in my chest. Wren is probably tucked into
my mother's bed, but I feel sick as I spring up, tugging my
clothes on and wincing as the fabric brushes the deep scratch
on my leg. I fasten my father's knife around my waist, cast a
sideways glance at the mirror, blow a dark strand from my
face. I stumble across the hall and into my mother's room.
It's empty. The bed is unmade, and there's no indent on the
left, the side Wren always takes, where my father used to
sleep. No mark on the pillow.

No Wren.

Voices spill out of the kitchen, my mother's and Otto's,
low and strained and lined with something worse, the kind
of thing that catches in your throat and bends your words
out of key. I hurry in.

"Where is she?" I nearly choke on the question. "Where's
Wren?"

And the answer is in Otto's eyes as he casts a troubled
glance my way, a look that has little sympathy, and more
than a touch of blame. He's leaning on the table, a mug of
something hot and strong in one hand. His other hand rests
on the rifle spread in front of him, where the morning loaves
of bread should be. My mother is not baking. She is standing
at the window, staring out and clutching a mug of tea tight
enough to turn her fingers as white as flour. The image
sways, and I realize my head is shaking back and forth.

And the silence in that kitchen, the absence of an answer
to my question, that silence is choking me.

I run to my mother and wrap my arms around her waist,
tight enough for her to know I'm here. Flesh and blood and
bone, and here. She squeezes back, and we stand there for a

suspended minute, clinging in silence. I try to breathe deeply, try to focus. I will find my sister, I remind myself. I will find my sister, I tell my mother silently. Cole and I will find the children today, and we'll fix this. I repeat this over and over again. Wren's not gone. It's just for a little while, just until we reach the forest.

My mother peels herself away from me and turns back to her work. She measures the flour in slow, steady motions, her eyes unfocused, the way she did in the days after my father's death. *Bring her back*, her knuckles press into the dough. *Bring my baby back*, she folds the words in.

"It was that witch," says Otto. And for a moment, only a moment, I think he knows the truth. Until he adds, "We should have held him down."

Otto sets the drained mug on the table, not with the usual thud, but a tense and quiet drop. He pulls his gun from the table.

"You still think it was Cole?" I ask, turning on him. "The one you tried to *kill*?"

"He attacked us," Otto says hollowly. "We had no choice but to defend ourselves."

"Did he attack you before or after you shot him?"

My mother's eyes flick up.

There's a dead pause before Otto says, "How do you know we shot him?"

"I heard Bo bragging about it." The words just bubble up. "Bragging about how you couldn't do it."

His fingers tighten around the gun and I turn away.

I have to get out of here.

"Where are you going?" asks Otto. I don't answer.

"Lexi," he warns. "I told you—"

"Then I'll face banishment." I cut him off. "When this is over."

When Wren is safely home. I'll face anything when she is safe.

"Lexi, don't do this," he pleads. He lowers the gun and it hits the table, metal scraping wood. The sound sets my feet in motion. I turn and hurry down the hall.

The front door is open, and the wooden crow that was once nailed to our door is lying, warped and broken, on the front steps. The moor-made Cole urged the nails from my window. It must have urged the crow from the door. The Near Witch knew I was trying to find the children. She knew I was in her way.

I cross the threshold, trying to remember the moment I came back through the window and into my room. I remember the pile of blankets. Wren must have been gone already.

I feel ill.

I'm halfway across the yard when fingers close heavily around my wrist.

"Where do you think you're off to?"

"Let go, Bo."

He gives me a slow curious frown, and his hand tightens.

An arm, Tyler's arm, closes around my shoulders from the other side. "I can handle this, Bo."

But Bo doesn't let go. Tyler pulls me closer, fitting me against his side. "I said I can handle this. Go tell Otto we're ready." Bo lets go, one finger at a time, that same amused expression on his face.

"Ready for what?" I ask, trying to pry myself free. I can't.

"How did things go so wrong?" asks Tyler softly, but his arm is still firmly around me. "You've made a mess of things now, Lex. The Council knows what you've been doing. They're furious. They're going to put you on trial. But we'll plead with them." His hand trails down my arm to my fingers, intertwining his with mine.

"This isn't about us, Tyler. Not at all."

"I'm so sorry about Wren," he says.

"I'm going to find her. I know where she—"

"In the forest, right?"

"Yes! Yes, that's exactly where." I disentangle my fingers and bring my hands to his chest. "I just have to go—"

"Lexi, we know about the forest, and there's no children there. We looked." His face darkens. "Lies won't help your *friend* now."

"Tyler, it's not—"

"The only thing hiding in that place is a witch. And we plan on fixing that."

"What do you—"

"We're ready," calls Bo as he comes back into the yard, Otto and my mother behind him. "Let's go."

"Where?" I ask, exasperated.

This is all wrong.

"We have to go to town," says Otto, slinging the rifle over his shoulder. "*All* of us."

Bo, Otto, and my mother walk ahead, but Tyler lingers a moment.

"I know you want to believe that witch, Lexi, but he tricked you. He cast some spell on you."

"It doesn't work like that, Tyler, and you know it." I try to push away, but he pulls me in closer, our noses almost touching. "Doesn't it?" he whispers. "Didn't he cast a spell on those children, on your sister too, luring them from their beds? He must have done the same to you."

"He's not the one doing—"

"It would have been better if he had just died," he says softly. "I never really knew it was him, you know. Until he attacked us. The look in his eyes, Lexi."

This is nonsense. Wren's absence and this sick procession to town and Tyler's arms, too warm around me, are all the stuff of bad dreams. I feel stifled again, twisted in too many blankets. I close my eyes, hoping to wake up.

"Don't lie, Tyler. Not to me—"

"How long did you know he was a witch?" Tyler breaks through.

"Does it matter?"

After a long pause, he says, "No, I don't suppose it does." He pulls me in the wake of the others, toward the center of Near.

"We'd better catch up."

*

All the villagers have gathered, and the three old Masters of the Council step up onto the low stone wall in the village square. I catch sight of Helena across the square and strain to get her attention, but she doesn't see me. Mrs. Thatcher is standing by my mother. She meets my eyes for a moment, but then Tyler pulls me against him, forcing us forward into the throng of tense, angry, tired bodies. But he stops in the middle of the crowd.

"They're going to arrest you," he whispers. "At the end of the meeting."

My heart lurches. The three Council bells sound, each a different pitch, and the square goes quiet. This can't be happening.

There's no echo when the Masters speak. Their withered voices grate against each other.

"Six days ago a stranger came to Near," announces Master Eli to the villagers, his dark eyes deep and narrowed in his face.

"That stranger is a witch," chimes in Master Tomas, towering over the others.

A murmur passes through the square.

"He has the ability to control the wind," adds Matthew, the sun glinting on his glasses.

"This witch proceeded to use this power to lure the children of the village from their beds."

"And he used the wind to cover his trail. This is why we have not been able to find them."

I try to pull back, away, but Tyler's arms are still around mine.

"And yesterday, when we finally confronted this witch, he used the wind to attack our men and escape."

The murmur grows louder, higher-pitched.

Several people ahead, and just shy of the wall, Bo, Otto, Mr. Ward, and Mr. Drake are huddled, muttering to each other, but I can't hear them over the crowd.

"What about the children?" calls out Mrs. Thatcher. A dozen voices shout in agreement, and the mass of people seems to surge forward slightly.

Matthew's withered blue eyes travel over the crowd and land on mine. "We have found no trace," he says, looking even older than he did when I saw him last. "We are still searching."

The crowd gives another surge forward, bringing me closer to the group of men by the wall, and I can just make out Mr. Drake's words. He's leaning in toward Otto, and he looks shaken, the way Helena did by the river. The way Edgar did when he fell in the square that day.

"You really think he's in the forest?" he whispers.

"Something is," grumbles Otto.

"What are we going to do?"

"Get rid of him," suggests Mr. Ward.

"That went so smoothly last time," interjects Bo, dryly.

"At least we know he can bleed."

"Won't miss again."

"Got to find him first."

Master Tomas's voice travels over the crowd. "This witch is loose. No one is safe until he is caught..."

The whole crowd clatters. Voices mix with the sound of feet shifting and grips tightening on guns.

They're hunting the wrong witch.

I press my elbows into Tyler and arch my back away from him, creating a small gap.

"...telling you, Bo," Mr. Drake says, "it's her. Me and Alan went back to that forest like you said, and we could hear her crows..." The men's voices begin to bleed together in the growing noise of the square.

"Matthew says it's her, the Near Witch."

Bo and Mr. Ward both let out bitter laughs.

"You can't actually be serious."

"The Near Witch is dead."

"One witch or another, it doesn't matter."

"But when Magda brought that charm, she said—"

"I say we take care of the sisters, too," says Bo. "Burn out all the bad at once."

"This isn't about them," cuts in Otto, glancing back.

"Isn't it? Didn't they harbor the stranger?" Bo says, his smile twisting. "Didn't they know all along what he was? They're just as responsible."

Tyler's grip has loosened a fraction. I manage to slide one hand between his body and mine.

"But what if the children are there somewhere, in the forest?"

They are, I think, *they have to be.*

My fingers close on the handle of my father's knife.

Master Eli's voice reaches me. "The witch was not acting alone." *No.* The crowd begins to whisper.

"We would have found the children," mutters Bo.

"You can't be certain," says Otto. "As soon as the meeting is over, we'll go to the forest ourselves. If something, or someone, is in there, we'll find out."

"And if not, we'll burn the forest down."

Master Tomas clears his throat. "There is a traitor among us."

My foot comes down on Tyler's, and he yelps, releasing me. Only a moment, but it's all the time I need. I slide the knife free, spin on him, then pull his body back against mine. The tip of the knife rests under his chin.

"Lexi," he hisses. "Don't do this."

"Sorry, Tyler."

I shove him back, hard, and run.

The crowd is thick around me, pressed close, and Tyler catches my arm just as I break through at the edge of the square. But his hand falls away suddenly, and he's sitting on the ground, dazed. A broad form stands over him. Mrs. Thatcher. Her large hands wrench him up by the collar.

"Show some respect, Mr. Ward," she says, turning him around. "Your Council is speaking." He tries to free himself, but she escorts him back into the crowd, glancing at me with only a strong look and a nod, and I'm gone.

28

I cut between the houses, weaving out of the town center. The wind rushes through my lungs as my feet find the path to the sisters' house. The fastest way. I never look back. Across the fields, through the grove, and up the hill, and all I can picture is the world on fire.

Magda is squatting in the garden bed, muttering something and looking more than ever like a large and very wrinkled weed. Dreska is leaning on her cane and telling her sister she's doing it wrong, whatever it is she's trying to do. I can just see buds and shoots poking through the soil. Several feet away, on the scorched patch of earth, a pile of stones that wasn't there before rumbles and shifts.

The sisters look up as I climb the hill.

"What is it, child?"

I stagger to a stop, breathless.

"Wren's gone," I gasp. "The Council's turned the village against Cole. Bo plans to burn the forest down. Now."

"Foolish men," says Dreska. Magda uncurls herself, turning her creased face to the sun as she stands.

"Where's Cole?" I ask, drawing deeper breaths.

Magda shakes her head. "He waited, but you didn't come. He went on ahead to the forest."

If I'd had any air left in my lungs, it would have been knocked out.

The forest.

Everything I hold dear is in those woods.

"Bring us the bones," says Dreska, glancing at the shifting pile of stones. "All of them. We'll have the rest ready."

"Run, Lexi dear," adds Magda. "Run."

*

I want so badly to stop running.

My heart feels like it will abandon my chest. My lungs are screaming.

I don't need air, I tell myself.

All I need is the image of Wren wandering through a forest on fire. The image of Cole surrounded by men, watching the world go up in flames again. The cocoon crumbling down over the witch's bones.

How far out are Otto's men? Does Bo have matches on him? The dead trees of the forest will go up like straw.

I crest the final hill, and there in the valley I see it, the tangled branches so close and dark at first I think they're smoking. I half slide down the hill to the cluster of trees jabbed into the earth, just as a gray cloak slips into the forest.

I plunge in after.

*

"Cole," I shout, upsetting a crow on a nearby branch. The gray cloak turns as I close the gap between us, and I practically launch myself into his arms before remembering his wound. His shirt is gone beneath his cloak, and his chest is a web of bandages, here and there a slice of dusty red seeping through. The pain lingers like a shadow on his face, and his fingers tighten around the handle of a basket at his side.

"You didn't come, so I thought I should..." He stops short, searching my eyes. "What is it? What's wrong?"

"It's Wren," I say, gasping for air. "She's gone." My chest tightens, and I can barely breathe. It is not the running, but the words themselves, sealing my throat. Cole pulls me in close, and his skin is cool against my flushed face.

"And the village," I say. "They all think—"

"Lexi," he says, keeping his voice even and calm, "it doesn't matter now."

I pull back. "Cole, they're coming now to burn the forest down."

His eyes narrow, but all he says is, "Then we'd better hurry."

He casts a last glance back to the edge of the trees and the hills beyond. The wind over the wild grass picks up, growing tangled and fierce. It grows and grows until the ground ripples this way and that. The world begins to blur. It's strangely quiet, this wall of wind, at least from our side.

"To slow them down," he says, meeting the question in my eyes. We set out, hand in hand, for the clearing and the bones.

"You've been practicing," I say, glancing behind us.

"I'm trying. I've got a ways to go."

"What were you thinking when you made that wall?"

"Not thinking, really," he says, without breaking his

stride. "It's just *want*. I want to keep you safe. I want to find the children. I want to put the Near Witch to rest. Because I want to stay." He looks down at the ground, but I can hear him add, "I want to stay here, with you."

I weave my fingers through his as the thickest part of the forest closes over us.

*

"Everything about this place, it's listening to *her*." Cole gestures to the entire forest, to the ruined nature of it. Everything is half rotted, half collapsed, like a spectacular grove fallen into total disrepair. "She must have been a very strong witch."

"But how can she control it? It's day. The sisters said she could only take shape at night."

"Take shape, maybe," says Cole. "But she is still here, and still strong. The woods obey her. They're enchanted."

I lead him through the sharp scrawny trees, my boots adding to the many sets of smaller feet still vaguely stamped into the soil. Otto's men have added prints, cutting their own road. Large feet clumsily dragged across the earth. No method, no skill. I try to follow the children's, but many of the small tracks are ruined. I look up at the thin light slipping through the canopy.

We've been walking for too long.

"It shouldn't be this hard to find."

"What are we looking for?" asks Cole.

"A nest of trees. A clearing. Even if the witch could move, those trees are old, deep-rooted." I look down at the half-smeared steps and stop. Set over the others, flitting and light, is a new pair of feet.

Wren.

Her steps are so light, they barely leave a mark, but I know them and the ways they move. I kneel, studying the strange little dance. She was playing a game. Not the circle-spinning game of the Witch's Rhyme, since that one takes a group, but one of her own games, the kind she played in the hall before bed.

"What is it?" asks Cole, arms crossed, but I hold up my hand. I stand and scan Wren's hops and skips and sideways jumps. Then I hurry along, following the strange steps that would never look like tracks to anyone but me. Cole follows silently behind.

At last, Wren leads us to the small clearing, the space where the trees have scooted back to make room for the earth, and the boughs bend low to form a kind of shelter. In the clearing, Wren's footsteps vanish with the rest, and I try to bite back the panic of having lost her trail.

"Wren?" I call out, but only the cracking trees reply. I circle the clearing, searching for something, anything, but there's no sign.

"Lexi," Cole calls, but he's not looking at me. He's looking back the way we came. I follow his gaze, but the woods are thick, and the edge of the forest is far beyond our sight. I wonder if the hunters have reached the tree line, if Bo is already digging out flint or matches or oil.

"They're coming," Cole says. "Where are the bones?"

"In there." I point to the mass of branches. On all sides above the nest, a dozen crows like black signposts sit and wait and watch with small stone eyes and beaks that glint even in the gray light.

Cole drops the basket and makes his way up to the cocoon, peering in between the crossed limbs. He looks as if he expects the cocoon to simply peel itself back and let us in, but the mass doesn't stir. If it did, I would trust it even less. He unfastens his cloak, letting it fall away and exposing the bandages that crisscross against his chest and back. The branches crack and snap in protest as he hoists himself through an opening, vanishing into the dark interior. Overhead, one of the crows flutters its wings.

"Wait." I hurry over, thinking of his wounds. "Let me do that." I keep my voice low, in case the men are getting close.

"I'm fine," he says automatically, his words muffled by the wall of sticks.

I find one of the larger openings, a place where the branches cross to form a kind of window. I peer down into the earthen nest, and the moss and rot make me feel ill. Cole stands in the center of it, up to his knees, and begins to dig. He hands me one bone after another, glinting and white as though they've been picked clean and bleached, despite the mud and moss clinging here and there. He searches in the semidarkness, and I lift the basket and climb the nest toward the top.

"Watch out," I warn, as I bring my boot down hard against the roof of branches. Most of them resist, half petrified with time. But several smaller ones snap, showering Cole with slivers of wood and shavings of light. The white bones glint where they jut through the earth, caught by the new beams of late afternoon sun. I resume my post, taking bones as he hands them up to me. Each one is a surprise of sorts. A thin finger. A splintered femur. A shoulder blade.

And then, a skull. He passes it to me, and I gasp as I take it, the half-crushed face blossoming with moss and weedy flowers. It's like a horrible flowerpot, roots escaping out the eye. So this is what they did to her, to the Near Witch, when they found the dead boy in her garden. I run my fingers over the ruined skull—the cracked cheekbone, the crushed eye socket—and shiver as I think of the hunting party dragging Cole out onto the moor.

"Lexi?" he asks, waiting to hand me another bone. "Are you all right?"

I take a deep breath, let it out, and place the skull gently into the filling basket. Through the trees the sun is crossing the sky. It took too long to find the bones. It's taking longer to collect them.

Cole continues to dig, but the hunt is getting harder, and minutes stretch between finds. A gun fires in the distance, and I spin, looking back, though all I can see are trees.

"How badly do you want this, Cole?" I ask. And he knows what I mean.

"With all my heart," he says, wincing as he passes me another bone. His hand grows thin around it, and I swear I can hear the wind pressing out against the rolling hills and the hunters. "But I can't keep them out for long."

There's a *click, click, click* overhead, and I look up to see a crow toying with a small bone, just like before. Only this time, I need that bone. I hop down to the ground, set the basket aside, and find a stray pebble, taking aim. This first rock falls short, the shot hurried and clumsy. The crow doesn't budge, doesn't seem the least bit disturbed by the assault. I hear my father's scolding even now.

Focus, Lexi. Make it count.

I slide the knife free, feel my fingers slip into the old grooves, before turning the weapon, pinching it by the blade. I stand slowly, measuring the distance. I raise the knife behind my shoulder, then feel the familiar release of metal past skin as I let go. The blade soars through the air, pinning the crow to the tree beyond its perch. It gives an agonizing caw, and then, to my shock, crumbles into a pile of black feathers and sticks and stones. Just like the wind-made Cole on the moor at night. I stare down at the heap, where the small bone waits like a crown, and pluck it off the top of the pile. I consider taking aim at the other crows, when I hear a flutter and a rustle, and the pile of forest things begins to piece itself back together at my feet. It assembles into a vaguely birdlike mass, except the beak is now a little off center, and one stone eye droops. The marred crow alights, and as it reaches its abandoned perch, it looks more bird than dirt again. I shiver, free the knife from the tree trunk, and hurry back to the basket and Cole, dropping the small bone in with the others and slipping my father's knife into the leather sheath around my waist.

Another gun sounds, this time not muffled by the wind. They're in the forest.

"We're almost done," Cole calls, his hands plunged to the elbows in the mossy rot.

My eyes dart across the horizon line, searching between the trees. I try to hear, to tune my ears to the sounds of feet and men, but no sound reaches me.

Cole hands me another bone. Some of the smaller ones are strung together by weeds and roots, weaving through the hollow middles like marrow. At least it makes them easier to find, I tell myself, cringing as Cole passes me a foot, most of the bones still connected, hanging in a limp cluster by tendril and moss. I load it into the basket and hop down to the ground, turning my back on Cole and the nest of trees for a moment. I think I can hear a man's voice, far off but on this side of the wind wall. Otto. Through the trees the autumn light is growing thin as the sun slips closer to the ground. The days have grown shorter as they've grown colder.

And then I smell smoke.

"Cole," I say.

"I know," he replies. "I'm almost done."

But something is wrong. Otto would never let this happen, not before he'd searched every inch for the children. The men and the fire are coming from different directions. Otto's voice winds in from the right, and thin trails of black smoke begin to waft in from the left.

I scour the forest floor, hoping once more to spot the children. My sister. My eyes run through the trees and down the trunks and over the dirt, and then, they snag. The dirt. The dirt beneath my feet is dry, matted with tendrils of weeds and patches of moss, settled. But a few feet away, beside the cocoon, the dirt is different. Freshly tilled. The witch's words rage in my ears. *Don't you dare disturb my garden.*

Oh no. No, no, no.

I fall to my knees beside the fresh earth, begin to dig with my hands, pushing the dirt to either side. There's nothing. Nothing. And then my fingertips feel something smooth and soft.

A cheek.

Cole calls out to me from within the huddle of trees, a question, I think, but all I can hear is my pulse and the Near Witch's words and the vague melody on the air. I hear him climbing through the tangled mass of tree limbs, trying to free himself from the nest. The wind and smoke sweeps through as I dig, unearthing a child's face.

Wren. She's not breathing. Her skin is pale, her nightgown spread gently around her, her hair still impossibly straight. No, no, Wren. We're supposed to be able to stop this. Supposed to be able to set things right. I stifle the urge to scream, and instead uncover her chest and press my ear against it, listening for a pulse. I hear it, slow and low and steady. My own heart lurches with relief as I pull my sister's shoulders from the earth.

"Help me, Cole!" I shout. And then he's there beside me, clearing the ground around her body, exposing her legs, her bare feet. Then he begins to push aside the surrounding dirt. Soon more faces appear. Edgar. Cecilia. Emily. Riley. Five children in all, tucked beneath the garden bed. I realize Cole is speaking.

"Lexi," he's saying. "Come." He pries my fingers from Wren's arms, and I realize I've been gripping, clenching. I can hear the voices now, growing closer. Smoke is filling the clearing, and I hear the crackle of burning wood.

"Lexi, take the bones, you've got to go."

I shake my head, brushing Wren's blond hair, caked in dirt, from her pale face.

"I can't. I can't leave her."

"The search party is coming," he says more forcefully. "You have to get the bones back to the sisters before the sun sets."

I shake my head. "No. No, the fire. I can't leave my sister."

"Look at me." He kneels down, his cool hand guiding my chin up. "I'll stay. I can use the wind to keep the fire back from Wren and the others, but you've got to run. One of us has to take the bones, and I'm not leaving you here."

My fingers loosen on Wren's body, but I can't let go.

"Lexi, please. We're running out of time." Nearby branches snap beneath heavy feet. But Wren feels like dead weight in my lap, so cold, and I cannot make my legs move. And then a crack so loud and close that it's amazing the searchers aren't there on top of us already. Fire licks the clearing from one side, men's voices call from the other.

"Go. Get to the sisters' house. I'll catch up." He looks down at the children, then back at me. "We'll all catch up. I promise."

The crows overhead flutter nervously, and I see the panic in Cole's eyes and let him guide me to my feet, my sister's blond hair sliding from my dress back to the dirt. I feel my legs again beneath me as I look up through the canopy and see that the sky is changing, darkening. Cole hands me the basket and lifts Wren into his arms. The wind curls up around him, around the other children. They begin to blur, but I don't know if it's from the wind or from tears, as I turn, gripping the basket of bones, and leave the clearing. The forest closes in a curtain behind me, and my world is swallowed by smoke and fire and trees.

29

I sprint through the dead forest, and the light slips lower and lower, impossibly fast toward the horizon. Something wrenches me back. My cloak has snagged on a low limb, and I fight to wrest it free. The limb snaps, and I stumble on.

I trust myself unto the moor... I try to recite my father's prayer, but the words feel hollow. I try a second time before abandoning the prayer.

Please, I beg the forest instead.

I break through the tree line and onto the open hills.

Please, I beg the sky and the tangled grass.

Please protect them. I cannot entrust my sister to the ground so soon. I cannot give her back to the moor the way we did my father. I cannot let Cole's world burn a second time.

From the top of the hill I see that the forest is engulfed in flames.

I clutch the basket as I run, the lower curve of the sun touching the hills, the golden circle skimming the wild grass. I fight the urge to look back, to slow down. I have to reach the sisters. The moor rolls away beneath me, and I imagine that I can feel a cool wind at my back, pushing me on.

I reach the last hill before the sisters' house. Just one more. One rise and one valley and then up, and I'll be there.

I am about to exhale when the ground gives a sudden lurch beneath my feet, and a fierce gust of wind tears through, ripping the basket from my hands. I hit the ground hard. Pain shoots through my head. White noise fills my ears. I wince as I try to push myself up, make it to my hands and knees before my head spins and I have to stop.

I'm still trying to figure out what happened when I see the basket of bones overturned, spilling white shards out onto the hillside. The ground ripples beneath me as I push myself shakily up. Something trickles down my face, and when I wipe it away, I find a dark smudge on my hand. The sun is bleeding, too, right into the horizon, and the whole world has turned a sickly red.

I turn around, looking down the hill, then up toward the top. My internal compass seems to have been knocked straight out of my head by the impact, and I am barely able to hear my own voice above the ringing in my ears. Up is good, I think slowly. I need to get up.

I fumble along the ground, scattered with bones, kneeling to collect as many as I can. Light explodes in front of my eyes, but I force myself to focus.

Several feet away, the basket twitches. Or rather, something *inside* the basket twitches just as the sun dips beneath the hills. An arm bone juts out, writhing as the moor climbs up around it, covering the eerie white in dirt and weeds.

I whisper a curse, staggering back from the forearm now

sliding across the ground and trying to connect itself to a stray wrist. It searches for fingers among the weeds.

Run, screams a voice inside my head.

I half crawl up the hill backward, keeping my eyes focused on the body picking itself up in front of me. The sun is now almost entirely out of sight. My retreat is too awkward, too slow, but I can't turn away from the thing before me, the wild grass crawling over the bones as they collect themselves. A foot finds a leg. Ribs find a spine. I manage to unsheath my father's knife as I stumble up the last hill. What I am going to do with it, I have no idea.

An arm, now fully assembled, digs into the basket and retrieves the skull, the wildflower still planted above the eye. And in the grass-covered palm, the dirt and weeds climb up over the skull, two stray stones clambering into the gaping holes where the roots wait like sinews.

I near the top of the hill by the time the witch recovers her head and turns it toward me. The skull, now growing grassy hair, still sits in the palm of her hand as the rest of her body assembles.

The Near Witch levels her stone eyes and opens her mossy lips and speaks in a windy voice.

"You ruined my garden."

"You stole my sister," I snap, raising the knife like I have a clue what to do with it.

The wind around us begins to blow harder.

"Hush, hush," she coos with her half-formed mouth, pieces of dirt crumbling from her lips. The ground shifts beneath me. My heel hits a new groove in the hillside, and I stumble back to the slanted ground.

"Quiet, little thing." She smiles, and the words are a tangible force, heavy in the air. They come over the wind like a spell, and before I can get up, the moor is upon me, roots and tangled grass climbing up around my arms and legs, pinning me to the ground. The brambles cut into my skin. I gasp as they tighten, and I saw at the roots with the knife, snapping them only to find a dozen more climbing up over my boot, my calf. My arms free, I hack at the weeds binding my ankles as the Near Witch approaches. She begins with a limp, her back leg still attaching itself, but as she draws near, her stride is as smooth as my mother's. Several weeds around my leg snap beneath my knife. She reaches out for me.

"I told you," she growls, her stone eyes glinting, her words traveling loud and clear through the air, "not to disturb my garden."

Finally the last strands break beneath my father's knife. Before they can redouble, I kick out as hard as I can with my boot. When it collides with the Near Witch, she stumbles back, half crumbles against the moor, still weak at the edges. But before she can fall down the hill, the grass and the dirt beneath coil up to catch her.

I reach the hilltop as she recovers. With every step, a few strands of the moor grow up, adding themselves to her limbs, thickening her.

I take another step back, and I can feel the hill slope down behind me. I dare to look back, and a small gasp of relief escapes when I see the low stone wall tapering off like a tail down the moor, and beside it, the sisters' house.

"How dare you."

I feel the words, the cold air against my skin. I spin, and the Near Witch is inches from my face, her mossy lips turned down in anger.

Her bone fingers, now covered in weeds, fly forward, closing around my throat. I clench my fist, feeling the warm wood of my father's knife, and bring it down in a single swipe, severing the witch's hand. It falls away, and so do I, tumbling down the hill several feet before I manage to stop. But she's already coming, putting her hand back onto her wrist. I manage to get my feet beneath me, sliding to the bottom of the hill. Glancing back at the sisters' house, I catch sight of a stone tomb, open, waiting. They did it. The structure sits, a rectangular vault, where before was only barren earth and that shifting pile of stones. Magda and Dreska made a house just big enough to hold the witch's bones. I've got to get her there.

I turn back to face the witch, and brace myself, but she stops moving. She pauses, for only a moment, as her eyes snag on the cottage and, beside it, the small garden, full of flowers, all in bloom, despite the fall chill. Half a dozen different kinds, in perfect rows. Clearly the sisters' craft hasn't withered away entirely over the years.

Something moves by the low stone wall, a flash of gray. It launches itself over and onto the moor toward me, traveling so fast it almost blurs.

"Cole?"

The word jars the Near Witch from her reverie, and her stone eyes flash to me, glistening. She lunges just as Cole reaches me, throwing his body in front of mine. And then a sound, a fierce crack, a dozen times louder than any breaking branch, loud enough to make the moors shiver and the witch turn, angry and fast, in the direction of it.

"Now, Cole!" I shout, and in that moment the wind tears through, catching the witch off guard. It forces us to the ground as the air slams into her, carrying her in one large gust past us to the garden and the tomb where her house once sat. The bones clatter against the stones of the tomb with such force that the structure collapses over them, a mound of rock and weedy earth, and bones somewhere beneath.

And suddenly, everything is quiet.

The kind of stifling quiet of blocked ears, booming pressure before sound returns. Cole's hands are on his knees as he tries to breathe. My head is spinning, and I sit, dazed, on the grass, watching as weeds begin to creep slowly over the tomb, blossoming wildflowers until the stone structure seems as old as the sisters' house, half eaten by the moor. It's over. I can't take my eyes from the small stone tomb, expecting it to shake, to crumble and unleash the angry, moor-made witch. But no sound, no motion comes.

And then I catch sight of the glinting metal back by the low stone wall, the source of the violent crack. Otto is standing, his rifle still raised against his shoulder, looking as singed as Cole. He continues to gaze down the barrel at the two of us, sitting half dead on the moor, and I can imagine him leveling the sight on Cole, for just a moment too long, wondering. Finally he lowers the gun, and Mr. Ward and Tyler hop the low wall and hurry toward us. Cole must have brought them. Behind my eyes the scene plays out, the fire spreading through the forest and his pleas for the men to come quick, to help him. Did they hesitate? Did they wonder?

I can see other men now walking up behind my uncle, and in their arms are forms, cradled and small. The children. Otto climbs the wall, too, as Magda and Dreska appear from their house and totter over. Magda's hand brushes the tomb as she passes it, looking pleased. Dreska follows behind, touching it once. Cole sits, breathless and pale, beside me.

"You made it," I gasp.

"I promised."

The sun is gone, and the night seems to have swept in, only the last edges of light strung across a few stray clouds.

And then Otto is standing over us. He gives me a measured gaze before turning his attention to Cole.

My uncle stares down at the pale and bloodied boy on the ground beside me. His face is just as dirty, his clothing singed. The two look as though they've been through the same battle. Cole looks back at Otto, not with anger or fear. What happened in the forest? Otto looks to the children, then to the stone tomb. After a long moment, his eyes fall back on Cole, who is shifting his weight, about to push himself to his feet. Otto holds out his hand, and Cole takes it.

The sisters are examining the children, all five set on the ground beside the low stone wall. They still aren't moving. Then Wren fidgets, rolls onto her side, asleep. Asleep. My head spins with relief.

When I look back at Otto, he has not let go of Cole's hand, eclipsing it in his own.

"Thank you," he says at last, so low it sounds more like a grumble than actual words. But I can hear it, and so can

Cole, and so can Tyler, judging by his hard expression. Otto's hand falls away, and Cole looks to me, and I cannot wipe the smile from my face. He steps to me, takes me into his arms. The wind curls around us. And for the first time in what seems like forever, everything feels right. In its place.

30

My father used to say that change is like a garden.

It doesn't come up overnight, unless you are a witch. Things have to be planted and tended, and most of all, the ground has to be right. He said the people of Near had the wrong dirt, and that's why they resisted change so much, the way roots resist hard earth. He said if you could just break through, there was good soil there, down deep.

There is a celebration in the town square the following night. The children are dancing and singing and playing their games. Edgar takes one of Wren's hands, and Cecilia the other, and they join the circle with the rest. Even the sisters have come, and are trying to teach the children new songs and some very old ones, too. I watch Wren's blond hair twirl as she flits from place to place, never landing for more than a moment.

My mother told her she wandered off to join her friends and fell asleep in the forest.

I told her the Near Witch stole her away in the dead of night, and her brave sister came to save her.

I don't think she believes either one of us entirely.

Helena is sitting on a piece of the wall that tapers off into the square, watching her little brother as if he might vanish at any moment, her eyes still nervous but her skin finally regaining color. I watch as Tyler slides onto the wall beside her, staring out at the children and trying to seem interested. Helena's face lights up, and I can see her blush, from where I sit across the square. Tyler seems content to be wanted so much by someone, even if it's not the someone he wanted, because when she shivers he slides closer and offers her a space beneath his arm. Helena beams and curls against his broad chest, and the two of them watch the children spin and sing. Now and then he throws a glance my way, and I pretend not to notice.

Near is still Near. It won't change by morning. It won't change in a day, or a week.

But there is something new—in the air and in the ground. Even as fall takes hold, I can feel it.

The Council still stands atop their steps, their bells ready in case they think of something to say. But Matthew is leaning forward, watching the sisters teach the children a song. His blue eyes dance from Magda to Edgar. Eli stands with his back to the village, talking privately with Tomas. Some people will never change.

The houses nearest the square have opened their doors to the village.

Emily's mother, Mrs. Harp, stands beside my mother, serving up bread and sweets. Another house is offering mugs of hot strong drinks, and Otto leans against a wall, surrounded by several other men. They talk and drink, but my uncle mostly looks out over the square with a mixture of relief and fatigue. And when none of his group is looking, I see him raise his glass to no one in particular, and his lips move quietly, as if in prayer. I wonder if he's praying for the moor, or the children, or my father, but it is short and silent, and then he is swallowed by the group of men as they huddle together and make a loud toast. Only Bo is missing.

I sit on another piece of wall, the last straight section before the sloping tail of it dives back into the ground. My fingertips play with Cole's dark hair as he stretches out on the stone surface, his head in my lap. I begin to tap out the beat to the children's songs on his skin, and he looks up at me and smiles and takes my hand, moving my fingers across his lips. Around us, the wind wanders through the celebration, swaying lamps and dresses.

I hear the three bells and look up, but it's not the Council preparing to speak. It's my uncle.

"Seven days ago, a stranger came to Near. And yes, that stranger is a witch."

A hush falls over the festival, his deep voice carrying over the crowd. Otto looks down, arms crossed across his broad chest.

"My brother told me that the moor and witches are like everything else, that they can be good or bad, weak or strong. That they come in as many shapes and sizes as we do.

"The last week alone has proven this. Your children are here tonight because of the Thorne sisters, and because of this witch's help." Otto's gaze settles on Cole, who's sitting up, propped on one elbow.

"Our village is open to you, if you wish to stay."

With that, Otto steps back, and slowly, all around the square, the celebration bubbles up again.

"Well," I ask, leaning over him, "do you wish to stay?"

"I do."

"And why is that, Cole?" I say, tipping toward him so that our noses nearly brush.

"Well," he says with a smile, "the weather's quite nice."

I pull back and scoff, but his fingers find their way to the back of my neck, wandering up through my hair, and he pulls me to him until our foreheads touch. His hand slips down my neck, between my shoulders, tracing the curve of my spine before it falls away. This time I don't pull back.

He plants a kiss on my nose.

"Lexi," he says.

He kisses my jaw.

"I want to be here."

He kisses my throat.

"Because you are here."

I can feel him smile against my skin.

The celebration fades away, and the village fades away, and everything fades away except for his hands finding mine. And his lips against mine. I pull back, studying his large gray eyes.

"Don't look at me like that," he says, with a soft laugh.

"Like what?"

"Like I'm not real, or not really here. Like I'm going to blow away."

"Are you?" I ask.

He frowns, sitting up and turning so that he can look at me.

"I hope not. This is the only place I want to be."

*

Later that night, Wren fidgets beside me in the bed, and the feeling has never been so welcome. I let her steal the blankets, let her build her nest, give her a soft, playful shove. I look forward to the morning, to her bread dolls and her hallway games. I look forward to watching her grow before my eyes, day by day.

Beyond the house, the wind blows.

I smile in the dark. There is no moonlight, no dancing images on the walls. Sleep will come soon. When I close my eyes, I keep seeing the witch's face, the crushed skull, the clumsy flowers spilling out. The way the anger melted into something else when she saw her home. Her garden. I hope she has found peace. I wonder if that is the thing I feel now, settling over me like a sheet, cool and comfortable. In this quiet place, I imagine I can hear my father whispering stories I've heard a thousand times. Stories that keep him close.

The wind on the moors will always be a tricky thing. It bends its voice and casts it into any shape, long and thin enough to slide beneath the door, stout enough to seem a thing of weight and breath and bone.

I will hold fast to this new story, too, tuck it away beside my father's bedtime tales, beside Magda's tea talk. I will remember everything.

My own voice slips in as the world falls away.

Sometimes the wind whispers names, perfectly clear, the way you might, on the verge of sleep, imagine you hear your own. And you never know if that sound beneath your door is only the howling of the wind, or the Near Witch, in her small stone house or in her garden, singing the hills to sleep.

ACKNOWLEDGMENTS

Belief is a contagious thing.

To my family, for their simple, unwavering belief that I was meant to write.

To my editor, Abby, for believing in my little ember of a book and helping me build a proper fire. (And to her assistant, Laura, for sprinkling nice comments in with the edits.)

To my agent, Amy, for somehow believing in me and my stories, no matter how off the beaten path I veer. (I'll still write that menopausal art school coven book one day, I swear.)

To the publishing gods, godsends, agents, and friends who believed I belonged, and helped my book on its way.

To my critique partners and readers, for believing in me enough to push me, and for carrying pins in case my head ever got too big.

To the online community of bloggers, reviewers, and friends, for believing in me from the start, and for making me feel like a rock star when all I did was string words together.

The fact is, I'm doing what I love, what I feel in my bones I'm meant to be doing, and somehow, impossibly, I'm being allowed to do it. Thank you.

THE
ASH-BORN BOY

by
V.E. SCHWAB

"Once, long ago, there was a man and a woman, and a boy, and a village full of people. And then the village burned down. And then there was nothing."

"How did you survive?"

"The fire was my fault."

1

The market coiled like a colored snake through the streets of Dale, patterned with the brown of the stalls, and the yellows and greens and reds of the things they sold.

People chattered, and children laughed beneath the rare blue stretch of sky, cloudless and perfect, and, bolstered by the sun, they darted between parents and booths, making up games as they went. A group played a messy kind of tag that involved weaving and racing, everyone both a target and a pursuer. A boy grabbed for a girl, who dodged desperately, clipping the edge of a fruit stand as she went. She recovered and ran on with a high laugh, but the stand, heaped high with apples, started to tip. The vendor turned, but lunged too late. The apples were already rolling, and the table was already falling, and he cringed away from the inevitable crash.

But it never came.

A hand caught the table's edge and steadied it. The apples settled, all but a small green one, which escaped, rolled to the lip, over, and into the rescuer's other hand. The vendor let out a sigh of relief.

"Master Dale," he said. "Good day, and thank you."

The rescuer, a boy of sixteen, brushed the apple along the sleeve of his cloak. It was a velvety black, just like his hair. "Please, Peter," he said. "That is my father, not me."

The vendor bowed his head. "Pardon, but I thought the son went by Master and the father by Lord. Have customs changed since I went to bed?"

"No." He bit into the apple. "But only my father's name is Dale."

The vendor cast a nervous glance around the market, unsure of what to do. All royals had two names, the one they were born with, and the one they took if they became a member of the ruling family. The first name could be anything, but the second was always Dale. It was the name of the city itself, and it was an honor. Peter knew that to call the boy anything else was a punishable offense, but he also knew of his temper, and even if he didn't believe the rumors—deals with gods or devils, or worse, witches—he didn't want trouble.

"Apologies, Master… Hart." He cast another glance around when he said the name, and this time swore he saw two people turn, an eyebrow lift, a word or two whispered beneath the din of the market.

The boy brightened. It was his mother's name, and it gave him some small pleasure to defy Robert by using it.

"Thank you," he said with a genuine smile. "And William's fine, really. Now, how much do I owe you?"

"Nothing."

He frowned, digging in his pocket. "Peter—"

"Don't matter what name you want to go by, William, I can't take money from you."

Will took another bite of the apple, and set three white

disks on the table with an audible *click*. "Then I will simply forget a few coins here. A harmless mistake." He drew a hand through the air above the market. "So many customers here today, you couldn't know whose coins they were."

He turned to go, and when the vendor opened his mouth to protest, Will cut him off with a backward glance, a smile, and a "Good day, Peter," before vanishing into the market crowd.

It was a hard thing, to vanish, especially when the people parted for him. Most of them didn't stare. No, in fact, they did the opposite of staring, averting their eyes and granting him too wide a berth for such a crowded place. It only drew more attention. Still, Will did his best to enjoy the apple and the blue-sky day and the fresh air as he made his way to the steps of the Great House.

The town of Dale grew more up than out, a tangle of streets and houses, squares and gardens, all piled on a hill in the middle of the moors. In a land of valleys, Dale was the tallest thing in sight, and the Great House was the tallest thing in Dale. The steps were wide and stone, and swept from the looming structure to the streets, a shallow landing halfway between. The house belonged to Dale, not to the town but to those that held the name and title. But the steps belonged to the people, and on blue-sky days when the sun warmed the stones, the steps were the most popular spot in the town. From them you could see the streets running down from the great house like roots, tapering into the fields below. Dale sat on a large hill, and it sloped away to every side. The valleys at its base were dotted with lakes, each reflecting up a bit of sky. Usually the lakes were gray, but today they were pools of brilliant blue.

Will found a spot on the steps and sat, his black cloak trailing over the stones like a shadow. The sun warmed the chain around his neck, the pendant safe beneath the collar of his shirt. He closed his eyes and listened to the thrum of people, and ran his fingers absently over a set of cuts on his right forearm. One was nearly faded, another was still faintly red, and the third was fresh, only a few days old.

"What's this? The prince sitting among commoners?"

Will's eyes drifted open, and he drew his sleeve down over the marks. "Are you calling yourself common, Phillip?"

The boy's face reddened. He was standing on the path at the foot of the steps, his blonde hair nearly white in the sun. Another boy stood behind him, and two girls stood out of the way, but clearly watching.

"Watch your words, *Master Dale*."

Will stood, and descended the steps to the path. Phillip was a year older, but no taller than him, and a bit stockier. "Don't call me that."

"Why not?" spat Phillip, drawing closer. The air that day was still, which was dangerous, because any unusual breeze, any gust, would be noticeable. "It's your name."

Will thought of the scars, of the pendant around his neck, of the dire need to keep calm, especially here. Anger seeped through him, but he kept his gray eyes level, intensely aware of the market's attention bending toward them.

"Your mother earned it," pressed Phillip, "when she climbed into bed with my uncle."

The air picked up around them now, rippling just enough for Phillip's smile to sharpen. Will's knuckles were white, but he didn't blink, didn't speak, didn't move. He didn't dare.

Phillip finally shook his head, and laughed. "What? Nothing to say? You really are callous, Will. I'd have slit your throat for talking that way about *my* mother."

At that, Will managed a grim smile. "I don't need to talk about her. Everyone else already does."

Phillip lunged, but Will had always been faster, and he dodged, and watched his cousin stumble forward against the steps. By the time Phillip found his feet, the eyes of the market were turning, the idle chatter dying as the crowd watched. Even Phillip knew better than to carry on now, but he let his friend, Ian, make a show of holding him back, while the girls stood and watched. One of them, Beth, was snickering, but the other, Sarah, looked sad. Will seized the chance, and turned away, letting Phillip curse him under his breath.

"You're nothing, Hart," growled Phillip, and those who could hear drew in a breath at the insult of the name. It was one thing for Will to insist on it. It was quite another for it to be hurled at him.

Will kept walking. His anger cooled as he climbed the steps, his fists unclenching and the blood flooding back into his knuckles. The sound of the market ebbed as he ascended. He brought a hand to the chain around his neck, and drew the pendant from beneath his collar as he made his way up, rubbing a thumb over the smooth metal face. Instantly he felt better.

"Master Dale."

His grip on control was thin, so he kept walking.

"Please wait."

He reached the top step.

"William."

He paused, and glanced back. Sarah was standing several steps below, breathless, her dress bunched in her hands. Her hair escaped in wisps around her face.

"Sarah," he said, softening. "What is it?"

She climbed the last few stairs and stepped up onto the path beside him. "It's just... I'm sorry... Phillip was being..." She brought her hand to rest against his arm and he tensed. Most people went out of their way to avoid touching him. "Phillip was being an ass." She bit her lip. "Phillip *is* an ass," she amended.

"You climbed the steps just to tell me that?"

Sarah blushed. "I wasn't sure if you knew."

Will *almost* smiled. "Alas, I did. But it never hurts to hear it again."

Sarah let out an easy laugh. Her gaze drifted up over his head to the Great House that rose behind him, and the sound caught in her throat. "Oh." She looked around at the path and the arching trees—brought into Dale as seedlings from the far-off forests—and the gardens that flanked the house, and the veil of low clouds, and woven through it all, the quiet.

"I shouldn't be here," she whispered. Her hand fell away from his arm, and Will was sad to feel it go. She twirled back toward the steps, but he reached out, and took her hand.

"Stay," he said.

"Are you certain?" Will nodded, and Sarah's smile was radiant. She wove her arm through his. "Would you show me the gardens?"

He led her through a vine-wrapped arch into his mother's pride and joy, the Great House gardens. They were not groomed, but wild, tangled and free as they might be on the moors, beyond the reach of Dale, where buildings gave way to valley and grass and, beyond the far rise, who knew what else. The sun was sinking now, the day losing half its light, hedges and trees blotting out even more to cast the gardens in shadows. Sarah pulled free and wandered a few steps ahead, turning in slow circles to take it in.

He liked that she liked it. These places where nature ate up everything, they were the only ones where he felt...

Sarah gasped, gleefully. "Is that...?"

"Shush," he whispered, even as his lips curled up.

"A smile, I see it!" she said in a dramatic whisper. "You know what I think, Will? I think you're not callous, or cold."

He forced his mouth back into a thin, grim line. "I fear you're wrong," he said. "I'm quite heartless." But even as he said it, the smile flickered back to life.

Sarah stepped forward, closing the gap between them. "I mean it. Why do you put on this act?"

His smile slipped. "I..."

Sarah didn't wait for him to think up a lie. Instead, she kissed him. And whatever lie he would have given, it died on his lips as they met hers.

A breeze caught up the loose strands of her hair. "Stop," he said softly.

Sarah smiled and leaned in to him, pressing her body flush with his. The air rustled the leaves and flowers around them, a low sound threaded through the breeze. She tangled her fingers in the metal chain of his pendant and kissed him deeper, and while he kissed her back, Will slid his hands up her arms, over the bare skin until he reached her shoulders. There he stopped, curled his fingers, and guided her body back, carving a space between them.

"Stop," he said, breathless but insistent.

She stopped, but the wind didn't. It was still picking up around them.

Fear crossed his face like a shadow, and he tried to calm down, but it was too late. Control danced out of his grip, and the wind blew through the garden. His touch on her shoulders lightened as his body wavered faintly.

"It's true," said Sarah in a hushed voice. "I'd heard rumors, but..."

He tightened his grip, despite his thinning form. "Which rumors?" he asked coldly. "That I sold my heart for this? That I made a deal with a monster? That *I* am a monster? A demon?"

"Or a god," whispered Sarah, and Will laughed bitterly.

"You only think that because you don't know..." He stopped himself. The people knew of witches in Dale, but only as the stuff of stories, and only as those who dealt in earth and stone and petty charms. Not wind. If any witches were fool enough to actually live here, he had never met them. His father made sure of that. As for Will... the sky was the realm of gods and godthings. And the boy whose temper seemed tethered to the air itself... they didn't know what to make of him.

"Don't know what?" pressed Sarah.

Will swallowed hard, and kissed her forehead. "I'm not anything but me."

She pulled back enough to look him in the eyes, and then

drew his mouth to hers. The wind whistled around them, and he tensed.

"Just let go," she said against his mouth.

He knew better. But the fight with Phillip had weakened his resolve and the strange glee in Sarah's eyes broke it, and so, even though his arm still burned from the last cut, he gave in. He guided her back against a hedge, and kissed her breathless. The wind sang through the garden, tangling in her dress and his cloak, whipping around them both as his hands, more smoke than skin, wrapped around her waist and her hands, flesh and bone, wrapped around his back and—

"*William.*"

The moment broke.

He pulled back, and the wind wobbled and fell apart at his mother's voice. She was standing on her balcony—the garden was hers, and her rooms overlooked it—and even though she couldn't possibly see Sarah from this angle, she said, "Miss Lowe, I think you best be getting home."

Sarah blushed, and ducked under Will's arm—which was solid again—brushing leaves from her skirts as she stepped into his mother's line of sight.

"I'll walk you—" started Will.

"I'm sure Miss Lowe can find her way to the steps," cut in his mother. Her words were harsh but her tone was warm, and Sarah gave a small nod.

"Of course, Lady Dale," she said brightly, as though she'd been given a reward instead of a reprimand. William often thought his mother had a kind of magic in her, too, not a talent for stone or water or air, but the things that flow *in* people. Sarah gave him a quick smile, and made her way out.

Lady Dale plucked a leaf from the lemon tree she kept on
her balcony, and dropped it over the stone rail. The wind
was nothing more than a faint breeze now, and it floated
toward the ground by Will's feet. He watched it land, and
felt tired, drained, half by the slip and half by the look in his
mother's eyes when he finally met them.

"Inside," she said. "Now."

2

His mother was still on the balcony when he reached the
room.

Her back was to him as she stood, watching the day bleed
into night, her hands resting delicately on the banister. She
looked regal. Lady Katherine Dale belonged in the Great
House. She always belonged. He was lucky, he knew, to take
after his mother, from her black hair—though hers coiled
and his fell straight—to her slim build, his real father only
showing in his eyes, which were a much darker gray than
hers. That mattered little, though, since he rarely met
people's gaze.

He crossed the room now, and came out onto the balcony
beside her.

"I heard about what happened in the market," she said
without looking at him.

"Word travels so fast," said Will, leaning his elbows
against the rail.

"Why do you do this?"

"It's a foolish tradition. And it's not my name. It's not anyone's name."

"I won you that name, William," she said, sternly. "You will take it."

Your mother earned it, when she climbed in bed with my uncle.

Will pushed off the banister and went inside. He was Lord Robert's son, and heir to Dale, but not by blood. His mother had arrived in the city pregnant, and wed Lord Dale within a month. And yet, the people of Dale seemed willfully blind to the question of his descent. Perhaps they thought the two had met before, beyond the town's edge, and William, conceived before rings, was still Robert's flesh. Perhaps they didn't care. Perhaps his mother had enchanted them, charmed them into forgetting. Only Phillip seemed intent on pressing the issue. The fact was, William was born in Dale, and was its heir, and to most, the legitimacy of his birth was far less scandalous than his power. That they whispered about in taverns and alleys, and sometimes even on the steps.

"One day, you will be *Lord* Dale," pressed his mother, following him inside.

"I do not want it. And I do not think the people want it either. They call me cold, heartless, empty," he said, feeding a stick to the fire that burned despite the season in her chambers. "Callous."

He stared into the flames.

"Let them think you callous, then."

"But I am not."

"But you *are* different. Whatever word they put to it, it's there. Inescapable. Let them think you callous and cold. Let them think you a monster or a godthing."

"They think me all those things, and yet they think me Robert's son. How is that?" he asked, archly.

His mother ignored the question, as she always did whenever he suggested her influence over people.

"Let them think you a demon or a god," she said. "Let them fear you. It does not matter."

"It matters a great deal to me," he snapped.

His mother sighed, sliding into a chair beside the fire. "The market is one thing..." And she didn't even know of the fight with Phillip, he thought. "...and then the girl in the garden. Sarah. Really, William? Showing off with magic?"

"I wasn't—"

"Surely there are other ways to woo a girl than to put on such displays," she continued. "And besides, Sarah belongs to Phillip. Is that what prompted this? To provoke your cousin?"

"Sarah might disagree, and believe it or not, I do not court my cousin's hatred."

"Maybe that's the problem," said his mother, quietly. "You do not think like a royal."

"I will never apologize for that. And Sarah simply asked to see the gardens."

His mother brought her hand to his cheek. "It's a game, Will. You know that, right? Getting a rise out of you. Goading you to slip. Phillip with fists and Sarah with kisses, but that's the only difference. You can't think she actually feels anything."

Anger hummed beneath his skin, but he knew it wouldn't take shape, not here. His mother's perpetual calm kept his power smothered. In its absence, he simply felt tired.

"This is the fourth slip this month, Will, and it's not half over."

Will thought grimly of the three marks already on his skin. Robert's calm, controlled voice filled his head—*the cut has to be deep, William, it has to hurt, you have to learn*—as his eyes dragged over the mantle, past books and trinkets to his mother's knife. His stomach turned as he reached for it, and took it up, his fingers shaking as he ran his hand absently over the flat of the blade. It was warm from the fire. He rolled his sleeve, studying the scars on his arm.

"Wait," said his mother. "Robert doesn't need to know. It can be our secret. This once."

Will brought the edge to rest against his skin.

"He'll find out," he said, holding her gaze. "He always does."

With that, he drew the knife across his skin, cutting deep. Blood welled instantly, ribboning down over his wrist. He clenched his teeth as pain burned up his arm, but he relished it, because in that moment, he felt everything. Anger and sadness and fear and frustration and want, all of it simple and mortal and human. There had been a time when he loved his power, a time when he had clung to it instead of trying to slice it out. That time was gone.

He felt his mother's hand, guiding the knife from his grip. She produced a rag, wiping the blade clean before returning it to the mantle. By the time Will staunched the blood and she drew a length of cloth from the drawer of a side table and bound the cut, the pain was fading to a dull ache. He watched the red seep through the cloth.

"You'll learn," she said softly.

Learn what? he wondered, eyes trained on the drops of blood that made it to the floor. Learn to control? Or learn to hide? Learn to lie? Learn to be the callous prince? What scared him most was that, in the wake of the wound, he did feel strangely empty. Hollow. His mother ran her fingertips over the pendant chain against his shirt.

"Dinner's soon," she said. "Go get cleaned up."

Will nodded, and left.

*

Will rounded the corner too fast, and nearly collided with a man coming the opposite way. He drew up short just in time. The man stopped, too, and straightened.

"This is a foul habit you have, of walking with your head down."

Will forced his gaze up from the man's throat to his chin, his nose, and finally the lower edge of his eyes. "I'm sorry, Father."

Robert Dale, broad-shouldered and severe, looked down at his son, resting his own gaze just above the boy's. The two hardly ever looked each other in the eyes, Will out of a sense of respect—enforced as opposed to earned—and Robert out of a sense of distaste, the boy's dark eyes being the most offensive part of him. Now Robert's attention drifted down to the bloodstained length of cloth on the boy's forearm.

"What happened?" he asked.

Will hesitated. He knew Robert did not mean the cut, but rather its reason.

"Phillip. He spoke ill of our family. It provoked me." It wasn't a lie, not entirely. Sarah had been the one to push him over the edge, but the slip had started in the market. And besides, Robert disliked his brother's son.

"Let me see," said Robert, gesturing to the bandage.

Will held out his arm, and Robert took it, undoing the cloth wrapped tightly around the newest cut. The bloody swatch of fabric drifted to the floor.

"It was foolish," added Will. "A minor slip. My temper got the better of—"

Pain exploded up his arm, cutting off his words. Blood ran between Robert's knuckles as he tightened his grip on Will's arm, the force reopening the cut.

"A minor slip is still a slip," said Robert calmly. "And you know better."

Will dropped to a knee, gasping. The air in the hall began to stir and he clutched his pendant with his free hand, desperate to hold onto control. If he slipped here, with Robert, a few cuts would be the least of his problems. Last time he was bound to his rooms for a week, the windows nailed shut as if the magic could be stifled out. And that was *after* Robert carved the line himself, cutting nearly to bone. His guards had broken Will's wrist while holding him down.

Robert's fingers dug in. "I will bleed this temper out of you one cut at a time if I have to. Do you understand?"

Will thought he might be sick. He nodded. "I do."

Robert let go, wiping his bloodied palm on his black pants. Will stayed on his knees, very still, as the breeze in the hall leveled, and died.

"Clean yourself up," said Robert, turning away, "and come to dinner."

*

Will made it back to his room, one hand on the silver under his shirt and the other hanging at his side, leaving a bloody trail. He made it across the threshold before the air arced around him, his whole form wavering as the wind slammed the doors and shutters, swept a pair of unlit candles from the shelves and a set of books from the table beside his bed. He'd long since learned not to keep fragile things. The gust had spared a wooden cup, and Will swept it from the table with his hand, and sent it clattering to the floor. He threw open the window shutters—he was not afforded a balcony; his father probably saw that as too much fresh air—and leaned out, drawing several long breaths. His arm throbbed. One line for each time he lost control. He looked around at the room, the floor now cluttered with debris, and knew this probably counted too, but his arm ached and his head hurt, and as he examined the space, he concluded that this had been an act of control rather than a lapse of it. He'd wanted the doors closed, and closed them. Wanted to ruin the order, and ruined it.

He stepped over the books, reached a basin in the corner of the room, and began to wash the blood from his arm, drawing water from the large bowl into a second, smaller one. It was a ritual he knew too well. He cleaned the wound and dried it, drew a fresh bandage tight around the cut and then tied it off. He flexed his fingers, making sure he hadn't cut deep enough to damage the tendons, and while his fingers ached with the movement, he knew he would heal. He always did. When he leaned forward to wash his face, his pendant knocked against the lip of the basin. He straightened, and took the silver piece between his fingers, turning it so he could see its face. A W was carved into the metal, half worn away from the years he'd rubbed his thumb over the letter.

He'd worn it as long as he could remember, not just a trinket, but a charm, a piece of petty craft, meant to calm him. Will didn't know if it really worked, or if he only believe it worked, or if those things were any different, but when he touched the metal, the power beneath his skin quieted. According to his mother, the pendant had belonged to his real father, the man that had given him his gray eyes, and his power, and his name. Not that Robert knew of Will's namesake, of course.

Of his real father, Will knew little, and wished he knew less. The man was a shadow, a ghost, a witch, sweeping through only long enough to seduce Lady Katherine, and vanish. His mother never spoke ill of the man, but Will couldn't help but hate him. If he hadn't left, his mother never would have wandered into Dale. Into Lord Robert's bed.

He rubbed his thumb over the W, and let the pendant fall back against his shirt.

The only things protecting Will were his resemblance to his mother and Lord Dale's pride. It wasn't simply that Robert Dale thought his nephew, Phillip, too weak to rule. Denying Will would mean admitting he was not flesh and blood, and that would mean acknowledging that his wife, Lady Dale, was not his. Had not always been his.

Will pulled the sleeve down over his bandaged arm. Robert saw magic as a sickness, and meant to bleed it from him. If it were that easy, thought Will, straightening his cloak, he would have emptied his veins for his father long ago.

But the wind did not run in William Hart's veins. It ran deeper, through his bones and between his muscles, rooting somewhere beneath his heart, or between his lungs, a place he could feel but never find. Wherever it came from, it couldn't be cut out, and that scared him more than anything. It was getting stronger—*he* was getting stronger—and the pendant, and the cuts, and the fear of Robert's wrath, none of it seemed enough to silence the magic.

He tucked the pendant back beneath his collar, felt his heart slow as it settled against his skin, and went to dinner.

3

Will was standing in the middle of the crowded market, and he couldn't move. His arm was still bleeding, a trickle of red running over his wrist and falling from his fingertips into the dirt. It dripped one, two, three times, and then the wind started. At first, only a tiny swirl of air, right around the red drops. Panic rippled through him, and with it, the wind picked up, whipping around his body.

And then, the people in the market stopped. All at once,

every one of them fell silent and turned to look at him. He tried to warn them to get back, but his teeth were sealed together and they just stood and stared as the wind grew. It ripped through the streets, singing as it toppled stalls and broke windows and buckled doors and tore at the people. The wind howled and spun faster and faster around him until the world beyond it blurred.

He was alone inside the tunnel of air, ears filled with the sound of the wind. And then the air turned sharp, and sliced at his skin, carving line after line until the wind itself ran red around him, and the howl became a scream and the scream was his.

*

William sat up, clutching his chest.

The wind in the room was gusting, tugging at his hair and the sheets, and he tore up from the bed and pulled on his clothes in the dark. A couple of rectangles of fresh air wouldn't be enough. He needed more.

He fastened his cloak, and set one foot on the windowsill. Judging by the sky beyond, there was still some time until dawn. His mother's rooms overlooked the gardens, but his were at the back of the Great House, with a view of the town's spine, a steep set of narrow paths and alleys cutting all the way down to the valley of lakes that stretched at the base of Dale, and the fields beyond. He climbed through, down three stories of vine and stone, his boots hitting the path at the bottom with a hushed thud.

Will pulled the hood up over his head, and wove his way through the darkened streets to the base of Dale. The buildings changed, growing shorter and older and farther apart, and the ground beneath his boots changed, too, went from rock to dirt, and then to grass. He hurried across a narrow band of green between two lakes, and did not slow until he reached the moors beyond. Vast expanses of grass, high as his knees. A breath of relief escaped as he waded through the fields. He was safe here. A breeze swayed the field, and he didn't know if it was his wind or the world's, and it didn't matter. The nightmare clung to him, but this wind was soft, gentle, soothing. Calm spread through his limbs, as tangible as anger had been the night before.

He turned and looked up at the outline of Dale, a shadow against the deeper dark of night, a mass flecked here and there with torchlight. From here, it seemed quiet, small. All his life he'd lived there, and still the moors felt more like home. His mother said that it was the wild in him, the open space calling. She said it was part of him, as much as blood or bone. Why couldn't she tell Robert that?

His arm felt tight, and he undid the bandages with slow precision. The cold air ran over the freshest cut, and the pain seemed to lessen. Will ran his fingers absently up his forearm, each mark less noticeable, tapering away to calm skin close to his elbow. How many marks had he made over the years? A hundred? More? None of them scarred.

Will redid the bandage, wincing as he cinched it, and looked off in the direction of the unrisen sun. Light was just beginning to prick the edges of the sky. He had time, and so he sank to the grass, the blades swaying as he stretched and tucked his hand behind his head, and took a long breath.

For his thirteenth birthday, he'd been given a tutor named

Nicholas Stone. Nicholas was an older man with a close-cropped beard and a faint but perpetual smile. He'd been hired to teach Will history and politics and logic, but a year ago, after Will's temper had slipped over a tricky concept and he'd emptied half the library shelves in a single terrifying wind, Nicholas added an element to their lessons. He set aside an hour every day to teach Will stillness. The two would sit on the library floor, or the floor of his room or sometimes, when the weather was nice, in the gardens, and Nicholas would show Will how to breathe, how to stay calm.

"Energy's like a knot," he'd say. "The more you force it, the worse it gets. You have to untangle it. Close your eyes, and breathe. Picture the knot untangling a little with every breath."

And it had worked. Will had laughed, amazed, and Nicholas had told him to remember the feeling. Memorize it. For the first time in years, he didn't slip. He went more than a month without earning a new mark.

And then, three months ago, Robert Dale had walked in on a breathing lesson. He accused Nicholas of encouraging witchcraft, and dismissed him on the spot. When Will defended his tutor, Robert struck him, hard, and Will struck back, not with his fists but with the wind. That was the day they broke Will's wrist, the day his father carved a line bone-deep into his arm, and that was the last time he made the mistake of slipping in Robert Dale's presence.

Will never saw Nicholas again.

He stretched in the grass as the sky grew lighter. *This is calm*, he thought, as his chest untangled. Remember this. Memorize this. But even as he thought the words, the ease began to bleed away.

These days, breathing didn't seem to be enough.

He took hold of the pendant.

This is calm, he thought, clinging to it.

This is calm.

Be this.

Be this.

*

The sun was too bright.

Will rubbed his eyes, squinting up at it for several moments before he realized—the *sun*. He sat up. It was full morning. He scrambled to his feet, grass clinging to his black cloak, and spun to face Dale. The lakes that circled the town's base were dappled with clouds and morning light, and the town itself was alive with movement.

Will cursed, and ran. He ran out of the field and along the stretch of land between two lakes, and up the paths and the alleys that led toward the Great House. It was too late and too bright to climb the vines back into the house. He'd have to take the front steps. He smoothed his hair and skidded out of an alley, slowing his pace to blend in—as much as he could—and was one road shy of the great stairs when a body blocked his way.

Phillip stood, arms crossed, half his face in the shadow of a house. For once, he didn't have an entourage.

"I was wrong about you," he said.

"Get out of my way," said Will, trying to gauge the time by the sun.

"You're not callous. You're a coward."

"What are you on about?" snapped Will.

Phillip stepped forward. A bruise was blossoming beneath his eye. "You can't even fight your own battles. You run to your father. Who runs to *my* father." He gestured to his face.

"So you come whining to me?" Will clenched his fist, and his arm ached. "And you *did* provoke me..."

"It's not my fault you can't control your power." Phillip shoved him. The wind rustled through the alley.

"Don't," warned Will.

"I don't fear you, cousin," said Phillip, shoving him again. "I don't think you're a god or a godthing or even a monster. You're nothing but a pathetic boy hiding behind his magi—"

Phillip's face snapped sideways as Will's fist connected with his jaw. He stumbled back to the dirt.

"I'm not hiding behind anything," said Will.

Phillip wiped a line of blood from his lip, and grimaced through reddened teeth. Will turned to go.

"Running away, as always," growled Phillip.

Will spun back to face him. "You didn't push me over the edge..." he said, coldly. "But I couldn't exactly tell my father the truth."

Phillip got to his feet.

"It was Sarah," said Will, forcing a cold shrug. "She just couldn't keep her hands off me—"

Phillip swung again, but Will spun easily aside, and caught his cousin in the chest with his knee. Phillip collapsed forward to the ground, coughing. And Will felt... calm. Not the calm he'd felt in the field but hollow. Empty. He wanted to relish it, but the path to the stairs was finally clear, and he was late.

"I warned you, *cousin*," he said, striding from the alley. "Stay out of my way." And to his surprise, Phillip did.

4

Will passed through the main doors of the Great House, rubbing his hand. Three men lounged in the foyer, all wearing the Dale insignia on their white cloaks. The royals wore black and their guards wore white, and the rest of Dale wore whatever it pleased. One of the guards, a broad-shouldered man named Eric, looked up as Will passed, quirking a brow as he took in Will's grass-brushed clothes and his messy hair and his reddened knuckles, but then he turned back to the others and resumed whatever story he'd been telling.

Will was very late. As he made his way to the dining room, he tried to rub the red from his hand and decide on a lie, a line, a defense. Through the doors, he could hear his mother's voice, soft and pleasant, and he was about to step through, when her tone changed.

"About William," she said, and he paused, fingers pressed against the wood. "He's trying. He really is."

"You're too easy on him, Katherine," said Robert.

"And you're too hard."

"Not hard enough. I'm doing this for him. For his future."

"I believe you," said his mother. Will didn't. "But," she added gently, "he looks up to you. He wants to please you."

Will didn't care about pleasing his father, only avoiding his wrath. "You show him only your might. But you have other strengths. Show him those, too. Believe in him, my dear. One day he will make a wonderful—"

Will didn't want to hear more. He pushed open the door. His mother's eyes lit up, and his father's narrowed.

"There you are," said his mother.

"Where have you been?" snapped his father. But then her hand found his arm, and Robert... *softened* was the wrong word, but a few of his edges smoothed. Will stood very straight and very still as Robert's gaze tracked from his bandaged arm down to his bruised knuckles. But when he spoke, all he said was, "Sit."

"I'm sorry I'm late," said Will, coming forward.

He kissed his mother's cheek and took his seat across from Robert, Katherine Dale between them like a bridge. Blissfully, his parents both ignored his bedraggled state, and began to talk of mundane things like weather and markets and a spring festival. Will picked at his food, and watched more than listened.

One thing was clear. Lord Robert Dale loved his wife. It showed in the way he held her hand, fingers tangled on the table. It showed in the way he kissed her temple, in the way he served her food. Will hated it, hated that one person could be two people, hated being constantly reminded that Robert didn't hate everyone the way he hated him. Worst of all was that, despite Robert's infamous pride, he didn't seem to love his wife the way he loved *power* and *trinkets*, owning simply to own. Lord Dale seemed to genuinely love her. Or maybe, Will consoled himself, he only *believed* he loved her.

Will knew from his pendant that belief was a powerful thing. As was his mother's kind of magic.

Will took up his knife, and winced, forgetting his arm. He nearly fumbled the utensil, and the chatter around him died.

"How are you feeling?" asked his mother, the way she might if he had a headache, not a piece carved out of his skin. The care showed in her eyes, though, if not her tone.

"Quite well," he said, but set the knife aside, and soothed his arm beneath the table.

"It's a lovely day," she said. "You should get some fresh air."

"Judging by his state," said Robert, "he's already had quite a bit of fresh air." But if he disapproved of Will fighting, he didn't show it, and Will himself was growing increasingly sure that Robert Dale *wanted* him to be a bully. Just not one who relied on magic. His gaze was almost, *almost* approving. "Still," he added, "I've got a errand you can run for me."

Will brightened a little. "Really?"

Robert nodded stiffly. "I would do it myself, but I'm leading a trip into the forests." The forests ran in a wall beyond the fields that ran beyond the lakes that circled Dale. "We'll need wood for the festival. As for the errand, I could have a guard handle it…"

"I'd be happy to run it for you," said Will, trying to stifle some of his excitement. He knew too well how Robert enjoyed crushing it.

"Good," said his father. "Eric will escort you."

Will stiffened. An escort? What if Phillip came back? A guard would make it look like he wished for—or needed—

protection. "Father, I hardly think an escort—"

"After yesterday's performance…" warned Robert, his fingers tightening on the knife in his hand, "…you can't expect me to let you go unattended."

"No," said Will slowly. "Of course not."

"I think it's good," said his mother. "You spending time in town."

Will nodded. "A ruler," he recited, "should be among the people, though not of them."

"Who taught you that?" asked Robert.

"You did." He watched his father's brow crease. "Or rather, the book you assigned this week."

Robert sat back in his chair. "Ah," he said smugly. "And how are your studies going?"

Will resisted the urge to inform his father that they would be better, if he still had his tutor. He wouldn't rise to the bait.

"Well enough," he said, pushing up from the table. "I'll go get ready."

"Do you have to go?" asked his mother, and Will paused before realizing the question was not directed at him.

"It's only for the day," answered Robert. "I'll be back tonight, I promise…"

Will rolled his eyes and closed the door behind him.

*

Will found Eric waiting for him by the front doors, a slip of paper in his hand. On it were the details of the errand. Will read through, and frowned. His father never would have done this for himself. He didn't really mind the mundane nature of it, since he enjoyed any excuse to be in town, but the way Robert had spoken of the chore, he'd hoped for something a bit more...

"Is something wrong, Master Dale?"

"No," said Will, pocketing the note. He held his tongue against the usual *don't call me that*, remembering his mother's plea, and set off down the path to the great steps. Eric followed several strides behind, as if his crisp white cloak didn't set him off against the crowd. But there was nothing Will could do about his shadow, so he made his way through the streets toward the leather smith. His attention flicked around as he walked, watching for any signs of Phillip. His cousin's temper rivaled his own, and he wasn't one to suffer quietly. Now he was nowhere to be seen, and Will didn't trust it. He reached the leather smith's, and paused before the door. He wasn't used to paying visits, certainly not on his father's behalf, and wasn't sure quite how to go about it, so he simply knocked.

An old lady answered, gray hair fraying out of her bun, and when she saw Will, she gave a little croak, and nearly fumbled the fabric in her arms. A man appeared beside her, equally gray and equally surprised.

"Master Dale," he said, nudging the woman away. "I wasn't expecting a visit."

"I'm here on behalf of my father. I believe you have some of his things."

"Ah yes, yes, yes, of course," said the man nervously before vanishing, only to reappear a moment later with a bundle. He offered the package to Will, and fumbled for a few moments, eyes down, before he gestured to his stomach and said, "Had to, you know, add a bit of fabric."

Will surprised himself by laughing. It just kind of escaped. The man chuckled, too, but the woman, who'd reappeared behind him, cringed visibly when the sound left Will's mouth. His laughter died, and he took the parcel from the leather smith's arms.

"Yes, well," he said, retreating into the street. "Thank you."

"Would you like some tea before you go?" asked the man, but the woman's eyes were still nervous and wide, laced with fear, and Will shook his head, said a quiet thanks, and left. He passed the bundle off to Eric, because if he had to have a guard, he might as well put him to use, and he was making his way back to the steps, his spirits sinking, when someone touched his sleeve. He tensed, expecting Phillip, but before he could pull back, an arm linked itself with his.

"Sarah," he said, startled. He drew back, but she didn't.

"Walk with me?" she asked. He didn't have much choice. Her arm was already threaded through his, the pale blue of her cloak flush with the black of his own, and the eyes of the town were on them. Refusing now would draw even more attention.

"What is it?" he asked as they made their way down the street. His tone bordered on rudeness, but she ignored it.

"Do you remember," she asked, "when we were little, and you used to make things dance? My brother showed me how to make sculptures out of paper, ones with wings, and you would set them into flight."

Will frowned. There had been a time when he loved his powers. When he hadn't be afraid to show them. When he'd been too young for Robert to think him dangerous. But that was a long, long time ago, and now, even mentioning them had consequences. He glanced back at Eric to make sure he hadn't heard.

"I miss your magic," she said. "You seemed happier back then."

He had been.

"Things change," he said.

"Will you show me again, sometime?"

The pain in his arm was too fresh. "If you knew what that meant, you wouldn't ask."

"It can be our secret," she pressed.

Will remembered his mother's warning. This wasn't just anyone on his arm, pushing him to use his powers. This was Sarah, who had hardly spoken to him for years. Sarah, who was Phillip's. Sarah, whose friend, he realized, was following them. Beth bobbed in and out of sight, clearly watching. Waiting.

"Tell me," he growled. "Is this a game to you? Getting me to slip?"

Sarah pulled back, as if struck. "What? No. I just thought…"

Will tugged his arm free. "And yet your friends are waiting for their show."

Sarah scanned the crowd, saw Beth, and scowled at her before turning back to Will, who was busy walking away. "I didn't know. I swear, Will." She touched his arm and he spun on her, the wind picking up.

"Just stop," he snapped. "Go toy with someone else."

Tears sprung to the edges of her eyes, and Sarah turned and fled down the busy street. Will watched her go. Had he been wrong? Had she meant no harm? How was he supposed to know? He rubbed his eyes, the wind beginning to ebb.

"That was cold," said Eric, behind him.

Will spun on his guard. "You're out of line," he snapped, and all again the air whipped up.

"Careful, Master Dale," said Eric, bringing his heavy hand down on Will's shoulder. "Your father will be wanting a report."

Will pulled free and stormed back to the steps, clutching his pendant as the mood coiled around him, inside him. *Untangle*, he begged as he climbed the steps. *Untangle. Untangle. Untangle.* But as he reached the top, he felt the power choking him. He felt helpless, hopeless. He wanted to scream. He was sick of smothering the magic and himself. He wanted to let go, not as he had in the garden, or in his room, but really, truly let go. Was there no way to be free?

And then he turned and looked out over Dale, and saw it.

Hanging dark over the distant forest, inching forward across the fields toward the lakes and the hill. Will let out an amazed exhale, and sent up a word of thanks to the gods and godthings.

It was hope. It was a chance. It was a *storm*.

*

Will loved the storms.

Dale was most often a gray place, well acquainted with clouds, and rain, but only the pale and steady sort. Still storms, he called them, because they were nothing but falling water. The hill on which Dale sat rarely saw true storms. Not the kind with sound and color. Not the kind with *wind*.

These storms were a gift to Will, a time when he could stretch and breathe and let go without the fear of a trail leading straight back to him. A time when he could be part of the wind, but not its center.

He spent the rest of the day watching the clouds spread, watching the sky darken, and waiting for the storm to come. Energy hummed beneath his skin, not anger, but excitement. He could feel the storm singing to his blood. By mid-afternoon the foul weather had reached the fields. The sky lit up, the air crackled, and no rain fell yet, but that was fine. He didn't need rain. Only wind. He imagined he could see the fields of grass, even from here, swaying with it, but Dale itself lay still around him, the storm hovering at its edges.

By late afternoon, Will was getting restless.

The forest parties were never back before dark, but at this rate, his father would reach Dale before the storm, and he'd lose his chance. Since the weather would not come to him, he'd have to go to it. And soon, if he stood any chance of making it home before Lord Dale. Will looked out the window and down, but Eric had taken up residence in the grass below, eyes trained on the distant storm.

He swore quietly and abandoned his room. He could hear his mother playing music below, in one of the rooms off the foyer, as she did whenever her hands grew restless, and Will made his way to her vacant rooms. There he checked the balcony, saw the gardens below empty of guards, and smiled. He had a leg over the rail, but hesitated. Retreating back into the room, he found a loose paper on her desk and wrote a quick note—*Need air.*

With that, he closed the balcony doors, and climbed down

an old, flowering vine, his boots hitting the ground with a quiet thud. He took an older, hidden set of stairs, avoiding the great steps, which, in the impending weather, were empty, but well-lit.

He hit the base of the stairs, and stopped. There had been a noise, an echo, like a second set of footsteps, but as he hovered in the dusk, he heard nothing but his own breath and the sounds of far-off thunder. Will picked up his pace, weaving through alleys toward the base of the hill. The promise of bad weather had driven the people of Dale inside, shutters fastened against the coming storm, and Will found himself alone as he hurried through the dying day toward the black clouds.

He was nearly there.

And then he heard it again, the sound of steps, and skidded to a stop.

The other set of feet didn't stop, and he spun around just as something very hard and very sharp caught his face. Light exploded across his vision, and then the world tipped violently, and went black.

5

Will's eyes began to focus, and the first thing he saw was a coffin.

It was sitting in the strip of land between two of the lakes, the lid askew. Several poles driven into the ground held torchlight, which danced over the metal lining of the wooden box.

The ground beneath his body was cold but dry. The storm crackled overhead and to the side. It hadn't reached him yet. He tried to put the world together, remembered climbing through the window, hitting the ground, turning, and then...

Will tried to move, and pain tore through his head. Dried blood crusted the right side of his face, and coarse rope bound his wrists together. He got to his knees but had to stop when his vision blurred.

"When we were little," came a voice, "Uncle Robert had all the books on witches burned."

Will forced his vision to clear, and found a shape, silhouetted by torchlight. A hammer hung in the shape's hand.

"Phillip—" he said quietly.

"Only a few books survived, because Robert let them. The witches in those books were said to wield earth and stone. But what of air?"

Will could make out three other boys, circling him on the grass. Phillip set the hammer on the lip of the coffin, and came forward.

"You know what I think, cousin?" he said, kneeling in front of Will. "I think Robert had the books burned not just because he hated witches, but because he was trying to hide something about them."

He straightened and turned away. Will struggled up, and one of the other boys kicked him hard, in the ribs, sending him back to his hands and knees. He gasped, but the air around them barely wavered.

"*My* father has a book on witches," said Phillip. "One of

the oldest books. Do you want to know what it says?"

Will reached his bound hands for the pendant around his neck. It wasn't there. Phillip held the chain up to the torchlight.

"Give it back," growled Will.

"The W," he asked, "does it stand for William? Or wind? Or *witch*?" He spat the word. "Because my father's book says there are as many kinds of witches as there are elements."

Will got to his feet, but two of the boys were there, and they grabbed him, and held him still.

"Don't worry, cousin," said Phillip. "I know what it does." He closed the gap between them, and the others tightened their grip on Will's arms. "It weakens you. And for that, you can have it back." He looped the chain over Will's head. And then he smiled, and punched him as hard as he could in the stomach. Will doubled over, and Phillip leaned in close.

"Haven't you wondered about the coffin yet?" he hissed, drawing back. "It's said that royals are given to the air, and commoners to the soil. And witches to the water." He gestured to the box. "In the old days, the coffins were made entirely of metal, because metal was made by men, and the witches couldn't use it. But it's been so long since anyone buried a witch, and we'll have to make do."

"You've lost it."

Phillip fetched the hammer from the lip of the coffin, and put his foot on the skewed lid. "I am the heir of Dale," he said. "By blood. I must protect my people from the evils of witches." His smile sharpened as he kicked off the lid. It fell to the ground with a heavy thud. "Load him in."

"Stop this," ordered Will as the boys dragged him toward the metal bed. "Phillip! Stop!"

He tore backward from their grip, but lost his balance and went down. Before he could get to his feet, they were on top of him, kicking and punching and dragging him to the coffin. The ropes cut into his skin as he tried to force them back, first with fists and then with wind, but it wasn't enough. Pain splintered his vision every time he moved. He could barely focus, and, for the first time in his life, the wind wasn't listening. He fought and it didn't. He screamed and it didn't.

"Save your breath, cousin. You'll need it."

Will's shoulder cracked against the metal lining of the box as they shoved him in. This couldn't be happening. Phillip wouldn't. But he was. Before Will could sit up, they'd hoisted the lid onto the coffin. The torchlight vanished, along with the world, and Will was plunged into a metal-heavy dark.

He banged his bound fists against the lid of the box as the hammer sounded, sealing the coffin shut.

"*No. No. No,*" he hissed under his breath. It was a nightmare. It was all a nightmare. He squeezed his eyes closed and tried to believe that it was all a night— the coffin shifted over the ground. His heart lurched. They were dragging it.

Will couldn't breathe. He could feel the wind pressing in against the coffin now, but it couldn't reach him. Pain and panic and fear tore through him and something howled in his ears as he shoved his shaking hands against the coffin ceiling but it was metal, too, and he was going to die in a box all because of them and suddenly he wasn't just afraid. He was angry. Furious. How could they? How could they do this after he had tried so hard not to hurt anyone, not to ruin other lives and they were ruining the sliver of his and—

The world shook.

The boards bent and wind rushed in through the cracks in the wood, whistled through the seams in the metal, and the whole coffin groaned around him, crumpling in for a breath before shattering outward. Wind that ripped the pendant from his neck, and heaved him to his feet, and curled around him like armor. His edges blurred into it. His skin wavered, and the ropes that had cut into his wrists now fell to the ground as Will's hands thinned. The wind gutted the torches but he could still see the coffin shards and the shapes of the other boys as they struggled to their feet, only to be forced to the ground again. Will's body rippled as he spun and saw his cousin on his hands and knees, and in that moment he wanted to crush him, crush the air from his lungs. The wind began to spin faster and faster around Phillip, and thunder crackled as the storm finally drew over them.

"What's the matter?" Will shouted over the tearing wind as Phillip gasped and clawed at the grass. "Can't catch your breath?"

Everything was blurring.

And then a light flickered in his vision. A torch. All the torches by the lake had gone out, but this one burned steady. Soon there were half a dozen torches, and with them, men. Something clicked in Will's head, sharp in the murk of anger. *The forest party.* The men were running now, down the strip of grass between the lakes, Robert Dale at the lead, and beside him, his brother, Ian. Phillip's father. Will faltered and so did the wind storm, breaking into gusts and then into a strong breeze as his father strode over the coffin debris.

"*What is this?*" roared Robert. "What happened here?" And for once, maybe because Will's face was bloody and his wrists were raw, his father turned his anger on the others. The three boys were still sitting, dazed, in the grass, but Phillip was getting to his feet, his own father half-dragging him up by an elbow. Lightning flashed overhead.

"It was a *coffin*..." growled Will.

"It was a *joke*," spat Phillip, still breathless. "We weren't going to put it in the water."

Will lunged at Phillip, but before he could reach, Robert's arm came around his shoulders, and held him back. When Lord Dale spoke, it was to his own brother.

"Take your boy home," he said, "before I kill him."

The man shoved Phillip in the direction of Dale.

"All of you," ordered Robert, as the other boys got up. "Go now."

Most of the forest party went with them, leaving only three of the royal guard standing torchlit among the coffin planks and curls of metal. Robert's arm slid from Will's shoulders. Will braced himself, but his father said nothing, only ushered him home with a nod and a look.

The two walked back toward the Great House in silence, Will waiting for his father's inevitable wrath. How much had he seen? The aftermath, of course, but what before? Behind his eyes, Will replayed the last time his father had witnessed his power. He rubbed his bandaged forearm, the newest cut hardly healed, and waited. But Robert still said nothing.

Halfway to the house, the storm finally broke over Dale. Between one breath and the next, the air went cold, an icy rain tumbling down over them. The wind picked up, but with no mind of its own, tugging at their cloaks and chilling the water on their skin. Will shivered, and quickened his pace. By the time they reached the great steps, Will was tired of waiting.

"I didn't have a choice," he said.

Robert didn't respond, and Will assumed that the rain had muffled the words until a few moments later his father said, "I believe you."

His tone was ice, but Will still wanted to crumple to the wet ground with relief. They kept climbing the steps.

"Where was your knife?" asked Robert.

He had given Will a blade two years before, but Will had never cared for weapons, and ever since he had started using it to carve lines in his skin, he'd grown infinitely less fond of the knife. He'd left it in his room as he always did.

Now, as they reached the top of the steps, he thought of the anger, the singular want in that moment, to crush Phillip. If he'd *had* his knife, would he have killed his cousin? It would have been so easy, so fast. Then again, if he had not seen the torchlights coming, he still might have...

"I didn't—" He nearly said *bring it with me*, but caught himself, and at that moment Eric met them on the path, eyes alight with torchlight and panic.

"Is Lady Dale with you?" he asked.

"No," said Robert, the rain pounding cold and heavy around them. "Why would she be?"

Eric's gaze flicked to Will before he answered. "She went looking for Master Dale."

Panic rippled through Will's chest. "How long ago?" he asked.

Lightning cracked across the freezing sky.

"Is she alone?" demanded Robert over the storm.

"She took two of her guard," answered Eric. "But none have come back."

"Send two more," he ordered. "Everyone else, get inside."

Once within, Robert took to pacing. Will looked through the windows at the worsening storm. This was all wrong.

"When did she leave?" asked Robert.

"About an hour ago, when she found his note."

Will cringed, and Robert stopped mid-stride. "What note?"

Eric frowned, and produced a slip of paper. "He left a note when he snuck out."

The air in the room seemed to freeze as his father turned toward him. "How did you end up at the lake?"

"They dragged me there," said Will.

"But not from here, so from where?"

He hesitated.

"I will ask you once," warned Robert, "so answer well. Why did you leave this house this evening?"

Before Will could speak, someone else did.

"I heard the Lady say it was the storm."

The voice came from an old woman in a crisp white cloak. One of his mother's attendants. "He went for the storm," she chirped again. "He wanted the storm."

Robert stiffened, and spun on his son. "Is that true?"

Will took a step back.

"The Lady knew the Lord would be angry," she prattled. "And so she went to find him first."

Will took another step back, and vowed to smother the old lady in her sleep.

"*William.*" Robert's knuckles went white on the grip of

the knife at his belt. "Did you seek out the storm? To what end would you…" But he didn't need to finish the question. He knew. It showed in the tensing of his jaw, and his grip on the knife. Will was too tired to lie, but knew better than to voice the truth. Still, Robert took his silence for confession.

"And I thought you'd learned," he said quietly as he slid the knife free. "Roll up your sleeves."

Will took a third step, and came up against a shelf.

"Hold him down," ordered his father as Will reached blindly back, and felt something sharp on the shelf. He curled his fingers around it as Eric strode toward him, but just then the doors flew open, and a damp guard announced, "She's here, sir. Lady Dale is back."

6

Robert and Will hurried to the foyer as Lady Dale and her guards strode in. Icy rain coated their cloaks like frost, their cheeks flushed and their hair matted to their skin from the storm. Will reached for his mother, but Robert cut him off, stripping her cloak and wrapping his arms around her in a single gesture.

"You are the life and death of me," he said.

She soothed him with a touch. But then her eyes found Will, and widened at the sight of him. Half the blood had washed away in the rain, but his face was still cut and his eyes hollow. She pulled away, and stepped past Robert toward him. Will hugged her close, shivering as his cheek met hers. She was cold as ice.

"I'm sorry," he whispered. He said it again and again until she ran her hand over his hair.

"It's all right," she cooed. "You're safe. I'm safe. You're here. I'm here." It was something she used to say, when he had nightmares.

"Katherine," said Robert. "Let's get you warm." She began to pull away. Will didn't want to let go, but she slid from his embrace. "In the morning, Will, you must tell me everything."

Will nodded.

"Come," pressed Robert.

"I'm well," she said, as she took her husband's hand. But she did not look it. Dread crept through Will as he watched them go. He stood in the foyer, surrounded by the guards, and felt... lost. Something was wrong. So many things were wrong, and he didn't know what to do, so he stood very still and waited. Everyone else waited, too, as if they could feel the wrongness taking shape.

And then, sometime later, Robert returned.

The look on his face was unlike any Will had ever seen. Anger he recognized, and frustration, but the thing threaded through Robert's features was fear.

"Father," started Will, but when Robert spoke, he did not speak to his son, did not even acknowledge his presence.

"Take him to his room," he said. "And make sure he stays there."

With that he turned, and left the hall.

*

Will's room had two locks, one on the inside, and one on the out. He listened to the outer bolt grate across the wood, and tore the damp cloak from his shoulders before sinking into the nearest chair, cursing the storm and Phillip and himself.

He did this. He provoked his cousin and left the note and chased the darkening clouds, and his mother... she was just cold, he told himself. Chilled from the rain. She would be fine. She would be fine, and Robert's anger would fade into relief, and in the morning they would unlock Will's door and he would go down and have breakfast, and sit across from his father, his mother between them like the bridge she was.

He closed his eyes, and sank back in the chair, and played the scene, listening to his parents go on about the spring festival, and the food, and the coming year, talking just to fill the quiet.

*

The guards did not unlock Will's door.

By morning, the storm outside had passed, but clouds still hung over the Great House.

Lady Dale was not well.

Will could feel it, even before he heard the news in the guards' lowered voices beyond his door. They said she had a fever and had stayed in bed, at Robert's orders. Will remained bound to his rooms, spared his father's wrath only because Lord Dale spent every moment with his wife.

"How sick is she?" asked Will through the wood of his door, but the guards beyond went silent. He asked again, but they refused to answer. They didn't leave, though. He could hear their shifting weight on the floor. And if he looked out the window, and down, his eyes met more white cloaks lurking in the yard beneath. He was trapped.

Will himself began to pace. He crossed the room a dozen times, and when that did not help, he reached for his pendant.

It wasn't there.

He cringed and closed his eyes, trying to remember. A glint of silver lost among splintered wood and bent metal. The lakeside. His gaze went to the window, to the sloping hill of Dale. It wasn't far, not really, but with a barred door and a guarded yard, the stretch of grass between the lakes was worlds away. The air wavered nervously around him and he clutched his hand into a fist against his chest as if he could conjure the calming magic from memory.

It didn't work.

That first day was torture, the passing of time marked only by the shifting sun and Will's fraying nerves. The air hummed as he paced, as he tried to read, tried to sleep, tried to do anything but think about the walls of the room and the many more walls separating him from his mother.

She would be all right.

Katherine Dale was strong, and it was only a fever. She was made of magic. She would be fine. Robert was making a show of it, of their confinements, to punish him.

Will watched the sun sink as he played out the scene a dozen times, tweaking his father's tone or his mother's words, but in every version she sat bright-eyed in her bed and chided her husband for being so silly. In some versions, she'd even laugh.

Will swore once or twice that he could hear it, but soon he realized that it was nothing more than the restless wind.

7

That first night, Will dreamt again of blood-streaked air. The wind around him laughed, and laughed, and the laughing grew and twisted with the tunnel of air until it coiled around him, rising into screams, and he woke.

*

The second day he lay on the floor and closed his eyes and tried to picture the fields, the swaying grass, Nicholas's lessons, while the pages of the books and the bed sheets all fluttered in the nervous air.

*

The nights were nightmares and the days were worse.

*

Will woke, and shivered, his breath escaping in clouds as he sat up.

The room was freezing, but he'd had to leave the windows open. The memory of what he did to the coffin was too fresh in his mind. He couldn't risk that happening to the Great House. The nervous wind was growing worse.

It was now the fourth day of confinement. Four days bound to his room with no pendant and no word of his mother and no visitors save the guard who delivered his food, coming and going in stony silence. Four days of waiting. Three nights of nightmares.

The cold air rustled around him, tugging at his clothes as he stood, and tangling in them as he crossed to the window.

The first thing he saw was the crisp blue sky.

The second thing he saw were the flowers.

His heart dropped like a stone.

People were setting flowers on the great steps. White wildflowers, the kind that grew in the fields year-round, bloomed even in the dead of winter, and because of that were seen as tokens of health.

Prayers for health.

The top of the steps were piled with the stems of small white blossoms.

No.

He looked down and found the set of guards beneath his window, silent and sober. He might be able to get *out*, but they'd never let him back *in* to see her. He spun and strode to his door.

"Let me out," he said, banging on it. He knew they were out there, the guards, he could hear them moving, hear them talking, but they never answered.

"Eric!" he ordered. Nothing.

"You have to let me see her!" he shouted, striking his fist against the wood.

The wind coiled dangerously around him and he rested

his forehead against the door as he tried to calm down. It didn't work. There were white flowers on the great steps. *White wildflowers*.

The wind kept growing. It began to tug at him, not just his clothes, but his *skin*. He held up his hands, and watched as his flesh thinned, the tips of his fingers threading like smoke through the air. Maybe... his gaze went to the gap between his door and the floor. Whenever he slipped, he felt the thinning, the running of his edges, but he'd always resisted. He'd been afraid. What if he let go, what if he vanished, and couldn't come back together again?

He had to.

His hands always came back. His body returned to body. And just as something in his bones—deeper, even— drew him into wind, he would have to trust it to draw him back again.

And so, the wind began to pull him apart. And as his body thinned, so did his thoughts, blurring in his mind. His pain and fear and anger weakened, his focus broke apart, and it felt *good* and he didn't care, didn't care about his body or his life or this town or Robert's wrath or his mother's sickness, none of it mattered, nothing matter—

Will came violently back to himself, and collapsed, gasping on his hands and knees. Back in his mind and his skin, he felt disgusted. How could he think that? How could he be—

The bolt slid back, and his door opened.

Will staggered to his feet and turned to find Eric waiting, flanked by two other guards in white. For an instant, Eric's eyes widened, and Will wondered if some part of him hadn't come fully back, but when he stole a glance in the mirror, he saw that he was fully there, if ashen.

"You've been summoned," said Eric at last. Will's hopes rose until he added, "Lady Dale is dying."

8

Robert stood before the door, arms crossed. When Will hurried toward him, the guards trailing behind, he did not move, did not look up.

"Father, what's going on? How is she? Eric said..."

"You're a monster, William." The words were said low, but Will still heard. "You know that. I don't care what word you use. A witch or a demon or a godthing. You're a *thing*. But a powerful one." Robert straightened, and stepped toward his son. His eyes were rimmed red when he met Will's gaze. "If you're so powerful, fix this."

Will's eyes widened. "I am no healer."

"You speak to the moor. Tell it to save her."

"Father, I can't—"

Robert took hold of Will's collar, and slammed him back against the wall. *"If you love her, make it save her."*

He let go of Will abruptly, and said, under his breath, "If you do not save her life, so help me, I will not spare yours." And then he strode away.

Will stood there, stunned. And then he heard his mother, calling through the door. He went in. And stopped.

Katherine Dale sat up in bed, her black hair clinging to her face with fever.

She smiled when she saw him, but it was thin, tired.

"William," she said. "You came." There was something missing from her voice, replaced by a faint sound when she breathed, a *shhhh* sound. He came to the bed, and kneeled, but when he took her hand, he nearly recoiled. Her skin was cold as stone.

"They wouldn't let me come," he said, voice hitching. "I would have come. I didn't..."

"Hush now," she said. "And listen to me."

"I didn't know."

"William. *Listen.*" He listened to the sound of her breathing and thought of Robert's threat. He bowed his head and tried to picture the sound in her lungs as wind, but it was useless. His power didn't work that way.

"Look at me," she said, guiding his chin up with her other hand. He met her eyes. There wasn't enough life in them, and he felt the panic welling in his chest. The air hummed, and his mother tightened her grip on his hand.

"Dale is your home and your inheritance," she said. "You must look after it. And you must be careful. Now more than ever."

"Please..." he whispered, but he couldn't finish the sentence. He didn't know how.

He heard the door open behind him.

"Tread lightly, my sweet," she whispered.

Will felt Robert's hand come down on his shoulder, heavy as a house. He stiffened, but held his mother's gaze.

"You should rest," said Will softly. He got to his feet and

leaned forward, placing a kiss on his mother's temple. It burned beneath his lips.

He gave her hand a last squeeze, and then let go.

*

Lady Dale was wrapped in black.

The pyre was erected on the landing halfway up the great stairs, and was made from the festival wood. All of Dale was draped in garlands. The Great House gardens had been stripped bare to wreath the city, blossom and wildflower and grass and stem woven together into streamers that ran from the royal house down the steps and through the streets, turning the hill of Dale into a bed of color.

They set the fire at dawn, Robert and Will standing at opposite ends of the pyre, the people gathered at the base of the steps. Will watched the fire reach his mother's black cloak, and pictured her burning beneath it, hair crumbling, skin peeling away like paper. The wind lifted, and he closed his eyes, but the firelight echoed against his lids. He dug his nails into his palms until they bled. Something new had come over him, something worse, more engulfing, than fear and anger and pain and panic and anything else he'd ever felt. Sorrow. The wind sang with it, low and sad, and the fire danced.

Will felt the weight of a hand on his shoulder, and opened his eyes.

"This is your fault," Robert said, his tone ice. From the base of the steps the two men must have looked like a family bound by grief. But Robert's grip tightened. "It should be you."

Tread lightly, my sweet.

Will bit his tongue, and tried to pull away, to take a step forward, but Robert followed, forcing him toward the lip of the landing. Will twisted out of his grip but his father grabbed him by the collar, his blood-shot blue eyes meeting Will's sad gray ones for only an instant before he threw him backward, off the landing, and down the great steps. He hit the first stairs hard, his shoulder cracking, before the air sprung up to break his fall. By the time he hit the path at the base of the steps, hands thrown out to brace himself, the wind had sprung up, coiled and cushioned his fall, his body seeming to hover a moment above the stones before dropping him. The people gasped, and drew back.

Robert stormed down the steps as Will struggled to his feet, tasting blood.

"This thing," announced Robert, "is not my son. He is a monster."

Will straightened, the wind churning around him, rippling his cloak. He took a step away and the crowd shifted, moving back to avoid him.

"He is a witch. He summoned the storm that—"

"Enough," said Will, clutching his shoulder.

"—killed my wife."

"That's not true," begged Will, the air whipping up around him. "I would never, ever..."

But whatever spell his mother had cast over Robert, over Dale, it died with her. His father's eyes were filled with hate, and the people stood and watched, but made no move. The guards, too, stared on. Will looked around, and saw Sarah, eyes wide with shock, and Phillip, smiling. His head snapped back to Robert when the crowd gasped, and saw that his father had pulled free his knife.

"Don't do this," said Will as the wind tore at him, his limbs thinning. "Don't make me—"

Robert lifted his blade. "You brought the storm," he growled, gesturing up the steps to the pyre. "You murdered her." He charged forward.

"*Stop*," ordered Will, and the wind responded, and slammed into Robert, sending him back several steps. But it wasn't enough to stop him. He bent his head and struggled forward, and this time when Will tried to retreat, a pair of hands shoved him forward toward his father and the knife.

Will took a breath as Robert slashed the blade across his chest. The people gasped. But there was no scream, no blood. Will's whole body wavered, like smoke, the knife passing straight through. Will looked down at himself, eyes wide.

"Witch," someone shouted.

"Demon."

"Stop," said Will.

"Monster."

"Murderer."

"Please, stop."

"Witch."

"Kill him."

And then, the circle of space collapsed, the people plunging toward him, and he threw out his hands and closed his eyes and screamed, "STOP!"

There was a sound like a large door being slammed, a heavy crack as the wind whipped into everything around him, and threw it back with horrible force. At the same moment, everything around Will went very, very still.

He opened his eyes.

He was standing in the center of a column of wind, a wall of air that whined and moved so fast that the whole world blurred beyond it, and he blurred within, his body thinning more and more toward nothing. A nothing that was safe, empty, a nothing without thought and feeling and pain and loss. He began to vanish.

And then, above the howling wind, he heard the first screams.

Threaded through the wind was something bright, all light and color, brilliant and hot, and Will realized through his thinning mind what it was.

Fire.

The wind had caught up the flames from the funeral pyre and spread them to the garlands that ran like roots through Dale.

Will, still fading, tried to pull himself back. The wind didn't listen. He kept fading and the fire kept spreading.

No. I didn't want to... He reached out, but his arms were smoke and air. He tried to break free of the tunnel of wind, but every time he moved, the cyclone only shifted, keeping him in the center.

I didn't mean to hurt... The screams grew louder, the air choked with smoke, and he tried to pull back, but it was too late.

The wind tore Will from his body, and his mind, and set him free.

9

William woke in snow.

The late afternoon sun shone down as he lay there on the
cooling stone path, and looked up at the sky, and watched
the white flecks float down around him, thinking how rare a
thing it was in Dale. It fell, and coated his skin, his hair, his
cloak. And then he took a breath, and choked, and realized
what it was.

Ash.

He jerked up, coughing, and then he looked around, and
saw that he was sitting in the charred remains of Dale. The
buildings, what was left, were blackened, stone skeletons
with the wood burned out. And all around, to every side,
were mounds of ash. Will got to his knees, and reached for
the nearest heap, and when he wiped away the film, his hand
met still-warm bone. A corpse. All the mounds were corpses.
Will staggered to his feet, and spun to look up the great
steps. His mother's pyre was gutted, burned to nothing, and
beyond it the Great House stood, a still-smoking shell.

And through it all, a deathly stillness reigned. No sound
but the settling of dust and the pounding of Will's heart, and
then his boots as they tore through the ruined streets and
down to the base of the hill where Dale gave way to the
lakes and the field and the moor. He reached the edge and
collapsed to his knees and retched.

There was a line on the ground, a seam where the singed

world stopped and the green one started. A crisp, clean, impossible divide.

The wind. It hadn't simply pushed the people of Dale back, it had trapped them in, confined the destruction to the hill, sparing only Will and the moors beyond. He shuddered, and wrapped his arms around his ribs. He made it to his feet again, and toward the nearest lake, the shards of the coffin still scattered across the grass. Among the warped metal and wood, he found his pendant, took it up, and carried it to the water's edge, where his legs gave way. He felt hollowed out as he closed his hand around the necklace, and pitched it into the lake.

His reflection rippled, but he didn't meet its gaze. Instead he forced his eyes up to Dale, the sun hovering above the ruins of the Great House.

He couldn't stay. He felt the wind, now gentle, brush against him, soothing. At first he resisted, but then he realized, with a hollow kind of grief, that there was no reason to hold back now. He could have power or people, but never both, and now the people were gone, and so he gave in, let the wind rise and fall with his breath, let it course through him as he forced his shaking body to its feet.

And then, he began to walk.

He walked until he was no longer the heir of Dale, or the callous prince, or William Hart. He walked until he was simply a shadow, a stranger, a ghost. Until his edges blurred and his body thinned, and he was nothing but a gray streak against the wind.

ABOUT THE AUTHOR

V.E. Schwab is the No.1 *New York Times* bestselling author of multiple novels, including *This Savage Song* and the *Darker Shade of Magic* series, whose first book was described as "a classic work of fantasy" by Deborah Harkness. It was one of Waterstones' Best Fantasy Books of 2015 and one of *The Guardian*'s Best Science Fiction novels. *The Independent* has called her "The natural successor to Diana Wynne Jones."

For more fantastic fiction, author events, exclusive
excerpts, competitions, limited editions and more

VISIT OUR WEBSITE
titanbooks.com

LIKE US ON FACEBOOK
facebook.com/titanbooks

FOLLOW US ON TWITTER
@TitanBooks

EMAIL US
readerfeedback@titanemail.com